THE WIFE OF THE EMIR OF FALLUJAH

HAMZA HENDAWI

Black Rose Writing | Texas

©2024 by Hamza Hendawi

All rights reserved. No part of this book may be reproduced, stored in a retrieval system or transmitted in any form or by any means without the prior written permission of the publishers, except by a reviewer who may quote brief passages in a review to be printed in a newspaper, magazine or journal.

The author grants the final approval for this literary material.

First printing

This is a work of fiction. Names, characters, businesses, places, events, and incidents are either the products of the author's imagination or used in a fictitious manner. Any resemblance to actual persons, living or dead, or actual events is purely coincidental.

ISBN: 978-1-68513-467-9
PUBLISHED BY BLACK ROSE WRITING
www.blackrosewriting.com

Printed in the United States of America
Suggested Retail Price (SRP) $19.95

The Wife of the Emir of Fallujah is printed in Minion Pro

*As a planet-friendly publisher, Black Rose Writing does its best to eliminate unnecessary waste to reduce paper usage and energy costs, while never compromising the reading experience. As a result, the final word count vs. page count may not meet common expectations.

THE WIFE OF THE EMIR OF FALLUJAH

CHAPTER ONE

Baghdad, 2006.
The birds were the first to react to the gunfire, making a noise like humans shrieking in horror. Several blasts followed in quick succession, and everything shook: the house, the trees, the fuel tanks in the front yard and the cars whose alarms went off, echoing the horror of the moment.

Everyone in the house had been gathered in the basement dining room at the back, where they were celebrating thirty-five years of service by the news agency's boss, Samuel Kennedy, an American. Such occasions offered a chance for anyone with a sweet tooth to gorge on cake or indulge in some career-promoting flattery of the bosses, especially Samuel, who never minded flattery so long as it remained a notch below shameless ass-kissing.

For this occasion, the company had provided the cakes – most of which were barely edible – and a selection of savory pastries, which were of equally poor quality. As the guests cracked open sodas, group photos were taken and the three house cooks briefly appeared, posing for photos with everyone in their matching white coats and hats. The three, all in their mid to late 20s, quickly returned to the kitchen next door where they were busily preparing dinner for the house's occupants and a very important guest, whose real identity had been kept secret to everyone except a select few.

It was shortly before sundown when that first burst of gunfire rang out. As the power went out, the room was briefly swallowed by darkness before the guests' eyes adjusted to the last dregs of light still coming from the window at the back.

Many of those present were Iraqis who would have normally been home by that time of the day but had stayed for the party. Some hit the floor face down. Others took refuge under the dining table. Most just froze in horror. One or two pressed themselves into the wall so hard that if it had had a crack big enough, they probably would have squeezed inside. All they could think of was staying as far away from the large glass window, the most likely source of shrapnel and bullets.

Before the news agency had moved into this house, it had been quartered on two floors at the nearby Palestine Hotel, a rundown establishment with scruffy rooms, terrible food and a swimming pool routinely filled with murky water. The expatriates among the staff shared stories about how they had spent long hours in their rooms thinking of the best place to hide if the hotel came under attack. They were undoubtedly a prime target: the company was American and headquartered in New York. It had a large office in Baghdad, just like other major foreign news organizations. They compared notes on how effective it would be to hide on the tiny balcony, in the bathtub, under the bed or inside the wardrobe. They often laughed about it, since none of these places were actually safe. But beneath the laughter was frustration and genuine fear. They drew no comfort from the absurdity, or stupidity, of their hiding options, and perhaps that was the reason they never quit thinking of possible hiding places anywhere on the two floors the company occupied.

Their constant search for potential safe spots in case of an attack was not borne of paranoia or exaggerated fear. Not at all. Deadly attacks were taking place every day in the city, and some of them were remarkable in their creativity and tactics. A donkey-drawn cart loaded with rockets primed and timed to go off was one of the most memorable. There were also a few double suicide bombings, designed to kill not just the victims caught in the first blast but also the people who came to rescue them. They targeted funerals where the relatives of an already-slain enemy had gathered to say their last goodbyes. Intact watermelons injected with poison for thirsty American soldiers were another novelty item. The range was wide and diverse. All were at once deadly and scary.

The house was ringed by blast barriers. There were heavy metal gates and, at any given time, about a dozen armed Iraqi guards on duty, supervised by British security consultants hired by the company for the Baghdad office.

But now that everyone was finally facing the danger they had feared for so long, they discovered that, ironically, there wasn't much anyone could do about it.

Some of the party guests started shouting prayers in Arabic, their voices shaky but loud. Some just screamed "What's happening?!" while Samuel pelted out his trademark "SHIT!" in his distinct southern drawl.

More blasts were heard. They sounded like RPGs or grenades going off against walls or vehicles. No one was sure. Dust began to fill the room as the walls shook from the latest wave of explosions.

One of the British consultants present ran out of the kitchen, grabbed his Ak-47, three spare magazines and a flak jacket from his room and headed quickly to the roof to find out what's going on.

"Everyone to the safe room," yelled another security consultant. "Come on!"

The "safe room" was on the other side of the villa's basement. It was located next to bedrooms mostly used by Iraqi employees, rotating expatriate staff and security consultants. The panic room had a steel door that may or may not have been bulletproof. It was certainly on the small side: maybe eight or fewer people could fit inside, standing room only. Its value had always been questionable: a few months back, everyone had been ordered to run to the room when mortars meant for the "Green Zone" across the nearby Tigris were falling short of their target, hitting the vicinity of the house on Baghdad's storied Abu Nawas street. As was often the case, by the time everyone was gathered in the room, the shelling had stopped.

Everyone started to run toward the panic room when Samuel, a short and rather chubby man close to retirement, tripped and fell. His passport, which he religiously kept in the chest pocket of his glaringly unfashionable short-sleeve shirts, jumped out as he made his way down to the floor. Acting like his life depended on having it on him at all times, he picked it up off the floor, slowing down those behind him and almost causing one of the security consultants, who had stuck by him since the first burst of gunfire, to trip and fall down too. When everyone reached the room, it became obvious that there would not be enough space there for everyone.

The Iraqis and a pair of non-Iraqi Arab reporters were the first to arrive, but they paused when they realized the room's space limitations, or maybe because they were never convinced that the panic room was actually a safe place to be at a time like this. Samuel confidently pushed forward, walked into the room and, when he reached the wall at the far side, turned around and took his phone out of his pants pocket.

"SHIT!" he screamed when he realized it had no signal. He stared straight ahead, wearing that stern, dead-man look he often had when he wanted to ignore people around him or silently express his disapproval.

The two security consultants who remained with the group stood outside the room like nightclub bouncers, making it clear they would be the ones to decide who got in and who didn't. They were big men, an ex-marine and a former paratrooper, and physically imposing. They and other members of the security team spent hours every day working out in the small gym at the end of the back garden. To the other employees in the building, especially the Iraqis, the consultants had by far the best deal in post-Saddam Baghdad. They were ridiculously well paid but rarely did much work. No one really had much confidence in the depth of their commitment. Their security assessments of the city's districts and roads were often based on second or third-hand sources. Still, they were expected to do what was needed to protect the expat staff during pickups and drop-offs at Baghdad Airport. That entailed driving on a road that had quickly become notorious for the frequency of attacks after the fall of the city to the Americans. But no one thought their handguns and AK-47s would be a match against bad guys with heavy machineguns, RPGs, or against a suicide car bomb. But at the end of the day, they made the expats feel a little less worried about their safety. Also, the British men were indispensable for insurance purposes: the company had to be able to show that, if required, it was taking every possible measure to protect its employees, or at least the expats among them, in a war zone.

It had become a running joke that the security consultants spent hours online looking for properties to buy in sunny places like Spain or Portugal with the huge money they were making in Baghdad. They spent an equally long time chatting online with their partners or children. Just to really rub it in, they were the ones who always got the girls, seducing the women reporters and producers who came to Baghdad on short-term assignments. With the hours spent every day in the gym, the three homemade meals they ate daily and the little work they had to do, they had every other male in the office – working long hours, eating meals at their desks – at a huge disadvantage with any female visitor who might be looking for a little fun at the end of a long working day. Baghdad, after all, was a city that offered little or nothing in the way of entertainment. Those among them who had no desire for a war zone romance made do with binge watching their favorite series on their laptops, or joined their expat male colleagues in drinking sessions that lasted till the small hours.

"George, Bernadette, Caroline, get in there quickly," bellowed John Lancaster, the most senior of the security consultants, his face stern yet failing to hide his own fear that the house was being targeted for a major attack.

"*Habiby, men fadlak,*" yelled George, using perhaps half the Arabic vocabulary he had picked in a decade working in the Middle East, as he made his way through to the inside of the room. Next came Bernadette, another American who never tired of declaring her admiration and love for Iraqis and their country. "Excuse me, please!" she said in her Disney princess voice that belied her heavy build, occasional bouts of passive aggressiveness or her thinly veiled sense of ethnic superiority.

Caroline was the last to answer John Lancaster's call, quietly moving toward the room, making sure she made no eye contact with anyone.

The Iraqis and the two Arabs realized at that moment that they had better find someplace else to take shelter until the attack was over. In some ways, they thought it was probably better that they were separated from the westerners. Maybe, just maybe, there was a way they could escape death or captivity if they were found alone by the attackers. There might just be an upside in not going inside the panic room.

They moved to the side of the doorway, not wanting to come face to face with the moment when John Lancaster or the other consultant slammed the door shut and left them standing there, abandoned. Waiting outside the room until John Lancaster did just that would directly confirm what many of them had long suspected: when push came to shove, they would not be treated the same way as their western colleagues. But that did not matter much now. It was all about survival now, not striving for equality.

But there was one person who was not willing to stay quiet. Not unexpectedly it was Mohammed, the penguin-shaped senior television producer who was in the habit of adopting a fake British accent whenever he wanted to endear himself to expat staffers, or to set himself apart from the rest of his fellow Arab employees in the office.

"Excuse me!" he screamed, his faux English accent on full display. "I am the senior TV producer and I must go inside too," he told John Lancaster. He did not wait for the Briton's approval.

No one – neither the expats huddling in the safe room nor the Arabs still waiting outside – objected to Mohammed's defection.

The Arabs, perhaps, were too preoccupied with their own fate to bother with Mohammed's. Hussein, a well-connected Iraqi reporter in his mid-30s, had the quickness of mind and the fatalism typical of devout Muslims to say as much.

"Whatever is meant to happen to us will happen. There is not much we can do. Let's just go to one of the bedrooms and stay put," he said, showing commendable composure. He put an arm around the shoulder of one of the two Arab reporters he was close friends with and gave him a gentle nudge toward the bedrooms next to the safe room.

They all stepped away from the door, expecting it to be slammed shut any second. Inside the room, George Pseridis looked like he had seen a ghost. Samuel's eyes were closed as he stood with his back to the wall. Everyone was silent, faces frozen in horror.

Just as the door was closing, another powerful explosion knocked everyone waiting outside the panic room to the floor, some with blood streaming from their noses and ears. For a second, it seemed like the house might be about to collapse on top of them. Some briefly passed out. Thick dust filled the building, combined with the suffocating smell of gas. As people started to slowly come round, a few tried to pull themselves to their feet but couldn't stand up straight. They leaned on the wall or on the panic room's door for support, coughing and retching. They managed to walk to the nearest basement room, went in and locked the door.

In the kitchen, the cooks could be heard screaming in terror.

There was another burst of heavy gunfire, followed by the buzz of helicopters hovering over the building.

CHAPTER TWO

Fallujah, 2004

A knock on Omar Al Rawy's house door late at night or early in the morning was neither surprising nor reason for concern. This time round, it was shortly after 3 a.m. and Omar was lying awake in bed. The room was at the back of the family's one-story house near the iron bridge on the road to Khaldiyah, some ten miles away to the west.

His mind was whirling with life issues: his store was not doing much business, despite being on the main street, and the frequent U.S. airstrikes were harvesting lives, including members of his own extended family and clan. But worst of all, Fallujah was under siege by the Americans, making it extremely difficult for people and goods to leave or enter the city. The influx of foreign jihadists into the city was another source of worry. They arrived by the dozen, crossing the Syrian border under the cover of darkness at remote desert areas. They included Yemenis, Saudis, Egyptians, Syrians, Chechens and Turks. At least the Saudis brought with them large stashes of US dollars, which they spent lavishly. They gave money to the poor and to fellow Jihadists who needed help. They ate kebabs and rice for lunch every day. The Yemenis were mostly tiny men with spotty beards, their sniper rifles almost as tall as they were. Some of the Egyptians and Syrians were in their 40s or early 50s, grizzled veterans of the jihad in the Balkans and Chechnya. They ate little, had no time for small talk and showed a tendency to lecture other jihadists at length on Islam and the tactics of war. Some of the jihadists were privately annoyed by how the Egyptians never stopped bragging about their battlefield valor, but they never showed or dared show how they felt.

"The Americans will severely punish us," Omar had been telling friends and relatives since the jihadists became the dominant power in Fallujah, where the first spark of resistance against the Americans flared just weeks after they captured Baghdad in April 2003.

Omar's fears were not unfounded.

The eyes and ears of the jihadists, deployed both in the outlying districts of Fallujah and inside the nearby U.S. military bases, where many locals had found employment, had been reporting that the Americans were gearing up for a full-scale assault. A large force of Marines was already assembling, these spies said. In Baghdad, politicians had been talking tirelessly about the inevitability of restoring government control over Fallujah. Their rhetoric ignored what everyone knew: that actual control was in the hands of the Americans, not Iraqi politicians and their parties. But that was just too embarrassing to acknowledge publicly. At any rate, the government stood firmly behind whatever the Americans had in mind for Fallujah.

"They mean business this time round," said a friend of Omar's who worked as a builder at one of the bases, when they talked on the phone. "There are so many soldiers now in this camp and the one next door. I am worried about you and your family. My mother, father, brothers and sisters, all of them, are now in Baghdad. If I did not have this job, I would not have been able to afford the rent in Baghdad. *Al hamdulelah!*"

Already, tens of thousands had fled the city. Those who stayed were either too poor to leave or could not tear themselves away from their homes. They thought that staying put would somehow ensure the safety of their property. But the biggest deterrent to fleeing was the ballooning rents and cost of living in Baghdad. Ramadi, the nearby provincial capital, was hardly a more attractive option, hit by frequent airstrikes and constant American house raids.

Omar was considered "old" to still be single at 27, in the city's conservative customs. A high school graduate who went straight to work selling and repairing second-hand computers, he had quickly shifted to selling mobile phones after they were first introduced to Iraq, just weeks after the arrival of the Americans. His store had done well at first, being located in the heart of the city and close to the local government offices as well as the city's renowned kebab restaurant, Haji Hussein's.

But the income from the store was barely enough to maintain the house that Omar shared with his diabetic mother and two brothers; Mohammed, who studied Sharia at a local college, and Abu Bakr who was hoping against hope to sit his final high school exams this year, despite the mayhem engulfing the city. He hoped to study engineering in Baghdad, but that would have to wait until some semblance of normalcy was restored to the country. Their father had died three years before, after spending a lifetime trading in virtually anything that would turn a profit. He had his spot on the commercial street, where he sold children's toys, clothes, Chinese-made blankets and electrical fans. Anything that might make some money, especially during the decade of U.N. sanctions that followed Iraq's invasion of Kuwait in 1990. His inventory in those desperate days leaned heavily on tins of cheap tuna, corned beef, rice and tomato paste. He sold second-hand clothes and plastic Chinese-made flip-flops. People had much less cash during those years, and he was forced to slash his prices just to be able to carry on selling.

"Thanks to Saddam, I can sell anything now. Literally anything!" he would whisper to his wife, fearful that his own children might disapprove of any sarcasm directed at the president. Or worse, that they might join in. He did not want his boys to meet the fate that awaited him if he were ever caught.

There was only one goal during those miserable years of sanctions: to make enough to survive. Anything else, like clothes or fresh meat for a special occasion, was covered by the little extra that occasionally trickled in from his cousins who had jobs in Saudi Arabia.

On hearing the knock on the door, Omar sprang out of bed and strode to the front door, passing through the inner courtyard where the family gathered before sunset, when the temperature became a little less unbearable, to feast on tea and dry bread sticks.

Omar unlocked the door without bothering to ask who was there. He already knew who it was. Montaser, the 12-year-old boy entrusted by Omar's childhood friends-turned-jihadists to deliver messages for them around the city. The boy, a pious Muslim who observed the five daily prayers and Ramadan fast, was indispensable to the jihadists' communication lines. He'd found himself in the vital but unpaid job after successfully delivering an urgent message from his jihadist brother to his comrades manning a forward position on the fringes of the city. The message warned the men on the frontline of suspicious movements by the Americans, suggesting an imminent attack. Their movements had been reported by the spies working odd jobs for the Americans. As it turned out, the Americans may just have been testing the jihadists' defenses or familiarizing themselves with the terrain. Word spread among the fighters about the message and the ingenuity of using a small boy to deliver it. The jihadists discussed it and then unanimously agreed that Montaser would be designated as the group's official courier. Poor Montaser had no say in the matter, but he did enjoy the attention the job brought him. For a 12-year-old, delivering simple messages, sometimes written on small scraps of paper, was the closest thing to landing the lead part in a thriller or a war movie.

Mobile phones in Fallujah, like elsewhere in Iraq, were widely available now and, despite the siege, there was a signal available most of the time. But the city's jihadists feared the Americans were tracking their devices, either with drones or warplanes flying over the city. Their fears grew deeper as more and more airstrikes targeted meetings of senior jihadists, killing everyone with a rocket or a precision bomb, as well as invariably causing a great deal of "collateral damage."

It was because of these fears that Montaser's job was deemed vital. Some jihadists credited Montaser with saving lives. When he heard that for the first time, he was filled with such pride that he found it impossible not to share with Mohammed, his childhood friend and school classmate.

"You are lying, right?" said an incredulous Mohammed when he was told about his friend's secret job. "Stop telling lies or we'll be in trouble with the jihadists."

Montaser found some relief in Mohammed's reaction: if Mohammed did not believe him, then he had not broken his vow of secrecy to the jihadists.

As soon as Omar opened the door, Montaser delivered his message. "Good morning, Haji, my uncle wants to see you right away."

"Where is he now?"

"He is at Sheikh Ibrahim's house."

"Fine!" Omar said. He asked the boy to wait, then went back to the living room to fetch a piece of candy from a cheap china bowl by the television set. He returned and handed it to the boy, then closed the door and went back to his room.

The call for dawn prayers was ringing out from the mosques as Omar washed at the basin in the inner court.

"*Allahu Akbar*," he said out loud. his voice filled with anxiety. He began his prayer on the Chinese-made, blue-and-green rug given to his father years ago by one of the cousins in Saudi Arabia.

CHAPTER THREE

Hassan Al Anbary was in his thirties but with his prematurely graying beard and shaven head could easily pass for forty or even fifty. He had graduated from the agriculture college in Baghdad before landing a job at the local government in Fallujah as a food inspector. The job's description sounded important, but in reality was little more than a dull desk job that paid very little and took up most of his day.

He spent his days at the scruffy office sitting behind a stained table in a room he shared with five others. He killed time reading the Quran over and over, as well as books on jurisprudence and the "*hadeeth*," or the sayings of the Prophet. He would occasionally leave the office to inspect butcher shops, bakeries or eateries for possible health code violations.

Hassan married a cousin when he was still in college and the couple lived in the family home in Fallujah. Back in those days, he used to come home from Baghdad every Thursday full of excitement and desire for his young and beautiful wife. He would leave Fallujah to head back to the capital soon after sunrise on Sundays, often exhausted after long nights making love to Safiyah, his wife. He barely knew her before their marriage, but he quickly fell in love. Their timidity and modesty around each other did not leave them for weeks after the wedding, including during their weeklong honeymoon at a small chalet by Habaniyah lake, not far from Fallujah. The uninterrupted privacy they had there did not help matters. But that was only to be expected: he was barely 20 when he married Safiyah. She was a teenager; and a virgin, like him.

For weeks, she would throw herself into Hassan's arms and the couple would spend an hour or longer kissing until their lips were sore and their mouths dried up. Initially, their kissing only meant pressing their lips against the other's, but that soon changed. They learned to lock lips and use their tongues. The kisses became wet too and aroused them more. Hassan's hands would make frequent but cautious trips up to Safiyah's breasts or down to her upper thighs. At first, it caused her to tense up but those forays soon became something she looked forward to.

But neither one, despite the burning desire they felt from their extended foreplay, could muster enough "immodesty" to take off their clothes and have a shot at actual intercourse. They never spoke about what was needed to be done either. Not that either of them had a clear idea of what to actually do. But Hassan did not want to hurry things up, or spook his bride. He knew it would eventually happen. Besides, Safiyah was the first woman apart from his mother and aunts that he had touched or kissed since reaching puberty. He was happy enough with the arousing novelty of a woman as attractive as Safiyah throwing herself into his arms and kissing him with such passion.

His wet dreams became more frequent, many induced by his penis accidentally rubbing against her body while they slept after an evening of unrequited kissing and touching.

Hassan's patience came in part from his strong sense of pride that he had married a girl whose beauty was spoken about in the family as a rare or divine gift. Her thick dark brown hair, soft creamy skin and slender figure made her look like the models on the cover of glossy magazines. Safiyah's beauty was matched by her gentleness, and she could converse intelligently, coming across as informed and somewhat well read. She and Hassan spent many hours of their honeymoon talking as they sat by the Habaniyah lake or walking along its sandy shores.

Hassan's weekend sojourns in Fallujah during his college days were divided into two main activities: talking to Safiyah and making love to her. The studying was all done in Baghdad, not in Fallujah. When he was home, it was Safiyah who consumed all his attention, nothing and no one else. They talked about so many things: Iraq's future, Saddam, what would they do if they travelled to neighboring Syria or Jordan.

"Hassan, I would like us to have two or three children, maybe two boys and a girl. And I want us to leave Iraq and maybe you get a job in Saudi Arabia or Kuwait and we all move there."

"It's difficult to see what will happen to us in the next few years. Let's just hope that we survive these sanctions and life returns to normal. But I don't see that happening anytime soon. I'm tired of this tough life. Had it not been for you, I would have probably done some crazy things to rid myself of despair."

"Hassan, why? Like what?"

"I don't know, I really don't. Maybe join the jihad somewhere, why not? Don't take this the wrong way. Except for you, my life is meaningless here. I want to fight for something. I want to be useful and make a difference. I don't see this happening here, do you? Not with this corrupt regime, anyway."

"But what about me? And why jihad, and not a job in the Gulf and a family? How could you even think of that? Have you no regard for how I will feel if you just go one day and leave me behind here. What am I, a mistress? We are building a life together. We are married and we've also become friends, companions and lovers, all under God's eyes. Fallujah is our home and if we leave it, we go to the Gulf to see if we can make money and come back and start a business here or at least buy our own house. If you leave for jihad in a faraway place where I cannot reach or see you, then I might as well die," she said, her eyes brimming with tears of fear and anger.

"May God show you the right way," she said.

"If my mind is made up to go to jihad, then it is the will of the Almighty," said Hassan.

In fact, his long Salafi beard and his diligent trips to the nearby mosque for dawn prayers had already invited a visit to the family home by Saddam's local security branch.

"Know this, if we have to come back to your house, it will not be because we want to ask more questions," warned the slender security officer with a rugged face and cheap suit. Accompanying him were several members of the local branch of the ruling Baath party in olive green fatigues and dark orange boots. None of the Baathists opened their mouths during the half hour of questioning. They just stared with menacing faces.

Safiyah had worn the hijab since the age of seven, and started wearing the niqab at twelve, just after she reached puberty. It was around that time that the family began to talk less of her beauty, at least when she was around, and more about her good manners, domestic skills and, of course, her commitment to the pillars of Islam, like praying and fasting the holy month of Ramadan.

She was nearing graduation from high school when she married Hassan and, despite her young age, she knew how to cook, clean, wash and do other household chores, much to the delight of Hassan's mother. But she never gave up on reading. She was keen on fiction and read almost everything by Naguib Mahfouz, Egypt's Nobel laureate, as well as the works of prominent Iraqi poets like Maarouf Al Rasafy and Mohammed Al Gawahry or social studies by Ali Al Wardi.

Safiyah's father was a police officer with the local force. He lost his job when Saddam's regime fell in 2003 and did not want to return to work when, a few months later, things calmed down a little and he was summoned back. The Americans in Fallujah tried to reorganize the force, bringing to the city seasoned police officers from the United States to train local policemen. Their objective was chiefly to use the force to gather intelligence on jihadists in Fallujah and possibly serve as a back-up fighting force against what the Americans had begun referring to as "the insurgency."

"I will not serve under the command of those Americans," Safiyah's father told his family when he announced he was taking early retirement. His pension was a handsome monthly stipend of $600, but until the pension checks started to arrive, the family, like tens of thousands of others across Iraq, would have to get by on very little. At first, he dipped into his life savings. When that started to run out, he borrowed. He did so frequently, and for small amounts. Finally, he began to farm the small plot of land he'd bought years ago just outside the city. He had hoped it would eventually be zoned for housing so he could sell part of it and use the rest to build a large family home that would bring everyone together under one roof.

He sold most of the produce at the local market for a tiny profit and kept the rest for his family to eat. The plan worked well enough for him to keep the family fed and clothed through the difficult times after Saddam's fall, when so many Iraqis were either left destitute or had to resort to selling off family heirlooms just to survive. And just like the case was during the years of UN sanctions, markets continued to be awash with treasured antiques, wedding dresses, tuxedos and unused wedding gifts. Books and paintings that had been in families for decades were carted off to markets but did not sell well. Families even hawked their furniture, but what really kept most afloat was not the proceeds from these sales, but the help of relatives overseas, some of whom had not been seen in Iraq for years but who sent back dollars home to desperate families.

***

Hassan Al Anbary had extraordinarily broad shoulders, giving him a distinctive look few people failed to notice. He squatted on a cushion placed on the floor listening to his closest aide, Ibrahim Habib, who had sneaked into Fallujah a month before from Samarra, his birthplace north of Baghdad and the site of a shrine to two, much-revered Shiite imams. The room was austere, just cushions lining three of its four walls and a few small tables standing on the green straw matt that served as a carpet. The yellowing walls were bare.

It was shortly before 5 a.m. when Omar, in jeans, off-white T-shirt and a pair of plastic flip-flops, walked in. He kicked off his footwear at the door of the "guest room" and quickly walked over to Hassan to shake his hand. But Hassan was not having it. He stretched his arms wide and gave Omar a hug, then placed three kisses on his right cheek. Ibrahim, the host, similarly hugged and kissed Omar. This was Ibrahim's home, which the Fallujah jihadists had found and rented for him when he arrived from Samarra. Ibrahim was widely admired for the military skills he acquired during years of service in Saddam's army, something that warranted the special treatment he received.

As was customary, the three men exchanged greetings and asked about their respective families, before Hassan abruptly ended the social pleasantries. The jihadists, he said, had detained an Egyptian married to a local woman, and who was believed to be spying for the Americans.

"What's his name?" asked Omar, hoping he might recognize the man. Hundreds of Egyptians had settled in Fallujah to work during the war with Iran, and some had stayed on after most of their compatriots returned home.

"His name is Mohammed Hassan. He is about 50: we began to suspect him after two of our brothers spotted him in the middle of the night climbing to the roof of the house of the martyr Tariq Fawaz. The brothers said he was on the roof for a few minutes and then climbed down and left," said Hassan. "We think he might have placed a chip on the roof to guide America's planes. And that's what exactly happened. There is not much left of the house except a mound of dust and rubble. There was little of the martyr's body left intact, but we buried what was left."

"So, what are we to do with him?" asked Omar.

"Listen, there was nothing of value or interest on Tariq's roof, or inside the house for that matter. So, what was he doing up there? We cannot apply God's prescribed punishment on him unless he first confesses to his crime or we find compelling evidence of his guilt. We could talk him into working for us while continuing to serve the Americans and have him divert American airstrikes to deserted homes instead of those occupied by jihadists. But he will most likely betray us to the Americans and they will hide him from us and later ship him to America to live there. We must get retribution for Tariq's life. He must have played a role in all the American airstrikes that killed so many of us. We just cannot let him get away with it. So, what do you suggest we do?"

"We must make him confess. If he does, we apply God's punishment. But what if he doesn't?" asked Omar.

"I don't know. Let us try first and, if not, we talk again," said Hassan. "Can you question him? I want you to do it because our brothers use religion too much when they question prisoners and that distracts them from their task. I want to know how he was identified by the Americans as a potential recruit, how they recruited him and how much they are paying him. I want to know everything, everything."

"But why me? We talked about this before. To me, you are brothers, childhood friends and members of my clan, but I don't want to be part of what you do. Do you understand? My heart is with you and I support you, but my interest lies elsewhere. It's not jihad."

"You are a brother and a friend and nothing you say or do will change that, nothing! But I want you to do this for good reasons. You have that natural intelligence and a genuine and thorough knowledge of Fallujah. That Egyptian will never be able to lie to you or conceal the truth from you. He will not dare make up a story that exonerates him or mitigates his crime. I am certain that he is guilty, but I want to know the details surrounding his guilt."

"Alright, when do I get to see him?"

"Now, if you like."

CHAPTER FOUR

The action began around eight in the evening, after Samuel filed the day's final story, usually a wrap-up of the main events around Iraq. As a wire agency writer, Samuel was highly skilled at this kind of story, churning them out day after day, functional and flawless. The bosses in New York loved them, but for most readers they were not the kind of stories that were remembered long after they were published. He had produced one of these wraps that night before immediately joining the customary Thursday evening party that entailed a hearty barbecue prepared by the cooks who stayed late for the occasion. A hard drinking session always went with the food.

As well as meat and chicken, the cooks grilled tomatoes and onions, two customary side dishes in Iraq. They served humus, taboula and a green salad. The patrons of these weekly get-togethers were mostly the expatriate staff who lived in the house, plus one or two of the Iraqis who lived in, unlike their compatriots who went home to their families before dark when the streets became significantly more dangerous.

Samuel, the Greek-American George Pseridis and the Croatian chief photographer Antonio Barselav were the party's main movers and shakers, steering the conversation, determining the pace of drinking and calling it a night when they'd had enough and were ready to go to bed. Joining them on regular basis was Mohammed, the TV producer who prided himself on being a tireless champion of Scotch as God's remedy for all man's troubles, and whose love for 1970s music was generally deemed excessive.

Carolina, the American photographer, rarely joined those drinking sessions, preferring to leave when she was done eating. She did that partly to spend time on her own during the short breaks between embeds with the American forces, but also so she could hang out with her Iraqi lover, a photographer who'd made his name in the agency by always getting to the site of bombings quicker than anyone else, thanks to his muscle motorbike and daredevil riding. Married with three children, he found it both fascinating and empowering that a western woman was interested in him, although he quickly realized the interest was almost purely physical. Carolina found many of the American soldiers she met attractive, with their rugged good looks and gym-honed muscles, but "dating" one during embeds would have been deeply unprofessional. The Iraqi photographer, who invented endless excuses to stay the night at the house when she was around, had to satisfy Carolina's bottled-up passion whenever she came back from those embeds with the military. It was a demanding task, but his strength was kept up by the sudden abundance of quality food in a kitchen staffed by three cooks. The long years of sanctions had reduced many Iraqis to eating little and what they did eat was mostly bad quality or fattening. That poor diet and the endless frustrations of daily life under sanctions left many, both men and women, with little appetite for sex. He had definitely been among them, as had his wife. Good food had restored him, and now his passion for sex matched Carolina's. It was dirty and lustful, very different to what he had grown accustomed to with his wife over the years. Carolina seems to have liberated him in bed. He liked that even as much as he liked her efforts to please him.

They both exercised great restraint to be quiet while having sex in one of the basement rooms, although some of the Iraqis living in the house could hear their groans and shared the story with others. It was a popular inside joke among the local staff, but one they did not think wise to share with the expatriates, since it involved one of them.

For the barbecue, everyone was seated on the terrace that looked out on the front yard and the concrete blast barriers that protected the property. The entrance to the house was to the right, a small passage leading to a giant metal gate that opened out onto Abu Nawas street and the Tigris river.

It was a pleasant evening, with a cool breeze drifting through the house wherever a window was open. The sky was clear, and only the occasional thud of artillery shells could be heard in the distance, just south of the city: Baghdad's nighttime soundtrack was defined by artillery rounds, the buzzing of low-flying helicopters on their way to and from the Green Zone across the Tigris, or the ambulance and police sirens. Occasionally, an American jet fighter screaming overhead would add another unnerving note.

Abdul-Rahman the cook had done yet another spectacular job that night, grilling to perfection the Australian steaks bought from the Green Zone supermarket and the local free-range chicken. He toasted the bread, a dome-shaped Iraqi variety called *samoon*, on the charcoal and later made tea infused with crushed cardamom: he left the teapot on the charcoal long after the tea boiled so it could simmer to gain more aroma. Everyone drank the tea extra sweet, regardless of the health risks involved. Those who smoked received an extra buzz from their cigarette while sipping the tea.

As at every barbecue, people gossiped about the company; the latest moves, management politics and, occasionally, redundancies. When everyone was done trying to impress with inside information or fresh gossip, the discussion moved to another familiar area: foreign correspondents' tales of heroism, guile or close brushes with death in trouble spots. The stories all highlighted the dangers, real or imaginary, that a foreign correspondent faced in the field. In most of these tales, the professionalism, connections and talent of the local journalists who provided the correspondents with invaluable insight and contacts in those places were acknowledged only in passing, while the focus remained firmly on the courage and quickness of mind of the storyteller, almost always a white man of European heritage who barely fathomed the nuances of local cultures and customs. Those were replaced by what they perceived to be the "magic" effect of the few phrases they managed to pick up from a local language to get out of sticky situations.

For example, George Pserides' favorite phrase was *"Habiby, shwayah, shwayah!"* which is Arabic for "my friend, take it easy!" He genuinely seemed to believe that it worked like magic every time he was faced with local men angered by his presence at the site of a bombing or an airstrike in those days after the invasion, when western journalists like him still felt safe enough to occasionally venture out and report from the streets.

Samuel knew much more Arabic than any of the other westerners living in the house, and appeared to understand a great deal of Egyptian and Lebanese Arabic. But he caught far less when the Iraqi dialect was spoken. Even so, he rarely said anything in Arabic: if he had spoken in a funny accent like George, for example, the native Arabic speakers in the office might not be able to stop themselves from laughing. That would not be good for his carefully crafted aura as the wise manager of a diverse and somewhat unsettled bunch of reporters in a treacherous war zone like Baghdad.

"It's no coincidence that I've been working overseas for this company for 30 years. It's my guile that secured me all these foreign assignments," Samuel, who hailed from a one-time slave-owning family in the American south, once confided to a reporter, while letting out one of his trademark evil laughs.

His gravelly voice, the byproduct of years of heavy smoking and drinking, his passion for fried chicken legs and his extraordinary work ethic made him a larger-than-life figure. That he was the quintessential old-school foreign correspondent was beyond doubt. Every now and then, he would say something slightly inappropriate about the native inhabitants of the countries where he'd worked in Asia or the Middle East, but never anything harsh enough to confirm him as an outright racist. He let out hearty laughs when he heard stories about people's hardships or brushes with death while reporting, but he never questioned or belittled the authenticity of their stories. It was just his way of interacting with subordinates. He was friendly with everyone but appeared to trust no one. His ultimate commitment was to please the managers in New York, and to control what they knew about the office, and about Iraq in general.

Despite knowing it was culturally inappropriate in the Arab world to show the soles of one's shoes to another person, he routinely rested his feet on his desk when speaking on the phone or chatting with someone in his office, and his everyday speech was laced with profanities. It was a subtle form of entitlement that told everyone, "I am an American and this is an American news organization, so I will be as American as I wish."

Inevitably, those barbecue and drinking parties drew out funny stories about the clumsiness or inexperience of some of the reporters who embedded with the Americans. There was the story Bernadette told about the first day of her embed with an infantry platoon south of Baghdad, when she fell face-down in a muddy field. Or the gentle and gifted Greek photographer who asked a hardened army sergeant with tattoos covering half his body about where he could "go peepeei!" drawing a massive laugh from the sergeant and a few other soldiers within earshot. Some of the non-Iraqi Arab reporters had their own stories too and they shared them, but less frequently. They were mostly funny and not about heroic acts or taking huge risks for the sake of getting the story. They only recounted them because, deep down, they wanted to belong to the war correspondents' club, even though they knew its membership was exclusively for westerners. The temptation to blend in with their western colleagues was a sort of sickness or insecurity. Sometimes they resisted and instead found the company of each other more rewarding.

The Iraqi reporters had far more interesting and relevant stories to share than their western bosses or their non-Iraqi, Arab colleagues. Some of them were grim life-and-death stories about the dangers they faced on a daily basis just going about their lives in post-Saddam Iraq. They also had harrowing tales about the dangers they faced during their country's long war with Iran, the first Gulf War and the years of U.S. air and missile strikes they had to endure after the liberation of Kuwait in 1991. These Iraqis risked their lives by just working for an American news organization in post-Saddam Iraq. Dozens like them had lost their lives because they worked for the U.S. military as interpreters or contractors, slaughtered by Islamic militants and their bodies dumped on the streets.

The Iraqis working for Samuel's news agency had to make up stories to tell their neighbors and relatives about who they worked for and what they actually did. They lived under the constant threat of getting found out and paying the ultimate price. The militants had their eyes and ears everywhere, and their punishment was swift and deadly. The Iraqis who worked at the agency were a mix of Shiites, Sunnis, Kurds, Christians and Turkmen. Under the new, post-Saddam sectarian order in Baghdad, the Sunnis and Shiites had the worst deal, with followers of both sects often falling victim to militants from the other side.

"I tell everyone who asked that I am Shiite because I moved with my Shiite wife into a rented apartment in a Shiite neighborhood. We are outsiders there, and vulnerable," a Sunni-born Iraqi reporter told his coworkers in 2004, two years before the sectarian divide morphed into a bloodbath between Shiites and Sunnis. "If I did not do that, the militiamen in the neighborhood would keep an eye on me, and if they did they would find out that I am working for the Americans."

He, like other Iraqis in the office, took many risks to report the news for their western bosses, most of whom had rarely ventured outside the heavily guarded house except when escorted by the British security consultants to and from the airport.

The stories the Iraqis told about what happened in their neighborhoods after dark grew increasingly worrisome; the terror attacks they accidentally found themselves in the middle of while on their way to work or returning home, the photographers who were harassed and beaten up by Iraqi police when they rushed to cover the aftermath of bombings. At times, American soldiers treated them roughly too, preventing them from doing their job or forcing them to leave under the threat of violence.

Somehow, the westerners in the office never seemed sufficiently moved by these stories in the way they would have been had it happened to one of them. It was almost to be expected for the Iraqis, just as it was for their peers in Lebanon, Syria, Yemen or Egypt, that they should experience such a harsh reality on a regular basis. It's their country, right? And they should be grateful for having landed relatively well-paid jobs when most of their compatriots were struggling to make ends meet amid the turmoil of post-Saddam Iraq.

The Iraqis rarely told their western bosses of the hazardous lives they led in their dusty and austere Baghdad neighborhoods, whose social fabric was being torn apart by the explosion of sectarianism after the fall of Saddam. They may have feared that stories of menacing gunmen roaming their neighborhoods, of fake checkpoints that could mean a premature death for members of the wrong sect, or the brutality of American soldiers raiding homes in search of militants would not interest their western bosses.

Deep down, the Iraqis suspected their bosses would only have a mild reaction to their harrowing life stories. They knew they must continue to endure for the sake of their personal safety and for their families, and so acted as if the dangers, heartaches and uncertainty in Baghdad were an integral part of their lives.

"I'm in a war zone, so please don't tell me that smoking is bad for my health," a visiting American reporter indignantly told an Arab colleague who offered him unsolicited advice to quit smoking. That American would spend four to six weeks in Baghdad without ever leaving the house, right up till the day he headed to the airport to fly home.

Iraqi staffers would often come up with the idea for a major story and report it out but somehow the credit, or most of it, would go to the western members of the staff who actually wrote it up after shepherding the reporting process. It was not that the Iraqis would not get any praise. They would, but their bosses would get an equal amount or, as was often the case, more.

"These guys have explosive stories inside their heads and they don't even recognize it," the visiting American old the Arab reporter who had advised him to quit smoking. "I need to sit them down and practically interrogate them to get those stories," he boasted, suggesting that without him, those stories would never see the light of day.

While sipping his third glass of Scotch, Antonio, the chief photographer, told Samuel he was looking at several candidates for the position of a freelance photographer based in Fallujah. He explained that it was becoming more and more difficult and dangerous, even for Iraqis, to work in Fallujah since the city fell under the control of the militants. It would be virtually impossible though to find a photographer in Fallujah with the skills to match those of the local staff photographers in Baghdad, he said.

"I'll be happy with someone with a basic understanding of news photography," he told Samuel, who had to sign off on any hiring.

Samuel, nodded in agreement.

"We have the budget, but we need to spend it on people who will enrich our reporting," said Antonio, whose work was his whole life after an acrimonious divorce a few years back. The breakup meant he drank even more than before, but it had somehow also deepened his compassion for the people he worked with in Iraq.

"We may have found our man in Fallujah, but I will need to meet him before I decide to hire him. One of our drivers, who is from Anbar, has recommended him. Says he is very well connected in Fallujah. We will try and bring him to Baghdad so we can talk to him," said Antonio. "He has no previous experience as a news photographer, but neither did most if not all the photographers we have hired here."

"It's important that we verify that he is not linked to the militants in any way and that he will operate outside their influence," said Samuel, who had been drinking for so many years he could hold a serious conversation even after imbibing large amounts of liquor.

"The Americans will know as soon as our Fallujah photos begin to appear that we hired someone there. Their next step will be to track down the photographer and try to establish through their own sources whether he is linked in any way to the militants. People think the military is as democratic or liberal as America's political system. It's fucking not. They hate liberal media like us, but they keep that to themselves. You can be sure as hell they will be all over us if they catch us fucking up."

The business side of things taken care of, the conversation turned once again to war stories, each getting longer and more elaborate as the night wore on.

At around one in the morning, Samuel began to feel hungry again, but by now he was too drunk and too lazy to go and fetch something from the kitchen downstairs. He did not want to ask anyone to fetch him food either. For one thing, there was no one to ask since the cooks had gone home hours ago. So, he mustered just enough energy to totter over to the table where the cooks left extra steaks in case someone got hungry and wanted to grill one more. He was annoyed to find that the little charcoal left in the barbecue tray wasn't hot enough to properly grill. He grabbed a steak and walked back to his chair where, to the shock of everyone still sitting there, he started eating it raw, one large bite after another. No one said a word, doing their best to conceal their shock and disgust.

Mohammed, the penguin-shaped television producer, was about to say something, but the stern looks he received from the others reduced him to an inaudible mutter. An eerie silence descended on the gathering, as everyone stared at their feet or their drink. The silence lasted until Samuel had finished the steak and wiped his mouth and hands with a paper towel from the plastic garden table next to him.

CHAPTER FIVE

Omar was sitting behind the store's counter when Sinan Habib, an office driver and a native of Anbar's provincial capital Ramadi, walked in with one of the two Arab reporters who worked in the news agency's Baghdad bureau. Omar was startled by their unexpected arrival. He knew that Sinan would soon come to take him to Baghdad, but he never told him specifically when.

After a series of the usual greetings and embraces, he asked how they had entered Fallujah when the city was sealed off by the Americans and the Shura Council jihadists.

"The Americans asked for our IDs," said Sinan, who had driven to Fallujah from Baghdad.

"They took down our details as well as the license plate number and let us go. As for the jihadists, we just told them that we were coming to see you! They let us pass when we mentioned your name. No questions. No nothing. But, to tell you the truth, they did not look happy or comfortable allowing us into the city."

Omar smiled to conceal his discomfort about the final part of this account. He might have said something if the Arab reporter was not there. It was the first time he had seen the man, and he avoided making eye contact with him, directing himself instead to Sinan, a distant relative through some obscure clan ties. They had met several times before at weddings and funerals across Anbar. Omar dragged out the conversation, giving himself time to come up with an explanation as to how the mere mention of his name was enough for armed militants to allow the pair from Baghdad into the city without as much as a single question.

Eventually, he could no longer ignore the reporter.

"My name is Mohammed Abu El Enein, I am a journalist from Egypt but based in Baghdad now," said the reporter. "I came to take a look at Fallujah and speak to a few people and then take you to Baghdad to meet the bosses as Sinan must have explained to you. Did we come at a bad time? You were expecting us, right?"

"No, not at all," Omar said, perhaps taking some comfort from knowing that he was Egyptian and, in all likelihood, a fellow Sunni. "Let me know if you need any help. I have a few things to do here and I will be ready to travel with you when you're done. So, go take a look and talk to people and when you're done come back and I will be here and ready to go."

Omar did not really have any errands to run. It was a slow day and all he needed to do was switch off the small generator, which he places outside the store on the sidewalk every morning, take it inside the shop and pull down the shutters. But he also needed to go and see Hassan Al Anbary before he left. He needed the jihadist's blessing. It was not something his departure absolutely depended on, but he knew he would be uncomfortable going to Baghdad without seeing him first, even if he planned to be back in Fallujah the following day. He was not just the "emir" of the Shura Council, he was a friend, a mentor and fellow clansman.

Today, he might be offered the job he had long dreamt of. A news photographer in an intensely and globally covered war for one of the world's biggest news organizations. Lady luck has finally smiled at him, or soon she might. But he often wondered whether Hassan really approved of him working for the Americans. Every time he mentioned it to him, Hassan looked less than pleased. He never really raised any objections, but his silence spoke volumes about how he felt about one of his closest friends abandoning the cause and pursuing a journalistic career, with the Americans no less.

It was too much for Hassan to take or explain to fellow jihadists in the city. But Hassan knew better than to try to talk him out of it. He knew of Omar's passion for photography, and he also knew of his aspirations to get out of the small and suffocating world that is Fallujah and begin a life in a much bigger city, a different country, anywhere really where life was a little less ordinary than here.

Omar waited a few minutes while Sinan and Mohammed disappeared in Fallujah's rag-tag market that was packed with shoppers with cars and motorbikes weaving their way through them. When he was certain they were gone, he switched off the generator, took it inside the shop and pulled down the shutters. He hurried off to Hassan's house.

The jihadist greeted him with a smile when he told him what had happened.

"So, is that it? Your mind is made up? I am happy for you, really, but I am also worried about you. Working for the Americans? You could not just land a job with, say, the Germans or the French?" Hassan said as the two squatted on cushions placed on the tiled floor.

"I cannot quite put my finger on it, but there is something very worrying about what you are about to do. It does not feel right, you know. But let us see. I will be praying for you, Omar, you're like a brother to me and you know that. I just wish …" Hassan paused as Safiyah walked in with tea for her husband and his guest. She knew Omar through Hassan, but never spoke to him or even looked him straight in the eye. She wore a loose and flowing black *abaya*, or robe, and a niqab, with only her eyes showing.

"*Salamu aleikoum!*" she said in a barely audible voice, attempting not to make eye contact with either her husband or Omar.

Hassan was startled, and a little annoyed, at Safiyah's surprise incursion into the guest room. For the wife of an emir of a militant Islamic group to enter a room where an "unrelated" man was present was taboo among jihadists. But that was Safiyah's work. It was a small but symbolically significant victory by the beautiful Fallujah woman, after all the endless hours of discussions with her husband who, astonishingly for a man of his religious piety and militant convictions, listened patiently to his wife, although he still felt a deep disappointment, even anger, over what he saw as her lack of total submission to him and his convictions. Safiyah refused to embrace the conduct and appearance expected from the emir's wife or even of any regular jihadist for that matter. She refused to wear the "armor," a heavy coat worn on top of the abaya and which completely concealed all bodily curves, unlike the *abayas* that could expose a woman's figure with the slightest breath of wind. She argued that the armor was unnecessary and might even encourage curious and religiously weak men to stare longer and imagine more intensely what might be underneath.

Hassan never completely accepted that argument but, like on so many other issues, he let her believe that she prevailed, for the sake of his own peace of mind. It was not because he approved of her views or that he was surprisingly tolerant for a man whose job was to show utter ruthlessness and oversee the occasional cold blooded murder. He humored her because he knew that if he did not, he was likely to lose access to her beautiful body, soft skin and the lust in her brown eyes when she desired him. There were times when she had denied him the passion he craved in bed, and just went through the motions while wearing a stony face and staring at the ceiling while he thrashed on top of her. She did that to punish him for being too rough in bed or insisting on having sex when she did not feel like it or was simply too exhausted.

Sometimes, though, Safiyah was just not in the mood for sex, or for anything else for that matter, because she was burdened by a deeply felt pointlessness over her life as the wife of a jihadist. At such times, she felt Hassan would not be around for much longer, given the dangerous path he had chosen. She almost felt like he was not worth investing in as a lifelong partner. She was never really comfortable with being tied down to a man whose life was so immersed in blood and violence. She had not always felt like that, certainly not during the early days of their marriage when they were magically bound by love and desire. But Hassan was not a jihadist then. He was just another Fallujah man whose secure and uneventful life hit a dead end at age twenty-five.

"*Allah kareem!*" – God is generous – Hassan would tell his wife every time he wanted one of their discussions to quickly end.

"Allah is indeed generous, so why cannot we humans seek to emulate his generosity when dealing with each other," she would respond.

On hearing her talk like that, he would lustfully smile and bring her close for a hug. But the smile would disappear once his head was rested on her right shoulder where she could not see his face. Replacing the smile was the haunted look of a man uncertain of what he was doing.

Angst; and the burden of having to keep so much to himself.

Hassan, too, had his demons.

His brand of love for Safiyah knew no bounds, but he often felt of late that the flame of their desire-filled love for each other had somewhat weakened by the tribulations that befell their hometown or the tempestuous nature of their relationship. What never changed though for him was the passion she showed him in bed when she chose to. During those times, she would whisper sweet nothings in his ear when she lied on top of him. She would loudly groan. But somehow, he felt but would not acknowledge that her passion was mostly to please herself not him. At times he felt she was fantasizing about another man while making love to him. The thought worried him; kept him up at night sometimes.

He deeply relished the passion and commitment of their sex, but he also began to sense that something was slipping away from their relationship. It started shortly after the American invasion when he decided to join the jihad against the occupation. He often caught glimpses of Safiyah's disapproval or unhappiness over the path he chose. In principle, she did not feel too strongly against fighting the Americans, but she felt uneasy, even resentful, about the horrific attacks by the jihadists against civilians or the execution of suspected spies or anyone who worked for the Americans. She often imagined fresh red blood dripping off her husband's hands when he came home. She had nightmares about him getting killed or captured. What was worse, however, were the visions she had of her husband killing another Iraqi, forcing him to kneel down before putting a bullet in the back of his head.

Divorce was out of the question, she knew that only too well. But that also left her with the most guilt-laden of wishes: That Hassan would be killed and she would be a widow free to make a more learned choice of a husband.

"Do you, really?" Hassan would earnestly ask Safiyah when she whispered in his ear how much she loved him while making love. He genuinely feared that Safiyah could see the inside of his soul. That terrified him. "What if she can?" he often asked himself, assuming, out of love, that his wife was so good and pure she could see through him. She did, but he did not know that because she hid it well.

Safiyah, in many ways, unwittingly provided him with a sort of a moral campus that vastly influenced his thinking but, curiously, not his decisions or actions. But beneath her compassion and love for her husband there was always that discomfort about what he did as the emir of the jihadists in Fallujah. Sometimes, she would stop what she was doing to watch him while speaking on the phone, barking out orders and showing a side of him that she was never on its receiving end. She felt Hassan could be heartless or even incredibly cruel at times. But she often pushed those thoughts aside and just went on with her life. But the thought of her husband taking lives or cutting off people's limbs made her heart heavy. His good temperament when with her and his care and love for her helped her ignore these nagging doubts about the true nature of her husband, but never for long. The doubts, fear in fact, always came back to haunt her.

In reality, her love brought out the best version of him, but that was something only she and maybe members of his immediate family experienced. And it was never enough. There was little or no sign of that when it came to his handling of the affairs of Fallujah, his group or the impending fight against the Americans and their Iraqi allies.

In their discussions, he and Safiyah firmly believed in the right of Iraqis to defend their country against a foreign occupier, America, by all and any means available. The aim was to drive them out. They both also believed that with an Iraqi government beholden to its American masters, the jihadists had to take the law into their own hands and produce a penal code of their own that, naturally, reflected the harshest interpretation of Sharia and included little recourse to appeal or a more thorough examination of the cases before meting out justice.

But she seemed to agree with him on these broad questions while under his influence. Hassan had a commanding personality. He easily steered Safiyah to his viewpoint, but she bounced back to her own convictions soon after Hassan was gone or the conversation ended. She had a mind of her own. In some ways, she seemed to accept Hassan, even love him, largely because in the narrow and limited world of Fallujah he's entitled to that. But the world of her own mind was much larger, more diverse and offered choices. Hassan did not qualify for that world she created in her own mind. He is too Fallujah, so to speak. He learned little at the university and what he learned was never put into use, either because the material he learned was mostly outdated or because he was never devoted to or believed in the job he landed after he graduated. He chose religion as his refuge, his mission in life and, accordingly, spent endless hours reading more and more books on Islamic teachings, the sayings of the Prophet and jurisprudence. Why did he do that? Possibly because it was a sure way for an ordinary man like him to distinguish himself in Fallujah's society; an easy path to local prominence. All he had to do was to read as much as he could and then sound authoritative when repeating things he's learned. In Safiyah's innermost mind, he was a man exactly like millions of other Iraqi men who shied away from challenges, any challenges, at a time when everyone lived in fear and selected to live quietly on the sidelines lest they unwittingly step into the brutal world that Saddam had set aside for those who dare dissent.

"So many wars, so many. When this one is over, we will not be the same people again," Safiyah told her husband once. "The war is eroding our generosity and compassion for one another. It's driving the best Iraqis out the country and is allowing the thieves to operate freely. Oh, how I wish we could leave and start over elsewhere. Maybe Syria or Jordan. I want you safely next me, so we can have children we can raise at a safe place," she said.

"If we all leave, there will be no Iraq left. Iraq will be finished," Hassan responded awkwardly. He always felt awkward when Safiyah brought up the subject of children. He knew it was on him that they did not have any. But he would not seek treatment, ostensibly because he believed that if God willed it, they will have children. No doctor could do anything unless God willed it. But a big part of his resistance to the idea of seeking treatment was his vanity. Hassan was a good looking man with an impressive physique. He was fully aware of that and chose to ignore the simple fact that good looks have nothing to do with the ability to impregnate Safiyah, or any other woman for that matter. Such was the extent of his ignorance.

"Haji, it's not like I am joining the American army," Omar told Hassan. "I will just be taking photos for an American news organization and I will not be joining the staff either. They will most likely dispose of me once there is no news out of Fallujah. So, please don't take this as something like treason or betrayal. It's a good step for me. We cannot all be jihadists, every man has his calling and I am trying to make news photography mine."

"I understand all that, Omar, I really do, but that does not make me worry less. The Americans will be watching you and they will probably try and track you down if they see unflattering photos of their troops or positive ones of us. Don't believe all the propaganda about American freedoms and rights. This is Iraq, not America!"

"I have thought about all this and I am aware of the possible dangers. But I want to take that risk and see. It might be the start of something good for me. Anyways, I will go to Baghdad today and meet them and see what they say. I will spend the night with relatives and return to Fallujah tomorrow. Don't start a war while I am gone. I need to be home with my mother and brothers when that happens and I want to be here to shoot it," Omar said, attempting a light-hearted joke, as he reached for the teapot brought by Safiyah and poured the tea into the two tiny, gold-rimmed glasses.

"Now, tell me about the Egyptian."

"Brother, he did it. He confessed in the end. He began by denying that he even went near the house, then he went on about how much he hates the Americans and loves Fallujah and its mujahideen. I listened patiently and silently. I did not interrupt him when he told me a long story about how he came to live in the city and met his wife. He would say things like 'I'm as Iraqi as anyone else here' and 'what concern you, concern me.' I kept a blank face so I would not betray what I was thinking. He kept on looking hard at me hoping to read my mind. He could not. I could see confusion on his face and maybe even panic. When he was done and had no more to tell me, I quietly told him that the video clip we have cannot lie and that it shows him clearly climbing on a water pipe to get to the roof. That alone threw him off. He realized he'd been caught lying. Then I ended the conversation telling him that our men in the American base near Fallujah overheard their officers speak with their translators about what he did. I promised him clemency if he confessed. He broke down and begged for forgiveness. I just left. Did you get the recording of the interrogation?

"Yes, I did but did not want to listen to it until I heard from you first. So, it's done by God's will. He will get what he deserves. He can only blame himself."

***

The Egyptian reporter took the back seat and let Omar sit next to Sinan, who was at the wheel of his battered blue Toyota. It was late afternoon by the time the two picked Omar up from outside his shop.

The pair first had had lunch at the city's famous kebab restaurant, Haji Hussein, where they ate copious amounts of meat, rice and vegetables cooked in tomato sauce. Since journalists began eating there in mid-2003, Haji Hussein's clientele had become very diverse. The restaurant attracted laborers, shopkeepers, artisans and small businessmen. Local Jihadists, distinguished by their attire, beards and walkie-talkies, were the latest addition to the restaurant's list of patrons. They said little to each other and left immediately after they were done eating. Mostly born and raised in Fallujah, these jihadists seem to have a knack for spotting outsiders from a mile away. The Egyptian reporter often recounted with concern that he received inquisitive looks from them every time he walked into the restaurant of late. Those looks were often followed by frowns of disapproval or suspicion. The Egyptian looked like any Iraqi, but maybe something about how he carried himself or how he dressed nevertheless aroused their suspicions. But he had often received inquisitive looks from the regular folks in Fallujah at Haji Hussein's way before the city became "Jihad Central." The city was deeply tribal and its residents, about 300,000, were a closely-knit community.

The three left the city without problems or delays. All they needed, it seemed, was for Omar to greet the jihadists manning checkpoints on the city's fringes and they would return the greeting and signal for them to move on. It was a fifty kilometer ride to Baghdad that normally took anywhere between one hour and ninety minutes given the delays at checkpoints outside Baghdad, and the frequency of slow-moving American military convoys that civilian cars needed to pull over on the hard shoulder for, waiting until they passed and keep a safe distance between them. Not to do so could easily cost Iraqis their lives.

The reporter was in a kind of a daze in the back seat from the huge meal they had eaten but he did not really fall asleep. How could he sleep with Omar and Sinan chatting non-stop, swapping information about relatives, fellow clansmen and life in Anbar under American occupation? Sinan was a proud Anbari but, unlike Omar, did not know a great deal about the vast province's clans and their ties to one another. Omar did, and he politely shot down every assumption made by Sinan about the strengths and weaknesses of various clans. With the conversation deadlocked by Sinan's ignorance about the tribal network in Anbar, he sheepishly moved to another topic: the Jihadists in Fallujah.

"So, what's it like in Fallujah under the rule of the Shura Council?"

Omar initially paused as if he did not wish to discuss the subject, not with an outsider in the back seat. But Sinan's silence left him no choice but to attempt an answer of sorts.

"The Americans have no right to be in Iraq," he began with a quiet voice that slowly gave way to an assertive tone, one suggesting a man of strong convictions. "They say they are here to free us from Saddam's dictatorship, but that's just a lie. Last year, I was with a friend in his car heading to Ramadi to pick up some stuff for my shop. We were stopped by the Americans a short distance outside Fallujah. Our papers were in order and the license of my friend's car was also valid. But they asked us to park the car on the side of the road and get out. They kept us for two hours squatting on the asphalt. They would look at us and laugh like we were monkeys in a zoo. There were about fifteen of us in total and we did not know why we were being detained, but it did not matter to them. Every time we told their Iraqi interpreter to ask them why we were being detained, the soldiers screamed at us and then just laughed. Even the way it ended was humiliating. They just got into their cars and drove away. They did not bother to tell us that we were free to go. They just left. Do you think there was any purpose for our detention other than to humiliate us? And that's just one example of what they do to us here. At nighttime, they raid homes on the strength of baseless information provided by their spies. In some cases, they beat the men in front of their wives and children. They turn homes upside down or kick house doors off their hinges. Our women don't have time to cover their hair or make themselves decent. Let me tell you, the Americans are turning many young men into mujahedeen because of what they do here. The mujahedeen are good Muslims, just like everyone else in Fallujah. History will judge them and it won't say they are terrorists like the Americans and their Iraqi allies say, but as patriotic and pious fighters who defended our homes and our honor. Allah is on their side. Do you doubt that?"

Sinan said nothing, so Omar went on.

"But I am not part of this jihad, not because I am opposed to it or have even the smallest reservation about it. My jihad, if you can call it that, lies elsewhere. I am hoping that if I land a job with that American organization you work for, I will be able to document the crimes of the Americans in Fallujah. It sounds like a lofty goal, but I think I can do it and I think it can be done. In the meantime, if my brothers in Fallujah ever call on me for help, I will do what I can to help them, but I am not going to fight. I sometimes interrogate prisoners for them, because they think I am calm and I quote the Quran and *hadeeth* less while asking questions," he said with a hearty laugh, appearing to think nothing of what he had just shared.

"May God be with you, but it will be unwise to share your thoughts on the Americans with the man who will interview you in Baghdad or say anything about helping the jihadists," Sinan said. "He's from Croatia, not America, but he has been working for the Americans for twenty years or more, so he might have become a little like them. They are all westerners, anyway. But other people in the office say the Croatian never supported the invasion. But just be careful what you tell him. You don't want to give him the impression that you support jihadists in any way or that you're zealously anti-American."

"I won't. I was just sharing with you my thoughts on what's happening in Fallujah because you are one of us," he told Sinan. He turned and spoke to the Egyptian in the back seat. "And you, what do you think of what's going on in Iraq?"

"It's a very big question and I am not sure I have a good answer to it," he said in a reserved voice, faking wisdom but in fact wishing that he had never been asked. He hated loaded questions like that.

"Things are not clear. Nothing is in black and white. The Americans have toppled a dictator, but they are considered by many in Iraq as invaders. The jihadists are seen as terrorists but, like you said, many see them as freedom fighters. The Shiites are a majority but the Sunni Arabs don't want to acknowledge that. They are a majority, I think, but after decades of repression, discrimination and exclusion they may not be ready to govern, but then who can say? Can you realistically expect them to step aside and allow the Sunnis to rule until they learn how to govern? Of course, not. I just don't know, but it breaks my heart to see thousands of innocent Iraqis caught in the crossfire and paying with their lives in a fight they did not start."

At this point, the Egyptian felt that he had said plenty and it was time to resort to some humor, if you can call it that, to ease his way out of a serious conversation.

"I can talk to you for a long time about Iraq's oil wealth and how it's squandered by politicians on fake or useless projects or stolen by con artists. One thing I know, though, I would be a very rich man now if I could land a contract to supply the Americans with anything they need here in Iraq or maybe if I have a factory that makes concrete blast barriers. Honestly, I am in the wrong profession at the wrong time here in Iraq. This is my bottom line. I want to get comfortable, not rich, just comfortable. The sad thing is that I won't be able to ever do that as a reporter. But Allah is generous."

It was almost dark when the car pulled over at the house on Abu Nawas street. The Egyptian reporter did not share what Omar had said in the car with anyone. Not that day, anyway. Maybe he was still processing the information, and his own thoughts on the Americans.

He did not know at the time, but what he had heard from Omar during the journey would one day be discussed at great length with two hot-shot New York lawyers who charged $400 dollars an hour for their clients in the States, and maybe four times that much in Baghdad.

CHAPTER SIX

Omar threw himself into his new job and relished every minute of it. He woke at sunrise every day to take advantage of the light that time of day, before the blazing sun flattened everything. His "everyday life" photos from Fallujah caught the eye of the agency's editors and were curated by some of the major news sites around the world in photo essays that received tens of thousands of views. He shot a lot, but only a handful would make the cut. Antonio was a tough editor who would never put out just any image. He rarely made any exceptions, not even for Omar's work from a besieged city that was capturing more attention every day in the United States, as everyone waited for the looming battle to break out any day.

"It is not enough that you are alone in Fallujah," Antonio would tell Omar on the phone through Fahd the interpreter in the Baghdad office. "You need to focus on quality. You cannot have me look at 100 frames every day and I end up using just five or six. They are focused and the light is good, but I need photos that speak to Fallujah's unique situation. Photos that tell a story."

The criticism did not anger or disappoint Omar, but he never fully grasped what exactly it was that Antonio wanted from him. However, his photos were slowly improving and Antonio was using more of them.

Knowing that the battle for Fallujah was imminent – the U.S. military had already asked the major news organizations in Baghdad to send the names and details of journalists who would be covering the battle -- Antonio was also coaching Omar on what to do when the fighting began.

"Your safety is the number one priority," he told him repeatedly. "By that I don't just mean keeping a safe distance from the frontlines, but also to not be visible at all to the Americans, making sure that you strike a balance between photographing the jihadists and not giving the impression in any way that you are associated with them. Civilians are important. We need bread lines while the fighting is going on. We need families gathered at home around candles when the power is out, or people frantically trying to get a signal on their mobile phones so they can speak to family and friends outside the city."

The more Antonio spoke of the upcoming battle the more concerned Omar became. It was a huge test for him as a news photographer, and one that might be coming way too soon. "I wish they would give me a few months before they start fighting," he thought "I want to be ready for that."

Antonio himself was under a great deal of pressure over the coverage of the upcoming battle. Two photographers, both Europeans, were accredited to cover the battle and would be embedded with the U.S. Marines.

"They are both excellent photographers. They are experienced and the quality of their work is very high. But unless Omar comes through for us, we run the risk of covering the war from the American side alone," Antonio told Samuel one evening over a cold Turkish beer in his office. "He has been good for us since he joined. His work is slowly improving and he understands better now what we need, although I feel that most of what I tell him through Fahd does not get through to him because the translation is bad or the ideas are too complex. Still, he is doing better, already."

"He needs to keep his head down when the bang-bang begins," Samuel told him. "We can't lose another one. We already lost three

Iraqi freelancers. That's three too many in less than two years. These things rile the bosses in New York, who just don't get it. They have no idea what it's like here for Iraqis who work for us. All three were killed execution-style when the militants found out that they worked for us. Believe me, I have spent hours trying to familiarize them with what's going on in here, but they still don't get it. In some ways I can't blame them. This war is nothing like other conflicts I covered. It's just way too evil and way too complicated."

"I know boss! I have been telling him to stay safe every day."

"His press card won't save him from the Americans if they spot him near their lines. In battle, they'll shoot first and ask questions later. They always do. The rules of engagement during battle put civilians in harm's way even when it's clear they are non-combatants. Just try to explain that to him in case he's one of those wannabe heroes I always feel sorry for. I really don't need to deal with more shit than I already have to. I barely have the time or energy to write the news. God almighty, this war is taking a toll on me and I'm not even fighting in it."

"We're all tired," said Antonio. "My average day is twelve hours on the desk editing shit and then shoveling it out. Been here for two months and I am fried. I don't get more than five hours of sleep every night and most of my photographers can't stitch together a simple sentence in English, let alone write it; and Fahd's English is not much better than theirs. I am spending a lot of time trying to coach photographers but I have a feeling only about ten percent is getting through to them, thanks to Fahd's terrible translation. But I cannot fire him and get someone else. He's got four kids and a sick wife. How can I?"

"Listen, let's not rock the boat now. We're going to have a hell of a big story once the Americans move in to retake Fallujah. It's going to be the defining battle of this war. Fire him if you still want to do that after things calm down. Don't worry about his wife and kids. They can survive on his government pension. It'll be tight but they won't go hungry. This is a business and we must remember that. We need to save where we can and need to make sure we are getting good value for our money. But, tell me, this guy in Fallujah, what's he like?"

"He's alright, I guess, but some of his photos make me a little nervous. Maybe even worried. They suggest that maybe he's too close to the bad guys."

"FUCK!" screamed Samuel.

"I know! There were some frames showing the bad guys praying in what looks like a home. They had their backs to the camera; and then there was that other one that showed another bunch sitting on the floor eating from a large dish of rice and meat. Only last night, he filed one of three jihadists in what looked like a foxhole on the edge of the city. It was taken at night. A beautiful frame, the three were looking at their mobile phones with the glare from the screens reflected on their faces. But it made me wonder: How can it be, given it is Fallujah, that he felt safe enough to go to the frontlines at night?"

"What do you think is going on?"

"I don't know, Samuel. It's another world out there in Fallujah and we don't understand even one bit of it. He is a homegrown boy and must be friends or a relative of some of the bad guys, if not many of them. To him, they may not be the bad guys we take them to be. It's difficult to say what is going on. The access is too tempting and it's producing results. Seems like his main concern is to get us photos that no one else can get, which is true, but without thinking of the consequences for him and us if we show the world the extraordinary access he enjoys. I have put out some of those daily life images of the jihadists and they got some very good play. One or two made it to the front page of the Times, so I can't really complain. The guy's photos are not technically great, but the stunning access they show more than makes up for that. What do you think I should do?"

"Don't put out too many of these. Maybe one or two a day. Use your own judgment. If you feel that some of the frames betray an unacceptable level of familiarity, kill them or just archive them. If in doubt, come to me. I'll be happy to look at them. We need to tread very carefully. The military is already on our case about a couple of stories we put out and the generals are challenging them. I am getting a call or two from the military every day. They are very persistent. I could use a break from all this shit so I can focus on reporting and writing the damn news," said Samuel, taking one last sip of his Turkish beer, which he drank straight from the can. He spat out the nicotine gum in his hand and placed it in the ashtray on Antonio's desk as he got up.

"Alright, Samuel. Let's hope this doesn't come back and bite us in the ass. I really want this battle to start and be over so I can go home and see my kid," Antonio said, trying to reassure the boss.

"You will. We will pull through this in the end. Just hang in there," said Samuel as he walked back to his office across the foyer. "God have mercy!" he yelled in desperation just before he disappeared into his office next to the small newsroom.

CHAPTER SEVEN

Safiyah had just finished making dinner when Hassan came home.

"*Al Salamu Aleikom*" he said in that deep, sweet voice that had earned him the admiration of many in Fallujah when he recited the Quran or sang the call for the dawn prayers. He rarely missed the dawn prayers at the Al Fateh mosque near his home. Often, the mosque's imam would wait until he came to ask him to sing the call for prayers, a request that Hassan never refused. In fact, he took pleasure in obliging.

"Your voice is so sweet and pious that I believe it gets men, women and children out of bed to pray. May Allah bless you, Hassan. People used to think that I had a good voice until they heard you make the call for prayers for the first time, remember? You were sixteen or maybe seventeen. They will have to do with my voice for the day's four other prayers, but for the dawn prayers, when the faithful need to arise and fight the temptation to stay in bed, they need a voice like yours," said Sheikh Abdullah.

Hassan's sweet voice was something that did not escape Safiyah's attention either. He routinely led her in prayers at home from early on in their marriage and he would recite from the Quran in a voice that sent a shiver down her spine and filled her heart with joy. She cherished the times when he was her "imam" in prayers at home. It was not often that he did that because his preference, and maybe duty, was to offer the prayers at the mosque. But the afternoon prayers on Friday were often performed at home and that's a time when she passionately washed and got ready to pray, knowing that she was in for a vocal treat. Often, that was also the time when she approached him after the prayers, throwing her hands around his neck and arousing him with gentle and slow kisses on his neck and cheeks. It was never more than a minute or two before their lips met and they kissed like they had never kissed before. At times, he would carry her to their bed. More often, he would hold her left hand and walk ahead of her slowly but deliberately, pulling her gently forward.

They have had fewer lovemaking sessions since Hassan took over the leadership of the jihadists in Fallujah. There was so much to do and little time to do it. There was the defense of the city to worry about, the collection and distribution of alms, ensuring that both men and women observed the strict dress code in public and monitoring prices in the city's steadily shrinking food markets. He also invested many hours and much effort trying to lift the morale of the jihadists. Footage shown by regional television networks of the arrival of American troop reinforcements was unnerving for some of them. Some even publicly questioned whether it was religiously acceptable for the jihadists to enter a battle they were virtually sure to lose.

"Would it not be better to save our resources for a battle we can win," was a commonly asked question by a small minority of jihadists.

Hassan has instructed loyal imams to focus the Friday sermons and the evening lessons at mosques on how a small number of the faithful won the first battle fought by early Muslims against infidels in seventh century Arabia.

"Talk to them about the angels that would come to the aid of the faithful. Tell them God will side with the faithful against the American infidels who invaded our country and forced their way into our homes," Hassan told a group of imams he summoned to one of the houses he has been moving in and out of to deny spies the chance to have him targeted in an airstrike.

This afternoon, Hassan's voice was exceptionally sweet although he would only say *"Allahu akbar"* out loud as it's customary for the afternoon prayers. But even that came out melodiously and heart-warming. For her, it was a turn-on, but not of the sexual kind. It was a spiritual sort of turn-on, one that smoothly morphed from the spiritual into a burning physical desire soon after the prayers ended.

Their lovemaking that afternoon was explosive. It was about 30 minutes or so before they climaxed, with both gently whispering groans in each other's ears as Safiyah, on top, gently moved forward and backward with Hassan's arms firmly wrapped around her lower back.

Hassan, as has been his custom, went quiet after. He would not say a word or show any affection. He felt a subtle kind of guilt that he enjoyed sex so much with his wife. Part of him saw it as a weakness. Too much worldly pleasure. He enjoyed Safiyah's pursuit of maximum enjoyment in bed. He also liked her trying to pleasure him, but he did not feel right about all this. He felt that having dirty and hot sex was not befitting a man of his position. After all, he was a jihadist who's asking his followers to forsake all worldly pleasures and seek martyrdom instead. And what about Safiyah? Where and how did she learn all that she was doing in bed? Should she be enjoying sex so much? Is that a weakness? What if he was away from home for a month or two, would she succumb to her thirst for sex and sleep with another man?

CHAPTER EIGHT

Omar got up before dawn, washed and read a little from the Quran before he prayed. He left home when it was still dark, got on the second-hand scooter he bought from a friend who left for Baghdad two weeks earlier to escape what everyone thought to be an imminent battle. Omar decided he needed a practical and economic mode of transport to travel around the city. His friend sold it to him for a fraction of its value, but he was glad to offload it for a reasonable amount of money given the circumstances.

It was a cold morning and Omar was wearing a black jacket he bought from Baghdad's famous Shorjah market. Second hand and smelling like a dirty wet blanket, he had to hang it on the laundry line in the backyard of the house for days to get rid of the smell.

His cameras were packed into a bag with a long shoulder strap. His destination, as was the case on previous days, was the jihadists' frontline positions facing the Americans. Photos from there scored big, he was told by Antonio. The frontline was teeming with foreign fighters. They had mortars, heavy machineguns, RPGs and rifles. Snipers were on nearby roofs and the stretch of desert in front of them was heavily mined. Many of the commanders wore Afghan tunics and baggy pants, carried binoculars and had Ak-47s strapped on their shoulders with two belts of ammunition and spare magazines. The atmosphere there was tense, especially at dawn since the commanders expected the

Americans to attack at first light. The fighters were sternly told to stay awake and that no change of guard at the frontline positions should be made until well after sunrise.

The local fighters warmly welcomed Omar when he showed up just as the sun was coming up. There were always hugs and kisses and sincere invitations for him to share their breakfast or have a glass of tea. Omar always politely declined. He knew by now that the perfect early morning light does not last long enough for him to waste time eating or chatting over tea.

"Omar, what are you doing with all these photos? By God, we will all end up in Guantanamo because of you?" one of the mujahedeen told him, drawing hearty laughs from a group of men that surrounded Omar that morning. They celebrated Omar's arrival every morning. He was a familiar face by now. A friendly one. His popularity among men his age in Fallujah was phenomenal. His football skills, shown for years on the city's empty land plots, earned him the admiration of his peers in a city that, like elsewhere in Iraq, was football mad. He scored with near impunity in those Friday afternoons when they played six-a-side. He stopped playing after he finished school and started working, but his legacy as a virtuoso endured long after he hung up his boots.

That popularity and the respect that came with it served him well in his new job as a news photographer. But he could not share with anyone who he really worked for. Only Hassan knew. He did not even tell his mother or his brothers. "I work for a photo agency in Germany," was his standard response. His selection of Germany was deliberate, not random. That country was not part of the U.S.-led coalition that invaded Iraq in 2003.

But the foreign fighters, especially the Arabs among them, were never comfortable with Omar shooting with his camera in their midst. Making them particularly irritated was the times when Omar went into a burst mode that made the camera's lens produce a noise akin to distant gunfire.

"Don't point that thing at me!" a burly and dark-skinned Saudi in his mid-40s once yelled at him.

"I don't know what others think, but if it was up to me, I would ban you from coming here. But I guess our Iraqi brothers know best. Still, there is something not right about you coming here and taking photos. What if the Americans see your photos? What if they get published in newspapers? We will be arrested and thrown in jail the minute we return to our homes."

"By God, you have nothing to worry about, our sheikh," Omar told the Saudi, Abu Soheib, trying to reassure him. "I will never deliberately harm you. You're a dear brother and we are glad you are here with us to fight the Americans."

"It's too much for me and my brothers here to do our jihad duty and worry at the same time about what awaits us at home if we survive this next battle," said Abu Soheib, who managed to wear a hint of a smile on his rugged face, which has a graying beard long enough it touches his chest.

"I am not complaining, thanks be to God for everything, but we are here for jihad for the Almighty's sake after we sacrificed our jobs and homes and left our families behind. I don't fear death. I seek martyrdom like every brother here, but that does not mean I am not afraid. I am. This battle will be the mother of all battles. If God has martyrdom written for me in his book, then I hope it's a quick and merciful death."

Omar was moved by the Saudi's words. His eyes welled up and he looked away from the man who just bared his heart to him so that he could privately regain his composure. He turned back to look at Abu Soheib only when he was sure the embarrassment of being seen crying has been avoided. But he could not see him. Instead he felt the Saudi man's arms locked around him.

"There is no God but God, and Mohammed is his prophet," Abu Soheib whispered in Omar's ears. "Fear not, brother Omar. We will be in heaven, and they will burn in hell."

"*Allahu Akbar!*" yelled Omar. Abu Soheib and some half dozen jihadists standing nearby joined in and they all chanted in unison at the top of their voice. They grinned as they chanted, as if they were celebrating a battle already won. They had barely stopped when they could hear others at a distance chanting *Allahu Akbar*. It sounded more like a plea for divine assistance delivered light-heartedly and with so much hope.

Omar took a few more shots before he got on his scooter and rode home. His mother and brothers were still sleeping, so he quietly went into the kitchen and made himself a pot of tea which he took to the living room along with a glass bowl of sugar, a tea spoon and one of those tiny, gold-rimmed glasses. His laptop awaited him in the living room, sitting on a table in the middle. Next to the laptop was a half dozen cheap china and glass bowls filled with plastic flowers coated in dust. He pushed the bowls to one side of the table, poured himself some tea, added sugar, stirred noisily and took one large and noisy sip before he reached for a brown velvet cushion, placed it on his lap and grabbed the laptop and sat it on his thighs.

Three hours went by before he finished filing his photos. A total of 25. He did not caption any of them, but Fahd, the interpreter in Baghdad, came on the company's in-house chat and asked Omar many questions about the photos. Omar was always patient when fielding questions from the interpreter, a retired army colonel pensioned off after Saddam's fall because of his track record as an active member of the now-outlawed and dissolved Baath party. Some of the questions were downright silly or totally unnecessary. Some appeared to assume that Omar was stupid or did not know what he was doing. He was new and had little knowledge of the finer aspects of news photography, but his access in Fallujah and a fair dose of beginners' luck made him the envy of every news photographer in Iraq.

"Was this today?" the interpreter asked, repeating a question he had already asked twice. "Do we know the real names of these foreign fighters?"

"They never say and even the Iraqi mujahedeen don't know their names" Omar calmly answered.

It was time for the noon prayers when Omar was done. He went out to a tiny mosque near his home. The number of worshippers praying there has been steadily diminishing as more and more people left

Fallujah in recent weeks. Today, the worshippers were barely enough to form two lines behind the imam.

There was not much to eat for lunch when he returned home. Not because Omar was not making enough from his new job to buy food. There was less and less food to buy in the market as the siege of the city became tighter in what was the final countdown to the battle. Most bakeries were closed, too. Long lines formed at all hours of day and night outside the handful that remained open. The bread was informally rationed to prevent hoarding and for everyone to have some.

For lunch that day, Omar had white cheese that was a little stale, two tomatoes and two boiled eggs. The bread his mother served him was about half the amount he would normally eat.

The family was also fast running out of diesel for the small generator that provides them with just enough power to operate the light bulbs and the small television in the living room. Omar spent his evenings watching Iraq coverage on Al Jazeera and Al Hurra Iraq as they slowly munched on greasy potato crisps that Omar secured two large bags of from a grocery store two days earlier. They washed them down with tea, which Omar's mother brewed with cardamom to give it that much more aroma. She made two pots that evening, perhaps knowing that no one would be going to bed early. Curiously, they watched the news in near total silence. No one said much and the little that was said was not related to the news they watched on television. They probably thought whatever they had to say would be an unwanted distraction and might even deepen the anxiety and fear their heads and hearts were filled with.

Everyone was startled when Omar's satellite phone rang. It was around 10 pm. He picked the phone up and headed to the front yard to get a better signal.

"It will most likely happen at dawn or shortly before that," said Fahd, the interpreter, relaying a message from Antonio in Baghdad.

"You know what to do, right? Keep your head down. Don't take any risks and for God's sake, keep well away from the Americans. Your safety is the most important thing, but please find a way of taking good photos. Keep your satellite phone fully charged at all times and keep it along with your laptop on you all the time."

"How do we know it's going to happen tonight or at dawn?"

"Never mind that. It is going to happen, that's all."

"Ok!" said Omar before he hung up.

With his head lowered, he stood there silently leaning on the wall next to the house door. So many thoughts rushed through his head. What would become of his mother and two brothers? Was he too wrapped up in his new job that he had overlooked arranging for them to leave Fallujah and go somewhere safer in Anbar? And how was he to take photos when the fighting begins? He had not done that before. He covered the aftermath of airstrikes or skirmishes on the outskirts of the city, but a full-fledged battle?

Then a more pressing question leapt to his mind: Should he tell Hassan that the Americans were to launch an all-out attack to retake the city in the next few hours? He could save lives if he did. After all, weren't the mujahedeen mostly friends and relatives? What would they think of him if they ever found out that he knew the time of the attack and did not share the information? Could he cold bloodedly betray the pious and kind men who had been sitting in those trenches on the city's outskirts for weeks, enduring the bitter cold of the desert and not knowing whether they would survive the battle? What about Hassan? Could he keep his mouth shut and risk a lifetime of painful regret and shame if Hassan was killed? And what about Safiyah, could he turn her into a childless widow and live with himself in peace after that?

CHAPTER NINE

Hassan had just finished eating a late dinner with Safiyah and was drinking a large glass of sweet black tea when he heard a frantic knock on the door. The house was dark except for the living room where he and Safiyah had eaten, squatting on the floor with the food placed on a white plastic sheet. A single bulb powered by a car battery was the only source of light in the room.

It was Montaser the messenger boy at the door.

"*Salamu aleikom*, haji," he said as he fished a small piece of paper out of his pants' pocket and handed it over to Hassan.

Hassan unfolded the paper and glanced at it before carefully folding it again and placing it in the chest pocket of his tunic.

"Montaser, listen to me very carefully," he said as he bent down to face the boy. "I want you to head back home immediately and stay there. Stay in the house with your family. No more messages for you to deliver around the city, you hear me? No matter what happens, don't leave your house ... Wait here for a second."

Hassan went back to his bedroom and came back with a red 50,000-dinar note.

"Take this. If the bakery near here is open and the line is short, buy some bread to take home and go to the grocery store after that and spend the rest of the money on whatever food you and your little brothers and sisters like. Don't spend it all on candy, you hear?"

"Thank you, haji!" said Montaser. Hassan bent down and pulled the boy close to give him a hug. Not accustomed to being shown any emotion from the mujahedeen, least of all the emir of the whole city, Montaser broke down in tears, something he had not done in a long time. Not crying was a big part of his obsessive struggle to look and behave older and tougher than his age.

"By God, I love you Haji, and by the will of God, you will be victorious."

"Go now, Montaser!"

Hassan watched Montaser as the boy made his way slowly to the street door. He opened the door and turned to look at Hassan again.

"*Salamu Aleikom*, haji," said Montaser, still sobbing, offering a faint smile and a half-committed wave.

Hassan waved back and murmured a short prayer, then stepped inside the house and closed the door behind him.

"What is it, Hassan?" shrieked Safiyah, her hands on her cheeks.

"Nothing for you to worry about. Everything is fine."

"Hassan, tell me. I know that something is going on. I need to know and you need to tell me."

"I am not one hundred percent certain and that's why I don't want to alarm you over nothing. When I am sure, I will tell you."

"No, Hassan, I need to know what you know now even if it's not certain. I beg you to tell me."

"Safiyah, this is not confirmed, but I just learned that the Americans might attack us at first light or earlier. And what I need to do now is not to debate this with you, but to do the million things I must do so that we are ready for them. There is very little time left, Safiyah, please understand."

Safiyah fell silent. She walked around the table in the middle of the room and went directly to Hassan with her arms stretched in front of her. She hugged him, gently at first. He wrapped his arms around her and squeezed. For a moment they felt like they were one, united by their love, their unfortunate circumstances and, now, the imminent danger.

"I love you!" she whispered, standing on her toes so her mouth was closer to his ear. She wanted to make sure that he had heard her. He did.

"I love you, too, Safiyah. More than you think," he said softly. "Will you forgive me and remember me kindly if I am martyred? That is what I need to know now."

"I cannot think of anything to forgive," she said, lying.

"You don't know everything, Safiyah."

"I can only judge by what I know."

That was another lie.

CHAPTER TEN

Samuel had returned to Baghdad from his Christmas break two days before. His travels over the holiday season were exhausting. He had flown to Amman, then London and on to Chicago where he picked a domestic flight to Raleigh, North Carolina, his ancestral home and the seat of his extended family. He left for New York on the 27th for meetings with top management to discuss Iraq and to perform a post-mortem on the coverage of the Fallujah battle, now generally viewed as the biggest and most defining moment of the Iraq war.

The bosses were happy with the coverage. They had special praise for the photos. They specifically mentioned the work of a French photographer who started an embed with the marines a few days before the battle began. A Greek photographer and a reporter also had embedded with the marines but were kept a safe distance away from the frontlines. The best of the Greek photographer's images showed wounded marines brought back to a field hospital before they were flown by helicopter to the main military hospital in the Green Zone in Baghdad.

"Not to take away anything from their work, but Omar's images from inside Fallujah made us stand apart from the rest. What access, eh?" said John, the global photo editor. "No one else had what he gave us. We need to think of giving him a bonus and set him up with a retainer. I have already discussed it with the folks in HR and finance and I think we can soon proceed."

"That's great!" said Samuel, although the idea of outside interference, even by senior editors in New York, in the affairs of his bureau made him fume. His idea of running the Baghdad operation was for him to have total control. That's not because he was a control freak - which he was of course – but because he firmly believed that the bureau could function efficiently only if he had that kind of control. The bosses in New York, even those who'd visited Baghdad once or twice since the war began, did not know anything of the complexities and the problems he had to deal with, day in and day out. In the course of one six-week stint, he would be dealing with kitchen issues, gasoline supply for the power generators, salaries for local staffers, money transfers, disagreements between the staff and ensuring good coverage of what essentially has been the world's biggest running story since 2003.

"Yeah, let's reward him for his excellent work and maybe offer him a retainer, too," Samuel said, grudgingly. "I will work out the details with Antonio when I'm back in Baghdad and he is back from his out," he added, trying to regain the initiative.

"That's good," said John with a sly smile. "Oh, I forgot to mention that a lieutenant-colonel from the Pentagon called our folks in Washington just before Christmas. He was a little unclear about his position at the Pentagon or what he really wanted, but he asked a few questions about Omar in Fallujah and how he came to work for us there. The staffer who received the call did not even know who Omar was, so he passed the call to the duty photo editor here in New York. He too did not know an awful lot about Omar either except that he had a handful of photos splashed on the front page of the Times before and during the battle. We didn't think much about it and I believe you were traveling the day the colonel called, so we just let it slide."

"That's fine, but I need to know about stuff like this when it happens," said Samuel, seizing the chance to reassert his authority.

"There is always something behind calls like these. Trust me, it's never good when the military calls to inquire about a journalist or a photographer in a war zone. We have had a series of run-ins with the military in Iraq over stories we ran. They can be a fucking nuisance. It's either they accuse us of not presenting the whole truth, like there is such a thing, or they have carefully gone over a story and found a small inaccuracy. We gave in once and had to issue an embarrassing correction the next day. God damn it! I know there will be trouble when I return to Baghdad. Let's hope it's nothing serious."

Later that afternoon, Samuel had a series of one-on-one meetings with the bosses when he made a point of expressing his disappointment over John's failure to immediately alert him to the Pentagon's inquiry.

"If I was traveling, he should have left a message on my mobile or shot me an email. I checked both during transfers when I had Wi-Fi. In today's world, no one is unreachable," he told them, deliberately exaggerating the problems John may have caused by not immediately letting him know about the Pentagon's call.

Samuel had not been himself since he returned to Baghdad from his latest out. The jet lag was brutal and his struggle to stay off smoking was making it much worse. He'd written nothing since his return, just spent his days catching up on admin work and editing routine stories. His wife of 35 years stayed in Chicago to visit relatives and was to later return to Amman, where they rented an apartment for her to stay in and use during Samuel's short breaks when they didn't fly home to North Carolina. She wanted to be as close as she could possibly be to Samuel, short of going to Iraq. She cared for Samuel more than anyone else, even more than their two children and four grandchildren. To Patricia, a petite lady who also came from Raleigh, Samuel was the love of her life. In fact, her only love. He was the quintessential "manly" man who combined knowledge, wisdom, success and good looks.

She'd recognized his rough edges from early on in their relationship, along with his bad temper and foul mouth, but she found ways and means of containing him when his worst version came to the fore.

Now, back in Baghdad, jet lagged, suffering the withdrawal symptoms bedeviling one-time heavy smokers when they quit and looking at another six-week stint in a war zone. Samuel was not a happy man.

The day was slow, news-wise, so Samuel went upstairs to his room after he ate lunch. He took off his shoes and lay down and was instantly asleep. He had been napping for 20 minutes when his phone rang. He opened his eyes and reached for his glasses on the bedside table. He clumsily put them on and looked at the phone's screen.

Unknown number.

"Hello, this is Samuel Kennedy," he barked.

"Samuel Kennedy, hi. Hope I am not calling at a bad time. This is Colonel James Mackenzie from legal in the coalition headquarters here in Baghdad. How're you doing, sir?"

"I am good, thank you, colonel."

"Well, I am gonna try and make this short and to the point. There has been, let us say, a specific incident involving our troops and one of your people during our operations in Fallujah. I am not authorized to say more at this point, especially on an unsecure line, but we will give you all the details that we can share when we see you in person. Can you come to headquarters at BIAP? Does tomorrow at 10 in the morning work for you?" the colonel said in a tone that sounded more like an order than a request.

"Sure," was all Samuel could muster as his mind raced in a multitude of directions, trying to figure out what the colonel was referring to.

"Great, thank you, sir! One of the guys in my office will call shortly to brief you on the pickup details. I think the standard practice is for you to come to the first airport checkpoint and we will have a ride ready to bring you here."

"Sure!" Again, was all that Samuel could manage.

"Super! See you tomorrow, sir. Have a good day."

"You, too, colonel."

Samuel's stabbed the red "end call" button on his cell phone

Sitting on the edge of his bed, he just stared for a few minutes at his feet and the black socks he was wearing.

"FUCK!" he screamed as he put his shoes back on and went downstairs.

He went straight to his office and found Antonio's number in Greece.

"So, when did you last hear from Omar?" he asked after a brief and awkward exchange of pleasantries.

"Maybe the final days of the offensive. I'm not sure what the exact day was. The Americans were in control of almost the whole city by then and I asked him to either stay home or find a way to leave."

"Not a word since?"

"Nothing. He filed very few photos after a week or 10 days into the battle. Looks like his freedom of movement and access shrunk as the marines took one neighborhood after another. Why, what's going on, boss?"

"I don't know. I am not entirely sure. The Americans might have detained him. I am going to find out more tomorrow. Anyway, can you be here tonight or early tomorrow? I need to know more from you and I need you to come with me when I see what this is all about tomorrow. The military wants us to go and see them at the airport. Well, can you?"

"Don't know, Samuel. Let me check flights and get back to you. I probably can. But this is not good. Not for the guy and not for us. Let me go and check flights now. There may be one to Amman in a few hours, I should not miss it if I can."

"Right, thanks Antonio. Let me know."

CHAPTER ELEVEN

Hassan had been very quiet and mostly unwell since he arrived at Mahmoudiyah, just south of Baghdad. His escape from Fallujah had been nothing less than miraculous after the marines closed in on his hideout on the fringes of the city late one afternoon. Hassan and a handful of his comrades could hear the marines screaming orders and profanities to each other as they took heavy fire from a house about 100 yards away. The marines' arrival was unexpected and clearly the result of accurate intelligence they received. The area, although on the outskirts of Fallujah, has been quiet since the marines sped through it in the initial stages of the offensive.

Encouraged by the fact that they were not taking any fire there, they just moved on closer to the city center, when in fact scores of mujahedeen were still hiding in deserted homes, plotting sneak attacks on the advancing troops. The houses were linked by underground tunnels wide enough for one person to squeeze through provided he was fit enough to crawl all the way to the last house on the far end of the district. The tunnels had been dug over months, with the mujahedeen doing 12-hour shifts in stiflingly hot conditions and in total secrecy. The one tunnel that led to a spot just outside the built up area in a thin strip of abandoned farmlands sitting on the edge of the desert may have been around 200 meters long.

Hassan and the men with him panicked when they realized the marines were so close, but they would have given their presence away by moving furniture and rugs to get inside the tunnel. The marines, now taking heavier fire from the nearby house, decided to call in an airstrike. They had to pull back to escape injury or worse by friendly fire. As they pulled back under cover of their own heavy fire, Hassan and his comrades had a small window to get into the tunnel and crawl away to safety. They knew that the large bomb the Americans were likely to drop might just wipe out the entire bloc. They had to act fast. Hassan was the second man to go into the tunnel. He and others crawled as fast as they could but were slowed down by other mujahedeen who were getting into the tunnel from houses farther up the road and making for the desert outside the city.

Not everyone was moving fast and not everyone was slim enough to easily squeeze through. But everyone was praying out loud as they crawled, asking for God's mercy and for the Americans to be vanquished.

It was approximately ten minutes after Hassan got into the tunnel when the ground violently shook and the tunnel filled with dust. Coughing, the mujahedeen continued to crawl, fearing that a second bomb could mean a slow death under the rubble of the houses above them.

Hassan emerged from the tunnel to see the early evening air filled with dust from the blast. A low-flying jet-fighter was circling above them, perhaps assessing the accuracy of the hit or searching for survivors escaping the scene. Hassan, now out in the open with about ten other men fully coated in yellow dust, yelled at everyone to lie flat on the ground and cover themselves with sand, leaving just enough space for their noses so they could breathe. They frantically followed his orders until all eleven men looked like small mounds of dirt, hardly distinguishable from the barren desert around them. The jet circled the area a couple more times before it flew away, but it was quickly replaced by what appeared to be a mopping-up operation by the marines, who fanned out in the area backed by Bradley fighting vehicles and armored Humvees.

Hassan and his men waited until darkness was complete, snoozing under the sand, reciting verses from the Quran or chatting to each other, all the while keeping an eye on the movements of the American troops. When night fell, they shook off the sand and headed to the desert. Luckily for them, the sky was clear, allowing the stars to illuminate the desert. They could not head to Baghdad to the east or west to Khaldiyah or Ramadi. Too risky. So, after debating the issue while walking in the desert, they decided that Mahmoudiyah, south of Baghdad, might just be doable. Six of the eleven, however, chose to try and head to Khaldiyah, arguing that they could cover the twenty kilometers before sunrise.

"By the time the marines wake up, we will be out of sight, hiding in one of our houses," said one of the six.

He was right: the marines in and around Fallujah were asleep. But not the American men and women at the control room of the armed drones patrolling the skies all night long from Florida or Qatar.

It was barely two hours later when all six who chose to walk to Khaldiyah perished in the desert, cut to pieces by two rockets fired in quick succession by a drone.

Mahmoudiyah, in contrast, was almost sixty kilometers away, but there were spots along the way where water, food and clothes could be found. It took Hassan and the group of four traveling with him about a week to get there. Once there, they headed under the cover of darkness to a safe house they had been told about during the pre-offensive planning sessions the Fallujah mujahedeen held.

The five were now holed up in a small apartment at a Saddam-era housing project. Hassan and the other four, all close aides, shared one of the 12 apartments in the three-story building facing barren farmlands. There was not much food available, although the apartment was designated by the mujahedeen as one of several "safe" houses for possible use in the case of an emergency. Water and power were off. They managed with the little water they had access to from four medium-sized tanks sitting on the roof. For power, they had a car battery and a single bulb, which they would only switch on after they made sure that the windows were perfectly covered with mattresses and blankets to escape detection by the Americans or their spies. Food was another problem. Whoever stocked the apartment was either in a big hurry or lacked any useful knowledge of what passed for a balanced, if austere, diet. It was either cheap cans of tuna or black-eye beans. The once fresh bread they had stored must have gone bad way before they even got there, so they had to ration the little dry bread that was available.

There were onions, rice and lentil stored in one of the cupboards along with cooking oil and salt.

The apartment had very little furniture beside single beds in the two bedrooms and the living area. Eight in all. The beds had cheap mattresses. There was no bed linen or pillows. Just a blanket spread over every bed. The blankets came in two colors, dark brown and dark blue. They all had a floral design. The small television set was lifeless, its screen gray from the dust it gathered over the days and weeks. The kitchen was very small, with just two tiny cupboards. There was a cooker powered by a gas tank, with a spare sat next to it. The sink was off-white marble with multiple stains. There were a handful of plates and glasses, a water kettle and six tiny, gold-rimmed glasses of the kind that Iraqis use for tea. One of the cupboard drawers had six large spoons and a single knife.

All the men stank by now; their hair looked like it had been covered by volcanic ash. Their tunics and baggy pants were dusty and smeared black and gray. The skin on their hands and feet was dry and blistered.

Hassan, as their leader, assumed the task of making the call for prayers. He did it in a low but sweet voice. They prayed together. To pass the time, they recited Quranic verses, which they had learned by heart. They all read well, but it was Hassan who recited it melodically in his deep voice, but fatigue and the bad diet left him without much energy, so he could only do it in brief spells. Diarrhea was another concern. Not a day went by without one or two of them having it. That, in turn, made the apartment smell even worse.

They took turns disposing of the garbage, sneaking out to look for a place where they could leave it without being detected. Mostly, they left it in apartments in their building, or in the one next door. Fresh garbage would be a giveaway. Burning it would be worse.

The battle for Fallujah was long and brutal. It never did go the Mujahedeen's way, not for one day, not ever. The overwhelming firepower available to the Americans and their unchallenged air domination made sure of that. Every time the mujahedeen thought they were on the cusp of a small victory and that they might have killed and wounded several marines, they would suffer heavy casualties from drones armed with rockets or get wiped out by heavy gunfire from attack helicopters. At times, entire mujahedeen positions would be vaporized by a single bomb dropped from warplanes they could not even see or hear.

One of the marines' tactics was to pull back and call in an airstrike every time the going got tough and they started to take casualties. It worked well for them. Their casualties were significantly light compared to what the mujahedeen suffered. But the marines' tactics caused large numbers of civilian casualties and widespread destruction in the city. For the Mujahedeen, it was another chapter in the annals of martyrdom that they could use in the future to energize their recruitment propaganda, when in fact the battle for Fallujah was one that they had absolutely no hope of winning. It was a lopsided fight. That did not mean that the mujahedeen did not show courage or some fighting valor. They did and even pulled off a handful of smart and carefully planned ambushes that killed and wounded marines. But that was never anywhere near enough to win the battle or to meaningfully slow down the advance of the Americans. Extreme caution and methodical mob-up operations by the marines – both designed to reduce their own casualties – combined to make the battle last as long as it did.

Hassan and his men thought differently. To them, that it took the marines weeks to capture the city was reason to hope that one day they would defeat the Americans in a battle that would be talked about for generations to come.

With little to do except pray, read from the Quran, keep the place as clean as possible and take out the trash, Hassan and his men were bored. When they sat down to talk, they almost whispered, fearing that if they spoke any louder, their presence would be detected by a passing U.S. or Iraqi patrol. Some of the conversations bordered on the philosophical or attempted to answer almost existential questions, like the future of Islam or whether ordinary Muslims the world over were ready to accept and live by their interpretation of the faith. They discussed how they could be better trained and armed and whether trying to function like a regular army was suited for them. Should the focus be on street warfare and sneak attacks rather than try and operate like the armies they were fighting? Should they control cities and run them like they did in Fallujah, or fall back on the old ways of operating as sleeper cells?

Hassan listened more than he talked during these lengthy conversations. The battle for Fallujah had taken a heavy toll on his jihadist convictions and sent him soul searching about whether armed struggle under the banner of Islam was effective or if it was in fact doing more harm than good to the cause. He was disappointed about the absence of any outpouring of sympathy for the mujahedeen in Fallujah. There were no street protests in the Arab world decrying the American attack like there were when Israel used excessive force against the Palestinians, for example. Did ordinary Muslims in Iraq and elsewhere actually hate them? If not hate them, were they indifferent to their cause? Were they not fighting against a foreign occupier? Could it be their reputation for being cruel and brutal to spies or Shiites that was denying them popular support? Fellow Sunnis should at least show them some support, but they didn't. They probably resented them just as much as the Shiites do, he reflected.

Hassan could find no satisfactory answers to any of the questions filling his head. He had been feeling isolated from the outside world ever since he took over the reins of power in the "emirate" of Fallujah the previous year. The people he met and interacted with were mostly like-minded. For years, he had not read a book other than the Quran, Hadeeth or Islamic jurisprudence. How could he possibly gauge the sentiment of Muslims outside the jihadist movement when almost his entire circle of friends, colleagues and family were linked one way or another to the mujahedeen?

But the one question that had been tormenting him the most was this: what happened to Safiyah?

***

Hassan and Safiyah had not seen nor heard from one another since the attack on the city began. That first night of the attack, he had taken her to her family home and said his goodbyes very quickly. Safiyah was heartbroken. She stood staring at the door after he disappeared into the dark streets of the city. She did not cry. She held back her tears. She wanted to be strong when she really was not at all. She wanted to be strong for him, although, at that point, it made no difference. He won't be there to see her, but she was convinced that she had to be strong for him, the husband she may never see again.

Her parents left the room for her and Hassan to be alone after he briefly explained to them that the battle could start at any moment. They wanted to give them privacy to say their goodbyes. But neither Hassan nor Safiyah needed privacy at that point. Hassan had been tense and agitated. Safiyah felt the hug they had at their home would have been the perfect goodbye. She could have used another one, of course, maybe even more, but Hassan did not look like he felt the same. So much weighed on his mind at the time.

Safiyah's parents came back to the room when they heard the door close. They wanted to comfort her, but she was not responsive to anything they said and did not hug her mother back, forcing the woman to pull back and burst into tears, not because her daughter rebuffed her affection but because she knew, as a mother, that Safiyah's heart was broken.

Safiyah knew all along that her husband's life would end abruptly or violently one day. That he could be arrested and put away for years. These thoughts were always in the back of her mind. Now that he had gone to lead his men in battle against a superior enemy, these thoughts overwhelmed her. And she stood there motionless and alone at the entrance of her family's home. Curiously, the thought of a life without Hassan somewhat appealed to her. It was not a thought she would entertain for long, but it lived somewhere in the depths of her mind. She felt that while she loved her husband, she deserved much more than the mundane and somewhat tedious and austere life he had provided her with in Fallujah. It was not greed, nor was it conceit. Just that nagging feeling that she deserved more or better, that she wanted to see more of the world, wanted a partner who was educated, interesting and engaging. Hassan was all about jihad and the teachings of Islam, but even that was subjected to his harsh and uncompromising interpretations which, in her view, did not fit in with the modern world. Not even some segments of the world in Fallujah.

To her, Hassan felt secure in his own thoughts and views because he was a member of a community that shared them. Not Safiyah.

It was not until twenty minutes later that she realized that she had been standing in the middle of the room, staring at the door. She slowly went and sat on one of the chairs and started to cry silently. The tear drops rolled off her face and fell on her chest and lap. She cried for a good half hour before she finally fell asleep. It was the kind of sleep that offered a reprieve from life's trials. She was asleep for close to three hours when, shortly after midnight, she was awakened by the sound of low-flying jet fighters screaming over the city, followed by loud blasts that could not have been very far from where she was.

"MOTHER, MOTHER!" she screamed.

CHAPTER TWELVE

It was around 9:30 in the morning when Samuel and Antonio arrived at the checkpoint outside of Baghdad airport. Antonio had managed to catch a 7 pm flight to Amman from Athens: he spent the night at the Queen Aliaa's airport hotel to add an hour or two to his sleep rather than do the one-hour-long journey to the city center. He was on the 6 am flight to Baghdad, also run by Royal Jordanian but operated by a South African company. It was a bumpy flight. Not a single seat was vacant, with half the passengers tough-looking men in their 30s and 40s who were joining the ever growing tribe of ex-servicemen from across the western world who now earned good wages as security consultants in Iraq.

Antonio did not touch the sandwiches they served. He was never a breakfast man, certainly not at 6:30 am. He tried to sleep but he could not. So he stared at the back of the seat in front of him, his mind blank except when the thought of what could be awaiting him in Baghdad burdened him. The 90-minute flight was smooth until the aircraft approached Baghdad airport. Then it began to fly in circles over the airport and the large U.S. military base next to it to avoid being hit by a missile. The "corkscrew" landing was a warzone tactic that is a substitute for the normal gradual approach that would see planes steadily lose altitude until touchdown. To do this in Baghdad at that time could have meant a hit by a projectile fired by rebels lurking outside the parameters of the airport.

Antonio was picked up by one of the British security consultants alongside an Iraqi employee. Instead of being taken to the house as was always the case, they took him to the nearby checkpoint to meet up with Samuel.

"I am glad you made it. Thanks!" Samuel said. "This is not going to be good and it has the potential to damage us one way or another. Already, New York is asking whether we screened Omar thoroughly enough before we hired him or whether we even attempted to find out more about him. I did not like that one bit, not one fucking bit, but they may have a point. It all happened very quickly in our rush to get someone inside Fallujah before the battle. But it's too soon to go into that now. Let's see what the military has to say and we can talk later."

Their military escort arrived right on schedule. A young lieutenant led a convoy of two Humvees with gunners on top. After a brief exchange of greetings and introductions, the young officer gave Samuel and Antonio a short briefing.

"It's a 10-minute ride to where we are going. We will be using the military road. You will disembark and take a ride in another vehicle that's waiting for us at the headquarters' checkpoint. Your cars will have to wait outside. You'll be escorted back to the checkpoint when your business is done. Do you have any questions?"

There was a pause.

"Alright, we should be on our way," he said, melodramatically pointing to the waiting Humvees, the armored BMW and Toyota pickup truck.

Like the officer said, it took the convoy about 10 minutes to reach the sprawling military base. The BMW and the Toyota went straight to the shaded parking spot outside the fence after Samuel and Antonio got out. As soon as the two vehicles parked, the drivers and the security consultants got out and stretched before they strolled together to a nearby spot where several wooden benches were arrayed under the shade of a stand covered by sheets of straw.

Samuel and Antonio got into a black SUV and were driven away to a building deep inside the base. The structure was nearly completely concealed by trees. There was a small green area outside with a few garden chairs randomly scattered, suggesting that the occupants of the building may be using the little space to cool off in the evening when Baghdad's winter can be refreshingly cold.

"Gentlemen, good morning! Welcome to our little home away from home! We are all living the dream here in Iraq!" shouted Colonel Mackenzie as he emerged from the main door of the building, a Saddam-era mansion that probably wasn't opulent or big enough for the personal use of the dictator but might have been good enough for senior bureaucrats and their support staff.

He shook Samuel's hand with exaggerated enthusiasm before he turned to Antonio.

"I am Colonel John Mackenzie from legal, and who might you be?" he asked.

"Antonio, I run photos in Iraq."

"Good to meet you, Antonio," the colonel said, again with affected enthusiasm. "Let's get inside and have a coffee. Colonel Alexander Fernandez will soon join us. He is the man in charge of this case, not me. We are both colonels, but he will soon make general. I still have a few years to go."

Samuel and Antonio said nothing in response to the colonel's attempt at conversation. They just produced cautious smiles before they started walking inside, where they delved into a corridor almost the entire length of the building before they were shown into a conference room filled with modern office furniture that was starkly at odds with the high ceiling, the massive chandelier and the ornate columns at the room's four corners.

Everyone took a seat, leaving the chair at the top of the conference table vacant for the more senior colonel who had yet to arrive.

The group had barely taken a sip of their coffee when Colonel Fernandez walked in. In blue and gray camouflage fatigues, he must have been at least 6.3 feet, with exceptionally broad shoulders and muscles bulging in the sleeves of his tight fatigues. His deep voice matched his imposing build.

"Gentlemen, forgive me for being a little late," he said, almost shouting. "My name is Alexander Fernandez. I am a lawyer by training, but I function here as a prosecutor. It's all about the law no matter which side you are on, right?" he said with an awkward chuckle.

"Alright, now here is what is going on," he began, his expression suddenly dead serious. He sifted through a file he took out of a camouflaged army bag. "Your man in Fallujah, what's his name? Omar, right? Well, we have good reason to believe he is a terrorist. We detained him in a Fallujah house with other terrorists during our mop-up operations along with one other terrorist known to us. It did not look like he was there shooting photos for you guys. We also believe that he has links to some of the most senior terrorists who ran Fallujah before we took it back. Our investigation is continuing but we are overwhelmed with the large number of terrorists we've detained and now have to question, as well as the tons of documents we seized. Then, we will still be left with the nearly impossible task of making any sense of it all. But it's not looking good for your boy. It's early days yet, but I can tell you now you will at some point need a lawyer. We will, of course, keep you posted. But you need to know that it's a long and complicated process. He may not appear before a court for months yet. That you're here and we are telling you all this is a courtesy because of who you are. We are not in the habit, neither are we obliged to, of informing next of kin or employers of suspected terrorists in our custody until a much later stage in the process. We are at war here and we are following Iraqi laws. We are just helping the Iraqi judiciary push through the process."

Samuel remained silent while the colonel spoke, just staring at him with a stone face that, he hoped, would adequately conceal his anger, frustration and fear over how this was going to play out. Many thoughts, most of them grim, rushed through his head. What will happen to Omar? Will they put him away for life? Execute him even? And what line will the bosses in New York take on this? They'll most likely look for a fall guy, he thought, and Samuel was to be the obvious candidate.

"Well, Colonel, thank you for letting us know. That's for starters. Now, about Omar, this must be one hell of a big mistake. I just cannot imagine someone like him leading a double life. It takes a very special man and years of training for anyone to pull off something like this. Omar is smart and a good photographer, but he isn't that man, not by a long shot. Is he a terrorist? I think that's preposterous. You have given us no details about the circumstances in which you detained him, but I am sure that there is a simple explanation for why he was in that house. Besides, the people he was found with, do you have evidence to suggest that they are terrorists?"

"Oh, yes, we do, don't worry about that."

"Well, can you be more specific?"

"No, I cannot. Not now, anyway. This meeting was not arranged to discuss or review the evidence or the details of the case. We asked you to come here so you know we have him and familiarize you with the gravity of his situation. We are doing you a favor. Like a heads-up, so you can hire a lawyer, maybe provide for his family, whatever it is that you need to be doing. This is it. We will get to the nitty gritty later when your lawyers will have access to the case file and see the evidence. But not now," said the colonel, visibly angered by Samuel's suggestion that the U.S. military got it all wrong regarding Omar.

"Fair enough, but can we see him now?"

"Not now. We will allow visits at some point, but not just yet. We are following the letter of the Iraqi law on serious crime and terrorism. I must be honest with you, these laws give us a fair bit of leeway to question, investigate and finally prosecute in a deliberate and thorough manner. No hurry. So don't judge our procedures by what we do back home. This is Iraq and we are bound by its laws and regulations," said the colonel as he rose from his chair, signaling the end of the meeting.

Samuel and Antonio got up too, shook hands with the two colonels and did away with the niceties as they made their way to the door. Colonel Mackenzie hurriedly followed them until they got into the black SUV. Samuel and Antonio waved politely to him as the car drove away.

CHAPTER THIRTEEN

The possibility of being detained by the Americans during the fighting in Fallujah was not something that Omar thought a great deal about. He never completely ruled it out, but he was convinced it was highly unlikely. During the early days of the offensive, he was able to roam around the city on his scooter, frequently stopping to take photos of the mujahedeen as they dashed from one district to another, offering prayers or gathered around a simple meal they ate while squatting on the ground behind sandbags or inside one of the houses they took over to rest, eat and sleep. He used his satellite phone to file to Baghdad, normally twice a day, once after his early morning outing and again shortly before sunset. He filed from home, where his mother and two brothers hunkered down for the duration of the offensive. Food was scarce, but Omar did not eat much anyway. He was overwhelmed by the excitement of his work, although it was tinged with anxiety over the safety of his mother and siblings as well as the fate of so many of his friends and relatives who were fighting the Americans. He was greeted warmly by the mujahedeen whenever he showed up. They did not consider him as one of their own, but something close to it.

"Haji, God bless you and your brothers in jihad," Omar would shout to the mujahedeen he knew as he dashed past them on his scooter. "Haji, do you and your brothers need anything?" he would ask the leader of another group. "Just command me and it will be done," he would add to a multitude of gratitude-filled shouts of "God bless you, Omar, but we are fine, thanks to God's mercy and generosity."

And Omar's photos were a big hit. The accolades flew in from all sides:

Antonio told him briefly about the praise he was getting but did not go into the details.

"There will be a handsome financial bonus for your work," Antonio told him a week into the offensive. "It's the least we can do for the work you have been doing and the danger involved. I cannot tell you how much exactly because that's still being decided, but I think you will be pleased."

"I am grateful for the opportunity you have given me and I will do everything I can to show my gratitude," Omar told him, although Antonio's translator Fahd rendered it as a simple "Omar says 'thank you'." Antonio would roll his eyes at the translator, struck by the huge discrepancy between the length of Omar's sentence and the brevity of the translation he received.

While high on the praise, Omar did not want to be complacent. He was thinking hard and long about what he could do to take his photography to a higher level. A level that would win him prizes. Maybe even a Pulitzer. He felt that he was doing more of the same every day. The photos were getting a lot of play but that's because the access was unique, he thought. What if he embedded with a band of mujahedeen as they plan, prepare and stage an attack against the marines and their Iraqi allies in the middle of the night? That would be a great photo essay, he thought. If that does not win him a big prize, then nothing will, he thought to himself.

He considered asking Hassan to introduce him to the "right" cell of mujahedeen. But, on second thoughts, he decided to look for one himself. He found his target in a mixed group of foreign and local jihadists. There were about 15 of them, including veterans from the wars in the Balkans and Chechnya. They were led by an Iraqi, a former army captain called Mohammed Saadoun, a native of Baghdad who had served in Saddam's elite Republican Guard. He found Saadoun and the group in a house on the eastern outskirts of the city. It was slightly damaged by an American airstrike at a nearby target two months ago. He only learned that the house was inhabited when he caught a glimpse of Saadoun and his men going inside shortly after dawn as he was roaming around on his scooter looking for photos.

He cautiously approached the house one afternoon. It was still light, but night was fast approaching. It was cold, too. That bitter desert cold in Iraq that, while a welcome change from the punishing heat of the long summers, becomes too much for Iraqis after sundown. Omar loudly cleared his throat several times to make his presence felt. "*Al Salamou Aleikom*," he shouted as he grew desperate to be noticed. A voice came from behind a wall or maybe a window.

"Brother, what are you doing here?" said the voice in a non-Iraqi accent. Maybe Saudi or Yemeni.

"It's Omar the photographer, I am here to see sheikh Mohammed Saadoun," he said. "Is he there?"

"What's your business?"

"It's a personal matter. He knows me, don't worry."

"Yes, he is here. Come in from the back," the stern voice commanded.

Omar went around the back and entered the house through a hole in the garden wall big enough to accommodate a fully-grown man. There were laundry lines and food leftovers scattered around the back yard, with a small army of flies feasting on the scraps.

A bearded man in faded jeans, a loose shirt and dirty trainers emerged from a door at the far end of the yard.

"Brother Omar, *salamou aleikom*, come with me," the man told the visitor while giving him a searching look, maybe to see whether he carried a firearm or a knife.

Omar followed him to a large living room furnished with green straw mats and several brown cushions. At one corner sat several prayer mats, with two copies of the Quran on top.

Mohammed Saadoun rose up to greet Omar, who leaned in for a traditional embrace and two pecks on one cheek. After a series of pleasantries and customary questions about family and children, the two men squatted on the floor. The man who escorted Omar to the room waited there long enough for the two men to settle down and then left.

"So, what is it that you want us to do for you?"

Omar explained to him what he was trying to do and gave him assurances that it wouldn't bring any harm to him or members of his cell. He told him that the photo essay would cast a positive light on the cause of the mujahedeen and shatter the stereotypical notion of them as evil men filled with hatred for humanity. He said it would be a total of twelve, maybe fifteen photos, but he would have to shoot many, many more and then start an initial selection process, with the editors in Baghdad doing the final pick.

"I will not show anyone's face. I will be shooting from behind you and if a face happens to appear in any of the photos, we can block it or not use the photo at all. I don't want to put anyone at risk, nor do my editors."

Mohammed Saadoun listened attentively but did not look convinced. And he was not interested in the technical details Omar offered as reassurances. Not that he did not believe him: it was more the burden of taking a civilian along on a combat mission and the extra effort needed to protect him if they were engaged in a firefight. But, he thought, Omar was a close friend of the emir of Fallujah so it would not look good for him to turn him down.

"Very well, brother Omar," he told his guest. "You are very lucky. We may have a mission tonight. It's not an easy one. In fact, it's very dangerous, but with God's grace, we will be triumphant. Are you interested?" asked Mohammed Saadoun, somewhat hoping the imminence of the mission would change his plans and send him away.

"Yes, I am," said Omar enthusiastically. "I did not expect to go on a mission that quickly. But, of course, yes, the sooner the better. It's God's will," he said with only a hint of hesitation in his voice.

"God willing, all will be well. Now, you need to get some rest and eat something, too, so you can be ready. It's a long walk to the target. The house is small, but I am sure you'll find a spot where you can lie down and sleep in peace. The kitchen is right here on the ground floor, when you are hungry, just go and grab something. There is not much to choose from, but you can also wait a little and eat with everyone if you're not hungry now."

Mohammed Saadoun abruptly got up and extended his hand to shake his guest's. The sudden move made Omar quickly spring to his feet and extend his hand to receive the handshake.

"On days like these, I have so much to do," Mohammed Saadoun said, his tone apologetic. "But you need to do me a favor," he said, his voice taking on a serious, almost threatening, edge. "Don't use your phone while you are here. In fact, I would like you to switch it off and take the battery out. Do the same if you have a satellite phone. I know you journalists like to be reachable at all hours of day and night, but these are dangerous times and we need to protect the lives of the mujahedeen."

"Of course," said Omar. "I will do that right away," he said as Mohammed Saadoun walked away.

Once alone in the room, Omar went to the corner near the shuttered window and squatted on the floor. He rested his hands on his knees and placed his head between them. The enormity and gravity of what he had just committed himself to do dawned on him and it made his head spin. A thousand questions raced through his head and each one of them seemed serious enough to unravel a man. He could not get his head wrapped around what was going to happen in just a few hours. Was it worth the risk? Should he shoot an email to Antonio to tell him? What if he was killed or injured? Worse, what if he was captured by the Americans?

But there was the upside, too.

He would go with the mujahedeen on their mission, take some great photos, come back and head home and file the images to Baghdad. Antonio would probably admonish him for not consulting him before going on such a dangerous assignment, but he would be pleased to see the photos for sure. It's a win-win situation for Antonio and the company. If something happens to him, anything, they could truthfully claim that he had gone on the assignment without their prior approval. If he survived and came back with compelling images, then everyone would be happy. All Antonio needed to do was to gently reprimand him and tell him never to do that again, before he dived into the treasure trove of images to pick out the best 12 or 15 frames, edit and caption them and let them rip. Prizes, many prizes, would be pouring in after just a few months, Omar dreamt.

But his heart suddenly felt heavy when he thought of his mother and two brothers. He had hardly seen them since the battle began. In fact, he'd seen little of them since he started working as a news photographer. His mother was happy that Omar brought home more money for the house's upkeep. She would thank him every time she saw him in the living room, working on his laptop. He would raise his head for a second to flash her a smile in acknowledgment of her gratitude. When he received his first salary, he told his mother he would keep the money in a kitchen drawer and that she should feel free to take whatever she needed to buy food and pay for other expenses. She said she would rather keep it in the top drawer of her bedroom cupboard.

"It's safer there," she argued. Omar smiled. "May God keep you safe and healthy for us," he told her.

It was completely dark when Omar peaked through the window's shutters. He could not see anything outside. Nothing. He realized he had missed the sunset prayers.

Switching on the flashlight of his mobile phone he found his way to a small bathroom on the ground floor, which had a toilet and a small washbasin. It did not smell too good but was not as bad as he had expected. He started the ritual washing, using the little water dripping from the sink's tap. He went back to the room and prayed on one of the mats sitting at the corner. He prayed hard. He teared up as he asked God in a low, trembling voice to protect him and his family. He asked Him to protect the mujahedeen and keep them safe. And he prayed for his late father. "Let him into heaven, oh God, for he was a pious and a good man who lived for his family."

The small bulb dangling from the ceiling went on just as he finished his prayers. Someone, he thought, must have turned on a small generator tucked away somewhere, or used a car battery. The room was dimly lit because the bulb was small, but there was enough light for him to switch off his flashlight.

He felt hungry, but he did not want to act on Mohammed Saadoun's advice and go into the kitchen and grab something to eat alone. He wanted to wait and eat with everyone. But where was everyone? He has been there a couple of hours now and he had only seen Mohammed Saadoun and the man who escorted him inside the house. They must be upstairs sleeping or readying their weapons for the operation. He started looking for the staircase leading to the floor above. When he found it, he paused for a minute, hoping that he would hear noises that would lead him to where the men might be. There was none. So he slowly climbed up the stairs, pausing every few steps to clear his throat in the hope that someone might hear him and approach. No one spoke and no one came to meet him. He could see three rooms upstairs, but only one had its door open. He started tiptoeing toward the open door. Leaning forward to see what or who was inside he found Mohammed Saadoun alone, praying. He was totally engrossed in his prayers. When he saw Omar at the door, he began to say his prayers in a voice just loud enough for the intruder to hear. Was he shaming Omar for his intrusion? Possibly.

Omar pulled himself away and, still tiptoeing, headed to one of the two other rooms. He knocked gently on the door of one. "*Salamou aleikom!*" he said just loud enough to be heard by whoever was inside the room. His greeting was answered by a faint voice. "Come on in, brother Omar," said the voice from behind the door, possibly the same man who had spoken to him from behind a wall when he first approached the house earlier that day. Omar opened the door and paused at its threshold.

There were six men, four of them praying separately. One was reading from the Quran and the sixth man was squatting on the floor cleaning his rifle with an oily piece of cloth.

"Brother Omar, we expected you to join us for the sunset prayers, but you did not come. Did you pray alone?" said the man cleaning the gun. Omar realized it was he who had spoken to him before.

"Yes, I prayed alone downstairs. I just did not know what to do or where was everyone."

"It's fine. May God accept your prayers. We are here and you will join us, God willing, for the evening prayers."

"God willing, I will."

The man who was reading the Quran paused, raised his head, and acknowledged Omar's presence with a gentle nod, murmured a greeting and showed a hint of a smile before he went back to reading. The other four continued to pray. One of them was silently weeping as he prayed, the tears rolling down his cheeks. He was a skinny man who could not be more than 30. He had a spotty beard. His face and hands were deeply tanned.

Omar watched him as the man with the familiar voice went back to cleaning and oiling his rifle with considerable care. The tearful man finished his prayers and for a few minutes paused as he sat on the floor staring at a spot right in front of him, trying to regain his composure now that there was a guest in the room. He stared at the spot on the prayer mat in front of him, like he was trying to decipher a text written in some ancient language that he alone could see. By the time he began to address Omar, everyone had left the room.

"Welcome, brother Omar! My name is Al Makki. I am one of the mujahedeen with God's help and blessing. I hear that you're coming with us on our next mission to photograph us. I don't exactly understand why you're doing this and I really must mind my own business, but I admire your courage and dedication to your work. May God deliver us all safely from this brutal war."

"Yes, brother, wars are never easy or merciful. They harvest the lives of good men, orphan children and widow women. But man has been fighting wars since the day of creation. Often, it's the only way to settle disputes and repel invaders."

"That's true. Take this war, for example, it has been imposed on us. The Americans crossed oceans and seas to come and invade the lands of the Muslims. We will not rest until we drive them out."

"May God bring us victory by his will and grace," said Omar, trying to wind up the conversation. He wanted to be left alone to wrestle with his own thoughts and worries, to ponder one more time what he was about to do that night. He wondered if he could still pull out without losing face. Was he being rash, carried away by his pursuit of professional glory? Did he want recognition so badly that he was willing to risk his life for a news photography prize? Was he being irresponsible, even stupid?

Omar's train of thought was interrupted by a voice calling from downstairs for everyone to gather for food.

Al Makki led him downstairs to the kitchen. Food was laid out on a table in the middle of the room and everyone was already gathered round. There were beans, bread, boiled eggs and tuna. Nothing green. The bread was stale and the beans and tuna came out of tins.

Mohammed Saadoun was there. He recited a brief prayer before everyone began to eat. No one appeared to be very hungry although their last meal was nearly twelve hours ago, an early breakfast they ate after a short nap that everyone took after the dawn prayers. There was an eerie silence as everyone ate. It was remarkable that eight men were gathered in one room and no one said anything other than the short prayer offered by their leader.

It was only a matter of minutes before everyone finished eating and started filing out of the room, except for one man who stayed behind to brew tea for everyone.

Back upstairs, they squatted with their backs to the wall, waiting for the tea to arrive. Everyone drank a glass or two, black and very sweet. They drank it noisily, as if they were savoring something dear to them for one last time. Something that they may not have again, or at least not for a long time.

Abruptly, Mohammed Saadoun pulled himself up off the floor, cleared his throat and made the call for the evening prayers in a voice that's gentle and low enough that someone standing outside the room could not have heard. Everyone got up and headed to the house's two bathrooms to wash. Omar went along and was allowed by the men to go first. They all gathered again in the room and Mohammed Saadoun led the prayers. He did not recite long verses from the Quran. He probably wanted to finish quickly so the men can have time to perform their own silent prayers or read from the Quran.

By the time everyone was finished, it was approaching ten pm.

"It's time to go, by God's will," announced Mohammed Saadoun, his voice more commanding now.

Everyone got up, picked their rifles, stuck ammunition magazines in their belts and dropped grenades in their pockets as they recited Quranic verses glorifying jihad, or whispering "*Allahu Akbar*" in barely heard voices.

Only three of the men had night vision goggles. The rest had to rely on the little light from the stars. Omar had nothing except his cameras and one long lens.

The men had been briefed on the mission in the morning, hours before Omar arrived. Mohammed Saadoun explained the target to them and what needed to be done.

The target was a joint Iraqi-American checkpoint that was about a 20-minute walk from the house. The Iraqis were members of the so-called "Dirty Division," an American-trained outfit made up of Saddam-era special forces who had been repurposed after the U.S. invasion as a counterterrorism force. The Americans invested much time, effort and money on the force in the hope that it could spearhead a concerted Iraqi effort against the militants with the U.S. military backing them up with air support and intelligence.

The jihadists moved in single file, keeping close to the houses. They were mostly in Taliban-style baggy pants and tunics, with trainers and a diverse range of headgear. They had no bulletproof vests or helmets.

The streets were eerily quiet, but they soon heard Iraqi soldiers shouting to each other, or maybe to civilians still out on the streets. The voices became louder, but the checkpoint was still out of sight.

Omar was the man before last in the single column. He kept shooting as the men tried to move in stealth. He also took photos of men, women and children looking out their windows, and men who stood outside their houses, maybe out of boredom. They saw the mujahedeen walking past but said nothing. The mujahedeen did not say anything to them either. The men quickly disappeared inside their homes once the column of mujahedeen had passed. They knew what was likely to happen next and they did not want to be caught in the crossfire or the subsequent manhunt.

The checkpoint was finally in sight. The men could also hear the noise of the small generator powering the floodlights, as well as the Iraqi soldiers speaking to each other at the top of their voice so they could be heard over the whirring noise of the engine. Immediately behind the checkpoint stood a Bradley fighting vehicle and an armored Humvee.

Mohammed Saadoun quietly gave the order for the two snipers in the group to start identifying their targets and wait for his order to fire. Omar was quick to photograph the snipers moving to slightly forward positions and stretching, belly down, on the dusty street with their rifles at the ready.

He then signaled to the rest of the men to continue to crawl toward the checkpoint without being detected so they could aim more accurately and effectively use their grenades if they needed to. He gave the signal to the two snipers. Seconds later, shots from their big rifles rang out followed by the almost instant screams of the Iraqi soldiers who had been hit. Gunshots rang out again and more screams could be heard along with the sound of engines revving to life. The Bradley and the Humvee started to move, but they were going straight ahead, not the street to the left of the checkpoint where the mujahedeen were. The marines at the checkpoint appeared to panic, screaming orders laced with profanities, but staying put behind the barricades and sandbags.

Mohammed Saadoun readied his RPG and aimed it at the Bradley before it disappeared out of sight. It was a good hit, right in the middle of the vehicle, which stalled for a minute, shrouded in white smoke before it quickly turned around and headed to the side street where the attackers were. Seconds later, the Humvee followed, with its heavy machinegun perched on top making a near complete circle. The gun's turret was now aimed straight at the mujahedeen.

The remotely controlled floodlights were now trained at them too.

Omar was trembling with fear but continued to shoot the firefight. His hands were shaking so much that most of the frames would probably be unusable. The blinding glare of the floodlights hit him straight in the eye and his panic grew when he could hear the engines of the two vehicles becoming louder and louder. Mohammed Saadoun shouted to everyone to pull back just as the Bradley sprayed the street with its large caliber bullets. Marines and Iraqi troops were cautiously walking behind the two vehicles.

Only four of the men and Omar responded to Mohammed Saadoun's order to pull back. They ran as fast they could, zigzagging but keeping close to the walls of the houses on their right. They delved into a side street to escape the gunfire and head for their safe house by a different route. It soon became clear that reaching the house without being detected would be very difficult, if not impossible.

"Kick house doors. If they open, we walk in and hide," Mohammed Saadoun screamed.

It was he who kicked the first door open. He walked in, followed quickly by the others. They took up firing positions by the windows, waiting for the marines to arrive. Minutes passed and no one showed up. They sat still, breathing heavily. They were thankful to have escaped what appeared to be certain death and were now inside a house unknown to the Americans. But the terror quickly returned when they heard a low-flying drone that appeared to be circling above the house. They held their breath, as if that might prevent the aircraft from detecting their presence.

Long minutes passed before the sound of the drone receded and the men could breathe easily again. They searched the house using their flashlights. It was deserted. The kitchen had no food, but there were some cans of beans and tuna in what appeared to be a storeroom. There was also rice and a large can of cooking fat.

The men had no desire to sleep or eat. Mohammed Saadoun said they should stay put until an opportunity arose to sneak back to the safe house, only a ten-minute walk away.

They stayed next to the windows, eyes peeled lest the marines find them and taking turns to guard the house. Two men on guard duty for two hours, while the other two sleep. Neither Omar nor Mohammed Saadoun was part of the rotation. Omar sat at a far corner away from the windows and started looking at the frames he shot.

The best frames were the ones he shot before the firefight began. The snipers, and the others as they crawled cautiously forward showed the tension before the attack began. One frame captured the moment just before the Bradley was hit by the RPG with Mohammed Saadoun's back to the camera and still holding the RPG rifle in a firing position.

He smiled to himself when he looked at the last one. His photo gallery will materialize after all. He began to think of what Antonio would tell him when he sent the photos. His gamble had paid off: he soon fell into a deep sleep, his body drained by adrenalin and hunger.

Mohammed Saadoun fell asleep too. The two men on watch duty struggled to keep their eyes open although the bitter cold of the night air helped them stay awak**e**. It was nearly halfway through the first watch when two muffled shots rang out. The two mujahedeen on watch died instantly, their bodies sliding down the wall they had been leaning against before they landed on the floor with a thud loud enough for everyone else in the room to wake up in horror. The two jihadists who had been sleeping next to Mohammed Saadoun reached for their rifles, but both were shot dead instantly with bullets that pierced their skulls. Mohammed Saadoun raised his hands in the air and cried "No kill! No kill!" as giant men in camouflage fatigues and night vision goggles stood over his head. Omar just stared aimlessly into the room, not knowing what was happening.

"Lay face down and stretch, you fuckers!" screamed one of the men in English as two other soldiers handcuffed Mohammed Saadoun and Omar behind their backs.

"You motherfuckers, we should just put a bullet in your fucking heads and get it done and over with now!" screamed one of the men as others used their legs to turn over the four men they shot to make sure they were dead.

"You are so fucking dead, you fucking cunts. You will be begging us to kill you when we start working you over," shouted another. "We are the army of the fucking USA you scumbags. We will always, always get you. Stupid fucks!"

Neither Omar nor Mohammed Saadoun understood a word that was being said, but the rage was unmistakable to both.

The calmer soldiers began to search them. Others were on their radios reporting the action and ordering reinforcements to secure their way back to the base.

They took everything out of Mohammed Saadoun's pockets, stripped him of his magazines' belt and his sneakers. They placed everything in nylon bags.

Searching Omar proved to be more interesting. One soldier looked carefully through his cameras and began to slowly scroll through the images.

"Who the fuck are you shooting photos for? Are you a fucking news photographer? Can someone get Ali, the fucking translator. This dumb fuck does not understand English."

Ali, an Iraqi in his early twenties, appeared two minutes later.

"Ali, ask this piece of shit who he is taking photographs for?"

Ali repeated the question in Arabic.

"I am a news photographer. I work for an American news company in Baghdad," Omar said in a trembling voice.

"Like fuck you do," said the soldier, a towering white beast of a man who appeared to be in charge. "I fucking hate journalists and I fucking hate photographers more."

He began to search Omar's khaki waistcoat, throwing everything that he found on the floor. Omar stood facing the wall, legs spread wide. The American was clearly looking for something.

"Aha, here it is!" the soldier shouted gleefully as he raised his right hand, clutching Omar's satellite phone.

"You should have switched it off, asshole!"

CHAPTER FOURTEEN

Safiyah's survival after two rockets hit her family home the night the Americans launched their offensive was nothing less than miraculous. It was almost like the rockets were meant to destroy the entire house except for the reception area where she had said her final goodbye to Hassan. The sound of the projectile impacting was deafening and the room she was in was instantly engulfed in a suffocating mix of dust and smoke. The spot where the first rocket impacted appeared to be a safe distance away from her. Maybe it hit the front yard or the house next door. She was startled out of her sleep and screamed for her mother before the second one hit just moments later, throwing her off the chair she was sleeping in. Her head slammed into the coffee table in front of her chair and for a minute or two she passed out.

She came round coughing violently, dizzy and disoriented. Her vision was blurred as she slowly opened her eyes, with her eye lashes and brows gray from dust. Her black abaya was also gray and her head cover sat askew, revealing unkempt hair. She tried to sit up, but her body would not let her. Her legs ached and her stomach was cramping.

She tried again, grabbing the table to support herself but the table tilted toward her and everything on top of it came down rushing toward her. She let go of the table and it fell back on its four legs. She needed something else to hold onto so she reached for the edge of the chair she'd been sleeping in and pushed down hard, groaning in pain until she was able to squat on the floor. She let out a scream. But what was causing the pain? She ran her right hand over her legs and looked at it. No blood. She did the same to her stomach, chest, arms and shoulders. Still no blood. But it felt like she was touching a raw nerve, especially her shoulders.

She was now desperate to get up. She reached for the arm of the chair again and pressed her other hand against the floor. She struggled but managed to stand up after several attempts. The pain was almost unbearable, but she did not scream again. Once on her feet, she felt dizzy and her legs wobbled. She quickly sat on the chair and felt she was going to pass out again, but she did not.

Safiyah looked around and, for a few seconds, she could not tell where she was. The walls were cracked. The short passage leading to the rest of the house was gone. In its place was a mound of debris. Above it was a large hole in the ceiling. It was like a sunroof, roughly and randomly cut open. The verses of the Quran written in calligraphy and framed were no longer hanging on the walls. The glass cupboard that sat on one side of the room was shattered and the two windows looking out on the house's front yard were gone.

Slowly it dawned on her: the house had been bombed. The Americans? Of course, who else. She survived. But her parents may not have been so lucky. She let out a scream.

"MOTHER! FATHER!" she yelled as she stumbled toward the mound of debris that blocks the passage leading to the bedrooms. Her parents were supposed to be in their bedroom. Frantically, she began to scoop debris with her bare hands throwing it behind her. Maybe they were still alive, she thought. It took her a few minutes to realize she was making almost no headway. She needed help, but who would be available to help her on a night like this? Slowly, she became aware of the frequent thudding noise rocking the city. The Americans were pounding Fallujah from the air and the ground.

She sat down next to the mound of debris.

"Mother, father! Where are you? Please, don't leave me!" she whispered to herself and began to cry.

She must have cried for a good hour before it occurred to her to venture out of the house and see if she could get inside her parents' bedroom through the window. She got up stiffly and walked with even more difficulty to the door. She opened it and stepped out. The first thing she did was to look up at the sky. It was lighting up at regular intervals as if the city was being lashed by an electrical storm. Every flash of light was closely followed by a thunderous bang. Most sounded like they came from far, maybe the fringes of the city. Others were unnervingly close, but she chose to ignore the obvious danger of being outdoors on a night like this.

The yard was strewn with debris and she almost tripped and fell on her face a couple of times. But she kept walking until she was outside her parents' bedroom. The window was badly damaged, but somehow it continued to cling to the frame. She picked up a slab of concrete from the ground and started to gently smash it against the window frame though she feared the glass could fall on her parents. But the window was not moving. She started to hit it harder and it finally gave way, but she could not clearly see the inside of the room. It was still dark and the power had been cut for days. "Mother? Father? Are you there?" She yelled. "Please, answer me, please!" she pleaded repeatedly. There was no response.

Safiyah's eyes slowly grew accustomed to the darkness but it was not until after dawn broke that she was able to make out what was inside.

"MOTHER! FATHER!" she screamed when she saw her parents' motionless bodies on their bed. Their heads rested on pools of blood, now soaked up by the bed linen. Their faces were covered by dust. Her father was in his home gallabiyah, the mother in a winter night gown and an old woolen sweater on top.

Safiyah let out a series of screams that pierced the early morning air. Ordinarily, a woman's scream would bring the neighbors running, eager to find out what happened and to see if they can be of any help. But no one came. Safiyah was left to mourn her parents alone. Not even her two sisters and brother were there. They had been dispatched to

Baghdad three weeks ago to stay with their aunt. The parents elected not to go because, ostensibly, they wanted to stay in the house to protect it.

Minutes went by and no one came. Safiyah stopped screaming and, despairing of anyone ever coming, she climbed through the window and into the room. She went up close to the bed where her parents lay motionless. Hesitantly, she reached to see if either had a pulse. There was none. She checked again lest she was not concentrating enough or that the pulse was there but very weak.

Now certain they were dead, she stood upright by the bed not knowing what to do next. The room was in a chaotic state, everything randomly thrown about; there were clothes, shoes, toiletries, towels. It looked like someone had opened the cupboards and the drawers, grabbed everything, and thrown them on the floor. Everything was covered in dust. Part of the ceiling had caved in, with a large piece of concrete now dangling perilously from a thin rod of iron.

Why did the Americans target our home, she asked herself. The house was not located in a frontline district nor was it known to be a jihadist hideout. So, why? It did not take long for a difficult-to-swallow idea to come to her. The Americans were tracking Hassan. They had followed him here and ordered an airstrike on the house in the belief that he was still there. But if they were able to track him entering the house, how come they did not know that he left a few minutes later?

The thought of her own husband causing the death of her parents was too much to bear. She tried to banish the idea from her head, but she could not. But even if that is what happened, how could she blame Hassan for their death? Maybe he should have thought about that before he brought her there. Maybe he should have used some sort of deception tactics to avoid detection. Perhaps entering one or two houses a safe distance away before coming to her parents' place would have been enough?

There was nothing that could be done now, she thought: her parents were dead and nothing would bring them back. What she needed to do now was to try to find help. She could not arrange a funeral for her parents. She could not even bury them in the cemetery in the northern part of the city where her father bought a tiny plot of land to use as a family graveyard. She would need to find someone to help her. That would be a useful first step.

She climbed out back into the yard and walked to the gate and went out. She could hear gunfire and the thud of rockets or bombs impacting. A dark cloud hung low over the city, moving slowly, perhaps the result of several fires ignited by the shelling. The morning air was cold, but she barely noticed. She was no longer unnerved or scared by the deafening explosions that sounded like they came from areas not too far away.

She must have knocked on the doors of at least fifteen houses before she gave up on finding anyone, and started walking back home. She knew what to do now and she was thinking of how she was going to do it.

Her father's garden tools would come in handy, but, just in case they were inaccessible after the bombing, she would look inside any house yard that she could get into to see if there is a shovel lying around. She found one in a house close to her home and grabbed it.

She would bury her parents. She would not have to give them the traditional wash that Muslims receive before they are buried. Martyrs are never washed before their burial, according to Islam's teachings, not that there was any running water in the house anyway.

Heading back to the house, she went straight to the section of the yard outside her parents' bedroom window. She started to clear the rubble, pushing it against the street wall away from the house. She took off her abaya, showing the colorful cotton dress with floral motifs she was wearing underneath; and attacked the ground. "Oh, God! Oh, God! Help me, please help me!" she yelled when she came to realize how tough the task was.

It took her several hours to dig a hole deep enough to bury her parents. Her dress was soaking with sweat and caked with dirt. Her headscarf had fallen to the ground and been swept away by the wind. It now sat between the inside of the street wall and a big slab of concrete, partially flapping, but unable to escape. What if a stranger walked by and saw the emir's wife with her hair uncovered and her dress hugging her slender body? She could not have cared less.

Hungry, thirsty and almost completely drained of energy, Safiyah dug deep into whatever willpower she had left in her and climbed back into the room. She went straight to her mother. Showing little reverence for death, she got a hold of her mother's lifeless hands and yanked the body off the bed. The upper part of her mother fell hard on the floor, but that did not stop Safiyah from carrying on. She dragged the body and placed it against the wall below the window. Bending down, she used her hands and her right knee to lift and support the body up to the window and unceremoniously heaved it out and inside the hole she had dug, the legs sprawling over the edge. Her mother was a small woman, and that helped Safiyah do what she needed to do. Moving her father was significantly more difficult, but she eventually managed.

Throughout, Safiyah wore a stone face. She knew they had to be buried before sunset as Muslim tradition dictates and she knew just as well that she had to find the strength to do that. Her mind was blank. She was not thinking of her loss anymore. The grief that filled her when she first saw their motionless bodies on the bed was temporarily gone. She could not think of anything associated with her parents. She was more like a stranger summoned off the street to bury two dead people without getting paid for the trouble. No emotions, just the sheer will to bury them.

With the two bodies now lying on top of each other and partially inside the makeshift grave, Safiyah leapt back out into the yard. She pushed the bodies down the hole and made sure their heads faced Mecca. She stretched their loose legs and placed their arms neatly by their sides. The two bodies were squeezed against each other. The grave was not wide enough, but thankfully it was long enough. Barely.

She took one long look at them before she moved away from the edge of the grave and picked the shovel up. She went to work with renewed energy and a sense of urgency while tears rolled down her cheeks. It took her another forty-five minutes to fill the grave with gravel and dirt. She used whatever was on the ground. When that was done, she hauled several slabs of concrete and large chunks of broken bricks coated in mortar and placed them on top of the grave.

Now that she was finally done, Safiyah was exhausted. An early evening chill was setting in as the sun started to go down and the sound of battle raging in the city rose once again. The sky lit up like fireworks. The whole city appeared to shake at short intervals.

She squatted by the grave and cried again, silently at first, and then hysterically. She could not cry for long. There was nothing left inside her. No energy, and she ran out of tears. She murmured some of the Quranic verses she had learned by heart over the years. She repeatedly prayed that God would have mercy on her parents' souls. She then assumed a child-like pose on her right side, placed her right hand under her head and slept.

CHAPTER FIFTEEN

Samuel had never been one to admit to his mistakes, and he was not about to start now. The Omar case has been weighing heavily on his mind since he got the call from the military and visited them the next day. New York had been on his case, breathing down his neck. They wanted answers he did not have, details he was not privy to; and they were pushing him to do things he could not do.

He was pushing back as much as he could, but the bosses were having none of it. They needed the information, they argued, so they could map out a strategy. They did not directly criticize Samuel's approval of Omar's selection as the Fallujah photographer, but there were vaguely phrased insinuations and thinly veiled digs at how he was running the bureau.

Samuel grudgingly tolerated the digs, which was unusual for a man like him. But he knew that the Omar affair had considerably weakened him. It started taking up entire afternoons and evenings, with calls coming in when New York woke up in the morning, which was around mid-afternoon in Baghdad.

At times, Samuel was tempted to shift the blame to Antonio. He was, after all, the one who hired Omar. Samuel resisted that temptation, although at times he would hint at it and Antonio would instantly become defensive.

"How can you screen someone from Fallujah? How should we have gone about it? It's impossible. We hired him when the city was a no-go area under the rule of the bad guys," Antonio, agitated and impatient, once told Samuel. "Even if we had decided to inquire about him in Fallujah, what did you expect people to say? Nothing. Or, at least, nothing useful."

Samuel would just nod and pretend that he appreciated Antonio's rationale, when in fact he was convinced that his chief photographer was largely to blame for hiring Omar without proper screening.

What really bothered Samuel was that he had been overwhelmed by fear that the Omar case would throw his career off track, maybe even get him fired. Although he was past 60, Samuel still craved new challenges and higher posts. He dreamt of being the Middle East editor, a job he had long coveted but was consistently overlooked for. He had not gone higher than bureau chief for decades. His first bureau chief job came when he was in his late 30s. Since then he had been a bureau chief in several places like Germany, Lebanon and Indonesia, but never in charge of a region. He never really knew why he was passed over for these jobs, but those who worked and socialized with him had an idea why. Samuel drank too much and everyone who worked for him knew it. And he had a temper. A really bad one. When he was angry, everyone knew about it right away. His thunderous outbursts were laced with profanities. He also had nothing but contempt for people in the company who knew less than him or had less experience than he did running a bureau or living outside the United States. Some of those he showed contempt for in the past had risen to key positions in New York and they did not forget Samuel's slights. He saw himself as some sort of a heavily decorated general who has seen combat in a half dozen wars, and thought little of his peers who made general without seeing combat.

"I want everyone to be quiet and listen without interrupting me for just one minute," he would sometimes command colleagues in the middle of a heated conversation. He was convinced that he knew better than everyone and people around him helped him think that. He had a sort of fans' club across the company. They were the closest thing in journalism to groupies.

Reporters, photographers and video journalists regularly quoted him, recounted funny situations in which he was involved or even adopted some of his favorite phrases.

The Omar saga was not easy for him to handle. He was holding his ground as well as he could in those lengthy conference calls with the New York managers. The criticism of his handling of Omar's hiring was there. Subtle, maybe, but it was there. He felt it and it hurt him so much that he could not hit back as he would have liked to.

Now there was a new development: two New York lawyers had been sent to Baghdad to build a case for Omar's defense if he went on trial. One of the two, Jim Spencer, was a former district attorney in Georgia who was in his early 50s. His time in the American South tempted Samuel to establish a bond with him, but that was not enough to make him happy about the presence of two non-company men in the Baghdad house asking everyone questions and not bothering to run anything of any substance by him other than logistical issues. The other one was a much older gentleman who had retired but did part time legal consultancy to keep busy. He was of Iraqi descent, spoke flawless Arabic and was popular with the Iraqi staff at the bureau. Mohammed Suleiman had moved to the United States with his family when he was barely 10 and was so bright he was accepted at Harvard's law school, where he had graduated with honors.

The two men conducted extensive interviews with anyone in the office who'd had dealings with Omar. They spent a great deal of time with Antonio, especially. They grilled him about his job interview with Omar, which lasted in its entirety less than 15 minutes. But they came up with a hundred questions to ask about that brief interview and all the telephone conversations he had with him through Fahd, the interpreter.

"So, did you get any sense of whether he was close to the bad guys in Fallujah?" Suleiman asked Antonio one afternoon.

"No, not at all, but he is a homegrown boy. Surely, he knows many of them or he's related to some of them. Fallujah, like the rest of Iraq, is very tribal. If you are not a relative or a friend, you are likely to be from the same tribe if you come from the same town or city."

"Yes, I know all that. But try and remember if there was even as much as a hint of him knowing them well. What about access, what did he say to sell himself to you as your best choice for a photographer in Fallujah? I mean everyone tries to sell himself as unique, special or gifted in an interview, right?"

"He only said he could have access to the jihadists that no one else has. That alone was enough for me to hire him. I did not press him on details. Remember, I was hiring a freelancer, not filling a staff position. If he could not deliver what he promised I would have fired him. He did deliver and his work was good. What he lacked technically, he made up for with the unique photos he filed."

"That's interesting," said Suleiman, skeptically.

"Listen, Samuel and I discussed his photos when they began to show an unusual level of familiarity with the jihadists. We were a little concerned, but we did not think it was something for us to worry so much about. We filed fewer of those photos and more of the good-but-not-so-unique ones. His photos were getting so much play, it was difficult to resist filing one or two of those potentially prize-winning frames he sent us. This is what we do. We want to have an edge over the competition and, just as importantly, we just did not know how close he was to the bad guys. Besides, I don't have much faith in what the Americans are saying about him. This guy is not a terrorist. He just used his contacts to get good images and he did that so well that we might very well win the big one this year."

Suleiman retorted: "Of course, you're right. But our views, yours and mine, on the case the military has built against him is irrelevant. If the Americans insist on due process, the Iraqis will make that just a formality and sentence people like Omar to death or long jail terms at the end of sham trials. The Iraqis control this. The Americans are just facilitators. They fight, detain jihadists, interrogate them for their own purposes and maybe hold them for long periods to get as much intelligence as possible out of them. Finally, they hand them over to the Iraqis. Justice in a war zone can be very tricky and your man has only himself to blame for the shit he's in."

The two lawyers appeared to make a point of conducting "flash" interviews with staff members about Omar. They were intense and, at times, heated, even hostile.

They did not have much to go with in terms of building up a solid defense argument to pass on to the Iraqi lawyer who would take up the case. But they persisted. Their Baghdad gig was too sweet to walk away from or let anyone take it away from them. The money was just fabulous.

"You were the first member of the editorial staff to meet Omar," Spencer, sitting at Samuel's office one evening, told Mohammed Abul Einein, the Egyptian reporter. "I know we have gone over this before, not once but twice, so humor us, please. It's important. What you heard from him during the drive back to Baghdad from Fallujah and what happened while you were there is more important than you think. So, what is your take-away from that conversation?"

"It is difficult to say, honestly. I believe he was closely linked to the jihadists, but I doubt very much he ever fired a weapon. But he could have done other things that would earn him a conviction on terrorism charges," said Abul Einein.

"Like what?"

"I don't know. I know for a fact that Antonio gave him a heads-up several hours before the marines attacked to retake Fallujah. Could he have passed on that piece of crucial information to his buddies? If he did, does not that mean he may have caused the loss of American and Iraqi lives since the jihadists would have been ready for the Americans when they came at them? I just don't know and I am not sure he did. He could have, but did he? But the Americans gave heads-up to the international media about the time of the attack. It was not an exact time but surely they knew or expected that that piece of information would filter through to Iraqis working for foreign media outlets, right?"

"Really? This little piece of information was never shared by anyone and we have been here for nearly a week now. But that's ok. We will deal with that later. But, now, why would Antonio do that you think?"

"Do what?"

"Tell him that the Americans were to attack in a few hours."

"I guess he wanted him to be ready and not be taken by surprise. Like make sure his phone and cameras are fully charged, for example. That he prepares himself psychologically. Don't think that Antonio was wrong to give him a heads-up. He had an obligation to do that for someone working for us in a war zone. Anyone would have done what Antonio did."

"Maybe you're right," said Spencer.

Suleiman sat there in silence behind Samuel's desk, listening and taking notes. He wore an expressionless face throughout. But anyone could tell that his brain was working at full throttle. Years of practicing law in New York had taught him to listen carefully and say little or nothing until he had a point to make or to steer the conversation in another direction.

That time had come.

"So, Mohammed, why did you never report back to Samuel or Antonio what happened at the jihadist checkpoints when you entered and left Fallujah the day you met Omar for the first time?" Suleiman asked.

Abul Einein's face dropped. His mind went temporarily blank. Was Suleiman trying to shift some of the blame to him? And how did he know about what happened at the checkpoints? The driver Sinan! Who else?

"Well, I did not think much about it at the time. I kind of saw the whole thing as the jihadists being helpful to a popular and well-connected local boy. I did not think it meant more than that and that's why, perhaps, I did not share with Samuel or anyone else. I kind of was glad that we may be getting a well-connected guy at an important place at the perfect time."

"I still think you should have said something. You're a journalist and what happened at the checkpoints, in my view, should have raised red flags. But I also understand why you thought it was unnecessary," Suleiman said, not sounding too convinced by his own words.

"Listen, you may not want to hear this or find it useful, but in this office it's best for someone like me not to share too many personal views, particularly on staffing and management issues," responded Mohammed, now a little edgy. "I only chip in when it has to do with the story or the quality of our coverage. Anything beyond that would likely be either frowned upon or rejected as inappropriate meddling. I spare myself the embarrassment of being told to mind my own business. Everyone was excited about Omar's work. When the photos began to come in and showed that kind of access, everyone was happy. Everyone was thinking of prizes and maybe even a Pulitzer. Do you understand any of this?"

"Of course!" Suleiman said, although he did not know for sure whether Abul Einein's question contained a subtle accusation of ignorance.

"Let's see how this pans out," he said. "It's difficult, if not outright impossible, to ascertain what Omar was really up to in Fallujah. We may be able to visit him soon. We will see then how much he will share with us. I am not hopeful that the visit will produce any game-changing information, but we will see. Thanks Mohammed. This was enormously useful."

CHAPTER SIXTEEN

It was nearly dawn when Safiyah finally opened her eyes. She was lying on her back with her legs spread wide and her arms thrown back. That was not a normal sleeping position for her, but a sign of her extreme fatigue. She did not move, although her eyes were wide open. Her mind raced to remember the events of the last twenty-four hours. The thought of her parents' violent death and the irreverent way in which she had been forced to bury them made her grimace and tear up. She looked at the grave she was right next to and ran her right hand on the part of the surface she could reach.

"May the Almighty have mercy on your soul and avenge your death," she said out loud as she tried to get up. Every bone in her body ached. Her eyes were swollen from crying. Her shoulders were so sore from all the physical exertion of the previous day. Her nose was blocked: she must have caught a cold from sleeping outdoors while sweaty in winter. She'd had nothing to eat for more than 24 hours. Not that she felt like eating, but the hunger left her totally without energy.

She finally managed to get up, leaning against the wall until her dizziness subsided. She walked into the house and collapsed on the same chair she'd been asleep in when the missiles hit. Surveying the wreckage, her heart felt heavy. She let out a loud sigh, and her thoughts returned to Hassan.

Where could he be now, she thought. Is he even alive?

It felt like she had not seen him in so long. She needed him now, or anyone else for that matter. She wanted someone to console her. Someone who could soothe her, maybe with a recital of Quranic verses to heal the soul. Hassan's sweet, deep voice could have done just that. Wouldn't that be the best thing to help her cope with the loss of her parents? But she could not just banish the thought that her parents' death was essentially caused by Hassan. His negligence cost them their lives. How could he not think that he was being tracked by the Americans? That they knew of him and decided to try and take him out? Was he too wrapped up in his jihadist world that he paid no attention to the safety of others around him? He was the emir of Fallujah, how could all this have escaped his mind?

Pushing aside the thought of Hassan, her mind turned to more immediate issues. Should she stay put at the house? Was it safe to stay here after the building had clearly sustained serious structural damage? The whole place could cave in and she would be buried under the rubble. Was it even safe to stay in Fallujah at all? Probably not, she thought. Maybe Baghdad, where she could be reunited with her siblings at her aunt's house in Azamiyah. But how could she leave the city when a battle was raging? Must give it a try, she thought, ruling out the option of attempting to reach some of her relatives in Fallujah. She was not even sure they were in town. Besides, she thought, would they be willing to put her up? The thought of providing shelter to the wife of the sheikh of the mujahedeen with the Americans now poised to retake the city could be unnerving. Some of them had been avoiding her and her parents for months because of Hassan.

Trying to get out of town on foot and then finding transport to Baghdad would be the best option.

She got up and looked for her abaya in the yard. It was still caught between a large slab of concrete and the street wall. She picked it up and put it on, went back to the house to fetch her sandals and left.

She had not been aware of the battle sounds since she woke up. She was immersed in her own thoughts. But the moment she stepped out, the potential danger of what she intended to do became clear. The ground was shaking. The sound of explosions was deafening. At a distance, helicopter gunships hovered over the city, firing flares and rockets. Intermittent bursts of heavy machine gun fire rang out across the city.

Safiyah felt like she would lose her nerve, but she was able to quickly collect herself. She began walking, finding some comfort in the notion that the battle was being fought on the city's outskirts.

She headed to the south, using side roads that appeared deserted. House doors were shut. Some had iron chains for extra security. No sign of life could be detected from looking at windows that were either left open by fleeing families or were smashed open by some of the larger blasts. The deserted streets scared her even though it was still morning.

The sound of the battle steadily grew louder as she approached the southern fringes of the city. She would stop and pause after every blast, trying to ascertain how close it was or whether she was unwittingly walking into the battle.

Unexpectedly, the scream of a jet-fighter swooping down forced her to the ground. A second later, the two-story house to her left lit up with a bang. The house was immediately engulfed in a giant ball of red and orange flame and a pall of black smoke rose above.

Safiyah let out a scream of pain. She was hurt and bleeding from her left thigh and torso. She screamed again when she saw blood seeping onto the ground. Her thigh was bleeding more than her torso. She pressed her left hand to the leg wound. The bleeding slowed but did not stop altogether.

She soon gave up on anyone coming to help or drive her to a hospital. She was silent, as though waiting to bleed enough to pass out and quietly die. The pain made her groan and she sat motionless; eyes shut. A few minutes passed before she heard loud engines, but she could not see anything. Suddenly, the lead Humvee of an American convoy came into sight, swinging out of a side street and heading straight for her.

The dust-covered convoy stopped just a few meters from where she sat.

"Move out of the way," yelled the gunner on top of the lead Humvee. "Move out of the fucking way," he yelled again. Safiyah did not understand, nor did she move. All she could do was tremble in fear. She had never come so close to American soldiers in Fallujah. She'd seen them many times from a distance, racing through the main road of the city in their vehicles. The helmets and the goggles concealed most of their faces, but she could roughly tell the ethnicity of the gunners. Black, white, brown.

Whenever the soldiers were on the ground in Fallujah and she happened to be in the vicinity, she went to great lengths to stay out of their way and sight.

"Are you blind?" screamed the gunner.

"She's hurt, man!" yelled another soldier at the gunner.

"Hey, John, get your bag and come here quick, man," he shouted at a medic riding in the fourth Humvee.

The medic came running to Safiyah. Other soldiers disembarked and went straight to the house, guns at the ready, to survey the damage and see if there is any useful material that can be retrieved and taken back to base.

"Don't be scared. I'm going to try and help you," John told Safiyah with an exaggerated but reassuring smile.

"Let me take a look, please," he pleaded as Safiyah tried to move away. He placed his hand on her shoulder and addressed her in a stern voice. "You let me help you now or you bleed to death," he said, pointing at the pool of blood beside her. "Do you understand? You will die if you don't let me," said John, mimicking death by slowly closing his eyes and throwing his head to the right.

"Ok, I'm not sure she understands; and she's badly hurt," the medic screamed to the others. "I need Hussein to translate," he said.

"Hussein!" screamed an older marine in the direction of the convoy. Soon, a 20-something man in ill-fitting military fatigues and a helmet emerged from the third Humvee and started walking toward Safiyah with some urgency.

"Tell her that if she does not let me help her, she will die."

Hussein translated.

"I don't care if I die, but I won't let him touch me. Tell him that," she said in a faint voice.

"Why? He is a medic. He will save you. Why die if you can live?" said Hussein, pleadingly.

"I would rather die. You won't understand. Are you Iraqi?"

"No, I am Lebanese, but I live in America."

"That's why you don't understand," she said, a hint of suppressed anger in her voice. She was silent for a few seconds, looking aimlessly at Hussein before her vision began to blur. Her head moved back and forth and then slumped backwards. John was quick to put his hand on the back of her head to stop it banging into the asphalt. Safiyah passed out. She had lost a great deal of blood.

John got to work quickly as he spoke to the older marine who was carrying a radio.

"I need transport and maybe a bird to fly her to Baghdad. This woman will die if she does not get to a hospital in the next 30 minutes," said John, clearly savoring another memorable war moment of trying to save a life. He placed pressure bandages on both wounds and pressed them hard with his hand to make sure they would stay.

John went back to his Humvee and returned with a stretcher. With help from Hussein the translator and another marine, he carefully lifted Safiyah on to it and together they carried her to the ambulance vehicle at the back of the convoy, marked with a red cross on white background on both sides. They secured her to the back of the Humvee with four olive green straps.

The convoy turned around and headed back to the base just outside Fallujah as the marine with the radio kept on talking to the command post.

"They'll have a bird ready in about 15 minutes and Ibn Sina is expecting her," he triumphantly announced. "That was not easy, boys. Getting a bird to fly an Iraqi civilian from a battle zone to hospital? We are making history!" he said, putting down the radio's hand piece.

Turning to the four marines in his vehicle, he said: "The boys at Ibn Sina will be pleased they decided to treat her when they see this eye candy we're sending their way." Everyone in the Humvee let out a hearty, vulgar laugh.

CHAPTER SEVENTEEN

It was late afternoon when Safiyah woke up in Ibn Sina hospital inside the Green Zone. The room had two beds, but the other was vacant. The room was small, but clean and neat. She had a drip in her left arm. She was in a blue, short-sleeved hospital gown, her hair was not covered.

She did not know where she was, except that she was in a hospital. But something more immediate and pressing than her location bothered her, and she started looking around the room to see what she could do to get help. There was a button on the side table. She pressed it and kept her finger there for a few seconds.

A nurse came in, an athletic white woman in her early 40s with blonde hair and a white dress that stopped just above the knees. She wore matching trainers.

"Hey sweetie, how are you doing? My name is Bridget and I am the head nurse in this wing," she said to Safiyah. When she received no response, she spoke slowly, articulating every word. "You're looking so much better now. We had to transfuse a lot of blood to you," she said, pausing in the hope she would get some sort of answer.

When none was forthcoming, she asked: "Now, how can I help you?"

Safiyah knew very little English and did not understand the question, but she knew what she wanted.

She pointed to her hair and made a sign to indicate that she wanted her hair covered and then ran her right hand down her left arm to suggest that she wanted to cover her arms as well.

The nurse did not get it at first but she understood when Safiyah repeated the two gestures.

"Oh, I see," she said, celebrating their first successful communication. "Of course, sweetie! I will see to it right away," she said before disappearing. She returned a few minutes later with a white scarf and a light blue cardigan that looked like a hospital issue.

"Here, let me help you put these on."

Safiyah surrendered. She was too weak to do anything, so she just let the nurse do it.

"There you are! That's better, right?"

Safiyah managed a cautious smile. She was grateful for the help. She mumbled a hesitant "thank you" in English that was barely loud enough for the nurse to hear it.

"You're so very welcome, sweetie. Now get some rest. The doctor will be along soon to check on you and then you will have to eat something."

Alone now and fully awake, Safiyah's eyes wandered around the hospital room. The walls were off white and there was a flat television screen hung on the wall next to the door, showing CNN International but with the volume on mute. There were a couple of chairs and two white side tables.

The floor was also off-white ceramics and the sole window provided a view of the manicured lawn outside. The buzz of low-flying helicopters pierced the eerie quiet around the hospital. A message would often blare out summoning staff to an emergency or requesting the presence of one or two doctors at a specified location. Sometimes, she would hear footsteps in the corridor outside her room. On occasion, it would be someone walking so fast they were almost running. On the side table next to her was a recent copy of Stars and Stripes, the newspaper of the U.S. armed forces.

The wife of the emir of Fallujah was being treated in an American military hospital? What would Hassan say? Should she even tell him? What if they found out who she really was when they ask for her personal details for their records? Surely the spies who worked for the Americans inside Fallujah had given them her name, and maybe even her picture. But what do they have against her? She was the wife of the emir of the jihadists, not one of his men. She never killed anyone. In fact, she never hurt the proverbial fly.

Her train of thought was interrupted when the doctor came into the room with the nurse in tow.

"Hello," said the doctor as soon as he entered the room, speaking Arabic with a slight accent that suggested his origins might be in Lebanon, Syria or Jordan. He wore army fatigues, with beige suede boots. His name tag read: Dr Khater Abu Suheil. He was in his mid-30s, tall, maybe six one or six two and his body suggested regular gym workouts. He wore an army cap that did not conceal his dark brown hair. His eyes were light green. Khater's good looks were made all the more attractive by the humility and modesty of his manner. Clearly conscious of his good looks, but not to the extent of being cocky or overconfident.

"My name is Dr Khater. I was the one who received you here on arrival and treated your wounds. I am an American, a captain from the National Guard, and I volunteered to come to Iraq, but I am of Palestinian origin. Born in Ramallah. Do you know where that is?"

Safiyah nodded and looked away with a look of affected contempt. That was the wife of the jihadist mode kicking in.

"I am told you were very close to where the airstrike happened. You're lucky to have survived with just a couple of wounds. Usually, people suffer much more or even die if they are that close to an airstrike. The medic who treated you at the site of the blast did a great job. Without him, you could have died."

Safiyah did not nod or say anything this time, but she listened attentively and in some wonderment at the man. Everything about Khater's looks and even the Arabic he spoke said he was an American, she thought. She began to examine him as he spoke to her. She noticed his green eyes, his imposing height and his slender yet muscular build.

"The marines thought it was their duty to help you and arrange for you to come to Ibn Sina. Have you heard of Ibn Sina before?"

Safiyah shook her head, still immersed in her bewilderment at the man addressing her in Arabic in an American military hospital. She continued to stare at him with a mix of admiration and curiosity.

"It's the biggest and best equipped hospital in Iraq and it's run by the U.S. military," he boasted. "We are in the Green Zone in Baghdad on the Karkh side of the city. We mostly treat military personnel or American contractors, but we make exceptions sometimes. You are one of those exceptions," he added with a smile. "Now, let us talk about your condition. You are out of danger, thanks be to Allah, but you'll need to stay here with us for a few days, maybe a week or 10 days before you can go home. We need to make sure the wound in your thigh is healing well before we let you go. We removed a few pieces of shrapnel from there, but nothing really big and they only left superficial wounds."

Safiyah was pleased to hear the good news about her condition, but she would not allow herself to show it. She felt awkward, even guilty, that she was lying in bed patiently listening to an American doctor, regardless of his Arab heritage, speaking to her at an American military hospital inside the Green Zone, the symbol of America's occupation of Iraq. Part of her wanted to thank him, but she convinced herself that it would not be right to do that. Dr Khater was, after all, an active participant in that occupation. He might have successfully treated hundreds of wounded American soldiers and sent them back to the streets to kill more Iraqis. He had perhaps saved her life, but that was his duty as a doctor. Not to do so would leave him in breach of his Hippocratic Oath. Besides, she thought, treating a civilian Iraqi woman must have made him feel good about himself. And after all it is God, and no one else, who wills whether we live or die.

But she felt she needed to say something. Anything, really. She did not want him to think that she was crazed or unable to say even a few words. Secretly, she wanted to engage him conversationally. She did not want him to finish what he had to say and leave the room. She wanted him to stay so she could look at him a little longer and, perhaps, savor his good looks. Who could tell when she would be able to see him again. But as she mustered the courage to say something, he asked her a question.

"So, what's your name?"

"Safiyah," she replied hesitantly as if she was not sure what her name was.

"That's one of my favorite names. My father's late aunt was called Safiyah. We believe in my family that she died of a broken heart when she lost her home in a small village near Haifa where she lived all her life. She could not handle her forced displacement in 1948: or maybe she just died of fatigue from that long journey on foot to the West Bank. She was fifty and my father told me she was also very fat," he said with a chuckle.

"I lost my parents just two days ago," said Safiyah, finally addressing the "enemy" doctor, but speaking with a disapproving tone. "They died when rockets hit our home the first night of the attack on Fallujah. I buried them with my own hands," she continued, deliberately avoiding a direct mention of who actually killed her parents. She thought if she did mention that the airstrike was carried out by the Americans he would take offence and maybe become less friendly, or just leave and not come back.

"I will mourn them until the last breath I take. I wish I'd died with them," she said, tearing up.

"Don't say that, Safiyah, you're young and you have your whole life ahead of you. Are you married?"

"I was," she said, her mind preoccupied with what would likely be his next question. "My husband died in a car accident," she lied, hoping that her untruth would steer the doctor away from finding out or suspecting that she was linked to Fallujah's jihadists.

"Do you have children?"

"No, I don't. God did not will it."

"Everything happens when God wills it," said Khater trying to show her that he too had faith in God and accepted his will, but he was also examining Safiyah. For a fleeting moment, he tried to imagine her in a western outfit, maybe a pair of jeans and a loose white T-shirt with her hair down. Maybe in a low-cut evening gown and a necklace of pearls attending a high-end function at the banquet hall of some luxury New York or Chicago hotel.

Khater could see some of her hair since the head cover the nurse gave her was not so tight. He could see her hazelnut eyes and he was instantly bewitched by them. He could see that creamy complexion on her bare neck. What if? He thought to himself before he snapped out of his brief daydream.

"Safiyah, everything will be good, God willing, and I will see you later today or tomorrow. Get as much sleep as you can. Oh, and eat as much as you can, too. You lost a great deal of blood and you're weak."

CHAPTER EIGHTEEN

It took Omar sometime before he began to grasp what happened to him the night the marines stormed the house where the jihadists had taken refuge.

He was blindfolded and handcuffed and thrown into the back of a Humvee. A marine fastened his seat belt for him and took the seat next to him. He and Mohammed Saadoun were taken to the U.S. base near Fallujah. The bumpy journey took about thirty minutes. Once there, his seat belt was unfastened and he was led down from the vehicle and into a grim looking, two-story building that appeared to be a makeshift jail. The marine guarding them was soon joined by another and the two led Omar upstairs. One of them nudged him inside a cell with a small, barred window close to the ceiling. The cell's metal door had a tiny square opening with a flap that slid to the right and which could only be used from outside the cell. Inside was a small washbasin, toilet and a narrow, metal-frame bed with a thin mattress on top. There were two blankets and a pillow that had no cover.

One of the two marines proceeded to remove the blindfold and undo the plastic handcuffs.

"I am a photographer," Omar said in heavily accented English, but enough for the marines to understand.

"Whatever!" said one of the two men as they walked out and slammed the door shut.

Omar stood in the middle of the cell staring at the gray door. A thousand thoughts raced through his mind. He was confused and felt drained. Everything happened so quickly. Just hours ago his mind had been focused on winning a photojournalism prize. Maybe several. Even amid the fear of accompanying the jihadists on their raid, he had been excited and hopeful. The adrenalin rush was immense. Now, he was here alone in an American jail cell, not knowing what would happen to him: It was clear the Americans suspected him of being a jihadist. But he could prove that he was a news photographer. His employers could just come over here and tell them that and he would walk free.

Was he wrong to take that risk for a photography prize that he might not even win? Did his zeal for his new job take him to uncharted waters? What would happen to his mother and brothers now?

Omar tried to comfort himself with the thought of Antonio going to the Americans and telling them that he worked for him. That thought provided him with a measure of solace. His detention would last a day or two, which he could easily endure. But how would Antonio know that he was detained by the Americans? The Americans would have to tell the company that they had him. Of course, they would have to do that.

Omar's racing train of thought was interrupted by the sound of the cell door opening.

"Your name is Omar Al Rawy?" asked a towering black marine as he looked at a folder he held in his left hand. Standing a couple of steps behind him was another marine.

"Yes."

"Ok," said the marine who proceeded to hand Omar a black blindfold he took out of his pocket.

"Put it on," he said. The marine saw that Omar did not quite understand so he used the hand holding the folder to gesture to him to put the blindfold on.

Omar did as he was told. The marine grabbed him by his left arm and led him out of the cell and toward the staircase. The second marine stayed back a couple of steps, keeping a close eye on Omar.

They led Omar to a door at the far end of the corridor. The black marine knocked twice and they went inside.

A captain was sitting behind a desk. Another two captains sat in armchairs in front of him.

Omar was made to stand right between the two officers in the armchairs. The captain behind the desk picked up the phone and barked an order. Two minutes later, an Iraqi in military fatigues walked in. A skinny, short man in his mid-twenties. He timidly approached the officers and greeted them with an accented "good evening, sir."

The greeting went unanswered.

"What's your name, age and profession?" asked the captain behind the desk. The Iraqi interpreter translated.

"Omar Al Rawy. I am 27 and I work as a news photographer."

"Who do you shoot for? And how long have you been doing this job?"

"I take pictures for International United News, the American organization. I have worked for them for several months now."

"So, what were you doing with the terrorists the night we captured you? You were with them during the attack on the checkpoint, right?"

"I was there to take photos and I went on the mission to take more photos," said Omar, his chest heaving and legs wobbly.

"Your activity that night means one thing to us. You were in cohort with terrorists and privy to a plot to kill American and Iraqi soldiers. That's terrorism. Clear cut terrorism."

"But I never carried a gun or fired a shot. I was doing my job," pleaded Omar, almost crying.

"That's not doing your job. You knew those guys were coming at us and you did not report that. You did not even walk away. You joined them. I don't care why you joined them. You did and that's all that matters to us. There is a line between good journalism and collusion with enemy combatants. You crossed that line and that led to the death of Iraqi and American soldiers. Their blood is on you. The law is clear. The Iraqi law, not ours."

It took the interpreter a few minutes to translate this to Omar. At the end, he just gave Omar the gist of what the captain said.

"I was doing my job, nothing more. I am new in this job and I wanted to do something big for the company I work for. I wanted to win prizes and I wanted to be a better photographer. I am not a terrorist."

"I think you are lying."

"No, I am telling the truth."

"Are you sure?"

"Yes."

"Then why did you alert the terrorists that we were about to attack Fallujah? Why did you send word about the attack to your friends? Was that part of your job as a news photographer? What you did that night cost us lives and you'll have to be held accountable for that. You should still consider yourself lucky. If the Iraqis were the ones who captured you, you would have been half dead by now from torture."

Omar froze when he heard the Arabic translation.

CHAPTER NINETEEN

Hassan's mind was made up to leave Mahmoudiyah. He felt it was just a matter of time before the Iraqis or the Americans found them. Staying too long in one place was bound to lead to that. He spoke about it with the four men who shared the apartment with him. They agreed but did not know how to safely get out of Mahmoudiyah. And where would they go that would be safe?

Going farther south would take them into Iraq's Shiite heartlands, a region that was uncomfortable to be in for ordinary Sunnis and deadly for Sunni jihadists. Baghdad, a thirty-minute car ride north, was the obvious choice, but the checkpoints on the city's outskirts were many and they could be detained in any one of them if they didn't have proper documents and a convincing story about their business in Baghdad.

"We need to get in touch with our brothers here in Mahmoudiyah and get them to provide us with documents and logistical support," Hassan told his men one morning. "I need a volunteer to do that."

"I will do it," said Ibrahim Habeeb, Hassan's closest lieutenant who came from Samarra in the north. "Just tell me what I need to do."

"Our guys here in Mahmoudiyah are mostly from the Al Gherer clan. They live on their farmlands away from the city. The legitimate owners of those farmlands have homes in the middle of the fields where they hide jihadists. You need to reach one of those farms and ask them whether they can help us get to Baghdad."

"Consider it done. I will go once I am ready."

"It is not going to be easy. Think hard and long about what you will do to get there," Hassan counselled him as the three other men listened silently, perhaps ashamed that they did not have the will or courage to volunteer for the mission.

When the day of the mission arrived, Ibrahim got up for the dawn prayers, which Hassan led as usual, and then shaved his beard. He changed into clothes brought by the man who regularly left them food and water. Ibrahim had asked the man for clothes that a farm hand would wear, as well as shaving gel, razor blades and a little cash. Ibrahim found everything he asked for at the usual drop-off spot, the first floor of the apartment bloc two doors down the street.

The clothes consisted of a pair of fading denim pants, a casual shirt, old trainers, socks and a change of underwear. Wrapped in an A-4 piece of paper was 50,000 dinars in small change and a fake ID card in the name of Ahmed Aziz, a resident of Mahmoudiyah, born July 1970.

Ibrahim's chief worry was getting out of the nearly deserted Saddam-era housing estate without being detected by a passing U.S. or Iraqi patrol or raising suspicion among the few residents still holding out in the complex. Most tenants fled after the neighborhood saw a series of deadly attacks by jihadists targeting U.S. troops, including roadside bombs that invariably killed or maimed civilians. The attacks had triggered almost nightly raids by the Americans searching for suspects and detaining dozens of fighting-age Iraqi males. The attacks and the raids combined to drive people out of the estate and move elsewhere in the country, mostly to nearby Baghdad or far-flung parts of Anbar.

Once out of the estate and inside the town proper, Ibrahim felt relatively safe. He walked for about 30 minutes to the town's usually bustling outdoor market, where vegetables, fruits, meat and live poultry were sold off rickety stands. The early morning hour meant that the vendors were ready and waiting for the day's first shoppers. Ibrahim had to start his journey early if his story about being a farm hand was to be believed. He walked briskly through the market, avoiding eye contact with the vendors and shoppers but greeting those who looked him in the eye. Not to do so would have aroused suspicion.

Mahmoudiyah is a traditionally Sunni town, with a small Shiite minority. But the number of Shiites had grown since Saddam's ouster in 2003. Poor Shiites from the south came to the town in search of jobs. Others rented homes in Mahmoudiyah but commuted to Baghdad where they took well-paid jobs as construction workers, helpers in eateries or found work in security companies if they had some military experience serving in Saddam's army.

Groups of Shiite militiamen also moved to the town, ostensibly to protect the Shiite minority there, but they soon began to operate as death squads, targeting Sunnis or hunting down suspected jihadists. Iraqi police, both the local contingent and the federal unit stationed in the town, looked the other way while the killings took place, either because they feared reprisals by the better armed and more mobile militiamen, or out of a sense of sectarian solidarity since they too were mostly Shiite.

Ibrahim cautiously asked for directions from travelers at the bus terminal, situated at an empty and heavily littered dirt plot across the road from the market. He boarded the right minibus and sat in the middle row and waited until all 16 seats were filled.

The vehicle pulled out and, just minutes later, the small and austere city dwellings started to give way to barren fields abandoned by farmers who had not been able to secure fertilizers or water to grow their crops since the U.S. invasion.

Ibrahim was dropped off on the main road and told where to go to find the "rest house" of the Al Gherer clan's chief. It was a ten-minute walk on a winding, narrow dirt road before he came to a one-story, off-white building with a courtyard the size of a basketball court. He pushed the metal door open and walked in.

To announce his arrival, he yelled "*Salamou Aleikom!*"

His greeting was answered in kind by a man in his early sixties who emerged from the main part of the house.

"I am Sheikh Assad Al Gherery," said the man as he stretched his hand to shake Ibrahim's.

"*Salamou Aleikoum*, Haji, I am honored."

"Come on in," said the man, in a gray robe, or thoub, and white headgear. He wore a pair of shiny black shoes that would have perfectly matched a dark business suit.

Ibrahim did away with any more niceties and went straight to the business at hand. With minimum details, he explained to Sheikh Assad the situation he and the other four men were in and why they needed help to move to Baghdad.

"We think it's just a matter of time now before we get found out and detained or worse if we stay put in Mahmoudiyah. The place is crawling with spies and Shiite militiamen."

"I understand, let me see what I can do, but I need a few days to consult our local brothers and see what's the best and safest way to get you to Baghdad."

"Don't take too long, Haji, we need to move fast."

"I will do what I can and as quickly as I can," said Assad, sensing Ibrahim's commanding tone and thinking of the possible reprisals he would endure at the hands of the jihadists if he did not act efficiently and quickly.

"Thanks be to God. Our business is done, but it would look odd if I were to return to our hideout now since I am supposed to be a farm hand. So, if you have a business to attend to, please go ahead and I will be here until it's a good time for me to leave."

"Listen, it's an honor to host one of the mujahedeen. Why don't you have a hot shower and change into a comfortable thoub and I will have some food readied and brought to you. Forgive me for saying this, but you look like you could use a home-cooked meal. What do you think?"

"Haji, this is very generous of you."

Sheikh Assad disappeared in an adjacent room and came out two minutes later carrying a fresh thoub, a white bath towel, a pair of plastic sandals and a change of underwear. He handed them over to Ibrahim and pointed to where the shower was and began to walk toward the door.

"I will walk over to the house and get them to start cooking. It will probably be rice with mutton, green beans and a salad. That's what we mostly eat this time of year. Is that fine with you?"

"God have mercy on your parents, haji. This is very generous. I will shower now and maybe lie down and sleep a little until the food is ready."

It did not take Sheikh Assad long to arrange a ride for Hassan and his fellow mujahedeen. Five days after Ibrahim visited him, a minibus arrived outside their building minutes after the muezzin's call for the dawn prayers rang out. It was still dark but daylight was not far off. The driver was a man in his early 30s. Seated next to him was a woman in her 60s wearing a black abaya and head cover. At the back seats immediately behind sat three more women in their 30s, wearing the niqab.

The driver immediately left the car and walked away, leaving the engine running. As soon as he was gone, Hassan, Ibrahim and the three other men emerged from the building, wearing traditional Arab robes and headgear, along with shiny black shoes.

The idea was for them to look like a family going to Baghdad to visit relatives on a Friday, when such visits are traditionally made. The car was loaded with fresh fruits and vegetables, the kind of present people living in rural areas would take to relatives in the city. Their destination was Baghdad's middle-class district of Dora, a Sunni majority area that is home to both an oil refinery and a power station. It lies on the Karkh side of the Tigris, the western and predominantly Sunni side of the capital.

The woman in the passenger seat was supposed to be the mother of the three women in the back, who were married to three of the men; Hassan, Ibrahim and another member of the group. The two extra men, both in their early 20s, were supposedly the brothers of the three younger women.

That way, Sheikh Assad reasoned, the Iraqi police or the Americans would have little reason to suspect them. They all had good forgeries of Iraq's key document, the "citizenship certificate," which served as an ID and without which no official business can be conducted anywhere in the country.

Sheikh Assad had contacted his wide and elaborate network of contacts in Baghdad's districts and the areas south of the capital to identify members of the clan serving in the federal police and manning checkpoints there. He then used emissaries, not phone messages or calls, to inform them of the car's license plate numbers, its occupants, and asking them to do what they could to facilitate their passage to Baghdad. He said nothing else. He did not have to. When Sheikh Assad commanded, clan members obeyed, or at least most of them did.

Sheikh Assad was a fair skinned man with a huge belly. He had been widowed about 10 years before, when his wife of more than 20 years died of stomach cancer. Given the poor state of medical care in Iraq under U.N. sanctions she never had much of a chance. The sheikh, still in his prime, remarried a year later and had three children with his second wife, making up a total of nine when counting the six offspring from his first marriage.

The Al Gherers had been at the receiving end of the wrath of the Americans since the start of the occupation. Many of them swelled the ranks of the mujahedeen in Mahmoudiyah and other areas south of Baghdad. They had been attacking American patrols with roadside bombs and were behind the near daily shelling of their large base in the area with Katyushas and mortars. The rockets and mortars rarely scored a kill, but there were enough of them to disrupt life at the sprawling base. The base's streetlights were permanently turned off, personnel were advised not to be outdoors longer than necessary and on occasion were ordered to wear helmets and body armor when out in the open.

Sheikh Assad was torn between the pressure put on him by local American commanders seeking the names of clan members who joined the jihadists, and from the young men who wanted him to openly declare his opposition to the American occupation. He was summoned several times by the Americans for questioning. On two occasions, he was escorted into a cell and left there until the next day to pressure him into giving them information. During those nights, he was given water and food but was never told why he was being held overnight or told when he would be released. That really bothered Sheikh Assad who, like any clan chief, had great pride and was quick to take offence.

"Those Americans just don't understand," he would say.

One time, he had a meeting with an American army colonel in the Al Rasheed hotel, in the Green Zone, where the officer asked him for a list of names of all the clan members who joined the resistance. Sheikh Assad could not do this even if he had such a list. He was intimidated and threatened by resistance fighters of all stripes in the area, who accused him of being an ally of the Americans or even an informant. They threatened to kill him after he was seen on several occasions going into the American base just north of Mahmoudiyah. What they did not know was that Sheikh Assad was trying to do business with the Americans. He was offering them a variety of services, including the supply of fresh vegetables and fruits and wheat-flour for their bakeries. Practically anything. But his failure to land a contract with the Americans deeply frustrated him: he knew too well that the Americans had a great deal of money to spend and Iraqis who were able to do business with them made a fortune. Those who manufactured concrete blast barriers, for example, made millions. Contractors who did restoration work on schools or health centers also made a great deal of money. Those who supplied the bases with bottled drinking water just killed it.

For Sheikh Assad, the resistance and the Americans were the same. He was convinced that both went to great lengths to make his existence miserable.

"Sheikh Assad, you are a sheep and the terrorists you are protecting are the wolves that one day will attack and eat you," the American colonel told him when they met at Al Rasheed hotel. "Be a wolf and tell us who they're and we will make sure that they will never hurt you. We know of their late-night visits to your home and the threats you get on your mobile phone. We can put an end to that, and I can guarantee you a building contract that will set you up for life."

"I am neither a sheep nor a wolf," Sheikh Assad said through the colonel's interpreter. Showing uncustomary bluntness, he added: "I just want to live in peace."

Now, as the car Sheikh Assad had provided for the jihadists began to move, Hassan and the four men with him prayed out loud, asking God to protect them and deliver them safely to their destination. They made no attempt to speak with the women and their supposed mother beyond the Muslim greeting when they got into the vehicle, with Hassan sitting behind the wheel. Moments later, Hassan made everyone say out loud their names, who they were married to, where they were headed and who they were meeting in Baghdad.

"We have about twenty minutes to go over the information. One slip or a moment of hesitation and we will all be in a lot of trouble," Hassan told everyone in the bus.

"We already have one big drawback and that is we don't have any children with us, which is odd. Now, take off your niqabs and let us take a good look at you. I know we are not supposed to do this, but this is an emergency and we are doing this for God and the Umma."

The three women immediately obliged. They looked very much like sisters. They were in fact two sisters and a cousin. Moreover, all three shared a look of deep alarm. Perhaps their alarm was caused by a combination of showing their faces to complete strangers, or the risk of being detained by the Iraqis or the Americans. None of the three was particularly good looking, and they all looked like they had not slept in days. One of them attempted a smile as she looked at Hassan, but he responded with a stern look of disapproval. The woman immediately wiped the smile off her face.

Ibrahim, who replaced the mother in the passenger seat, looked at the woman who was supposed to be his wife for the day.

"Show me your hair, too. I want to be able to recognize you if they detain us, separate us for a few days and then bring us together again. The hair will help me better remember how you look."

The woman looked at her mother, who nodded her approval. The daughter took off her head cover. Her black hair was long and shiny. It stopped halfway down her back. She adjusted it, to bring more hair to the sides of her head and down on her shoulders. The hair transformed her into a fairly good-looking, if somewhat rugged, woman. Ibrahim immediately felt a stir in his groin. He was getting an erection from just looking at her. When was the last time he saw a woman with her hair and face uncovered? Months, maybe longer. He could not remember. He was too wrapped up in this unexpected moment of joyful, yet unfulfilled, lust. He'd had his fair share of romantic escapades in Baghdad when he served as an officer in Saddam's army, often taking his breaks in the capital. But those days now felt like ancient history. He had become religious during the final years of Saddam's rule when the late dictator's "faith campaign" was in full swing, restricting the sale of alcohol, closing nightclubs and raiding whorehouses that had for decades been deliberately ignored by authorities, so long as they operated discreetly. His piety morphed into religious and nationalist rage after the Americans invaded. The very thought that non-Muslims ruled Iraq was enough to bring out the most extreme feelings in him. The idea of jihad appeared to be the only choice open to him, given the momentous events in his country. He wasted little time before he began to make discreet inquiries in his hometown of Samarra about which group to join. He knew that his military background would serve him well and perhaps even make him a prized member of the resistance. In the end, he chose not to join the Baathists and went for the local branch of Al Qaida.

But right now, on this perilous journey to Baghdad, all he could think of was this woman and the sweeping lust he felt. He was looking so hard at her that it felt he was undressing her with his eyes, imagining how she would look without her abaya and whatever else she was wearing beneath it. He was so engrossed in his sexual fantasy that he initially did not notice his erection.

"That's enough! Cover yourself!" he angrily yelled at her.

He felt guilty for allowing himself to slip and look for so long at a woman he was unrelated to. But he was not blaming himself for his lapse of "morality." It was she who led him into this sin, he thought, forgetting that she showed her face and hair at his and Hassan's request. He also was worried that Hassan may have noticed his erection and his lust for the woman. He placed both of his hands on the general area of his groin, pretending to be adjusting his underpants.

They hit the first checkpoint ten minutes into their journey. It was manned by federal Iraqi police. The cops just waved them on without searching the vehicle or asking for identity papers. Everyone in the car was happy, but Hassan, Ibrahim and the three other men knew the checkpoints would become more thorough as they get closer to Baghdad, especially the last one leading to the district of Al Jadriyah, whose opulent villas and mansions were home to dozens of top politicians as well as the headquarters of one of the country's most powerful Shiite parties.

The line was long and chaotic at that last checkpoint, with some motorists trying to jump the line, only to be yelled at by the Iraqi policemen to get back. It took Hassan and his company about 30 minutes creeping forward before an Iraqi policeman began to examine the faces and the vehicle. He slowly circled it like a predator in the jungle. He was dressed in the blue and gray camouflage of the federal police, armed with an AK-47 and a pistol strapped to his right thigh. A cigarette dangled from the corner of his mouth. He wore a menacing look, but Hassan kept his calm. Ibrahim was calm too, but not everyone else was. The women breathed heavily, and the men fidgeted in their seats, not knowing where to look or what to do.

"Stay calm. We will get through this by the will of God," Hassan said just before he rolled down his window.

The policeman approached Hassan with his right hand stretched in front of him.

"Citizenship" he asked as he examined the passengers.

"Peace and mercy," Hassan greeted the policeman before he reached for his chest pocket and fished out the document. "Here you are, *seidi!*"

The policeman carefully examined it, then looked at Hassan several times.

"Move out of the line, go to your right and wait there," he ordered. As Hassan pulled over the policeman followed the vehicle, calling to a younger colleague to join him. When the other policeman approached, he whispered something to him before he started walking toward the checkpoint about twenty meters away.

The younger policeman looked nervous and possibly trigger-happy as he watched the vehicle from a safe distance. He had his eyes fixed on Hassan, who was motionlessly staring ahead of him.

The older policeman returned with a man in civilian clothes, but with a pistol wedged in his belt.

"Everyone must step out of the vehicle," barked the menacing policeman, his Ak-47 at the ready. The man in civilian clothes took his pistol off his belt and held it like he could shoot at a moment's notice.

Hassan and the others stepped out of the vehicle, all looking alarmed. That's it, they thought, it's years and years in jail or a death sentence.

"Take out your citizenship certificates, all of you," yelled the policeman again, his voice betraying a hint of fear.

"Anmar!" shouted a police captain as he quickly approached the tense standoff.

"Anmar, what have you done now, old friend?" he said with a nervous laugh.

"Do you know him?" the security man in plain clothes asked the captain.

"Anmar and I grew up together in Mahmoudiyah, playing football and harassing girls," he said with a chuckle. "People used to say no one is as mischievous as Anmar Ghazi and Ahmed Samy. But I had not seen him in a long time."

The plainclothes security man signaled to the captain to move aside so they could talk without being heard by others.

"We became suspicious when we saw three men and their wives traveling to Baghdad for a family visit but without a single child between them," he whispered in the captain's ear. "Anyone in my place would stop and investigate."

"Listen, I had not seen Anmar in a long time, maybe years. Let me go talk to him," said the captain as he walked toward Hassan, still standing with everyone else on the side of the road under armed guard.

"So, Anmar," he said deliberately raising his voice for everyone to hear. "Who did you leave the children with?"

"They are both unwell, so we left them with my mother. We had to. There was a death in the family a month ago but we could not go to Baghdad and offer our respects and condolences because the roads were either unsafe or blocked. We just could not postpone that duty any longer. My wife's two sisters have no children. They were married a little more than a year ago," said Hassan, offering a well-rehearsed explanation.

"Ok, that explains everything," he said reassuringly. "Now get back inside the minibus and wait," said the captain as he walked back to the plainclothes security man, who was now sucking hard on a cigarette.

"It's all good. His two children, two boys, are sick and they could not postpone this visit any longer. There has been a death in the family and they are late offering their condolences. The other couple have just married, no kids. It all makes sense to me, but you can run further checks or question them further if you wish, but I think you will be wasting your time. I vouch for Anmar and his passengers. They are clean. He is not the kind who will get involved in anything bad."

"I will take your word for it," said the other man, signaling to Hassan, who was looking out the window, to move on.

"*Salamou aleikom*," shouted Hassan from the window before he rolled it up and drove away slowly.

"That was a close call, but God was on our side, as always," he told his passengers.

"*Allahu Akbar!*" said Ibrahim.

CHAPTER TWENTY

It took the two New York lawyers a week and endless calls to secure a visit to Omar at his jail near Baghdad airport. The company had to try to pull strings in Washington, where Pentagon and State Department officials were reluctant to be involved in what they considered a terrorism case in faraway Iraq. Samuel also spoke to several generals in Baghdad, none of whom he had ever met in person since he rarely left the office. They too were not keen on getting involved.

"That's out of my hands," one general told Samuel after he gave him an extensive brief on Omar's case. "Legal operates independently and entirely outside my chain of command. You'd better approach the Iraqis. At the end, they will be the ones who make the decision whether to put your man on trial or not, not us."

Samuel was deeply disappointed that his weight as the bureau chief of a major American news organization in Baghdad was not enough to get an army general to embrace the company's cause over Omar. The lawyers sensed that Samuel's hands were tied or that he just did not have the contacts to make a difference. They used their own networks back in New York and elsewhere to see if someone knew a senior officer serving in the military's legal in Baghdad. That took days, but they eventually found one, and that caused Samuel considerable embarrassment. The man was a two-star general in Baghdad who went to Yale with one of the lawyers' contacts in New York. That contact spoke to the general in Baghdad and explained Omar's situation. "All they need is to visit their man, that's all," their contact told the general.

"Your request sounds easy but it really isn't. Let me see what I can do. I don't call the shots here. Not all of them, anyway. The rules are rigid and our Iraqi counterparts are closely watching us to see if we slip. You know how it is, it's like a minefield and the stakes are high. The country has been torn apart since we got here. We are not realizing any of our objectives. Like I said, let me see what I can do."

The general got back to the lawyers' New York contact a few days later.

"They can visit next week. Ask them to bring their own interpreter since we have none to spare. Four people can go. How does that sound?"

"Sounds great! Thank you so much. I will tell my friends in Baghdad. They will be pleased."

The lawyers were brimming with pride and a sense of achievement on hearing the news. The bosses in New York were beginning to wonder whether the incredible number of dollars they were paying the pair was money well spent. They wanted to get the word out that their man was being taken care of, and that the company did not abandon him to the seriously-flawed Iraqi legal system.

In a bid to maintain its image as a diverse and inclusive company, the agency dispatched a top writer to Baghdad to write stories about Omar. The outcome was a series of labored stories heavy on quotations from legal experts, but which did not directly address the question of what was Omar doing with jihadists when they carried out a deadly attack on an Iraqi-American checkpoint. The articles strived to highlight cases where Iraqi courts had acquitted terrorism suspects only for the U.S. military to continue detaining them. They also quoted top legal executives from the company saying the military did not have sufficient evidence to detain Omar, let alone file terrorism charges against him.

The articles were hardly convincing to anyone who knew a thing or two about Omar or how things were done in a war zone, where the line between combatants and seemingly ordinary folks could sometimes be blurred. The writer asked the Iraqi reporters to interview spouses of Iraqi men acquitted by the courts but remained in U.S. detention. Those interviews yielded predictable quotes about the injustices committed by the Americans and the suffering of families. They did not conceal the actual purpose of the stories: showing that Omar was unjustly detained, or that there was no credible evidence against him.

The two lawyers decided that Samuel and the bureau's best interpreter should accompany them to visit Omar.

"I want nothing to be lost in translation," Mohammed Suleiman, the Iraqi-American lawyer, emphatically told Samuel. "I don't want the gist or summary of what Omar has to say. I want the nearest thing to a verbatim translation. This is important. We may not see him again until he is up in court."

"We will take Mohammed Abul Einein," Samuel responded in a tone that betrayed he felt offended by being told what to do by the lawyer. But another little chip off his authority did not matter so much at this point. It had been happening for weeks. He decided not to openly protest.

"That's a good idea. He will be perfect for the job."

Suleiman, Jim, Samuel and Abul Einein woke up at 6 am the day of the visit. They met in the kitchen although it was too early for the cooks to be there, so they separately made coffee and cheese sandwiches. Suleiman fished out several cucumbers and tomatoes from the fridge's bottom drawer and carefully washed them before he dried them with a clean kitchen towel, sliced them and placed them on a plate. They ate in silence, partly because it was too early to converse, but also because they were burdened by just how long and momentous the day promised to be.

"We are ready for you, gentlemen," shouted John Lancaster, the chief security consultant, bursting into the room. "We leave in five," he said, heading back out again.

The breakfast party looked at each other.

"I guess this is it," said Samuel with a sigh. "Let's see how this goes," he added as he slowly got to his feet. With equal reluctance, everyone else stood.

They left the compound in two armored vehicles, a blue BMW and a white pickup truck. The drivers were Iraqis. Seated next to them were the British consultants; Lancaster and another one, John Richardson, a former marine in his late thirties.

The drive to the first checkpoint on the airport road went smoothly. Not much traffic this early in the day.

They were met on the hard shoulder by the Americans, who arrived in four Humvees. After a brief exchange of pleasantries, the two company cars followed the Humvees to the base's gate, about ten minutes' drive. At that point, each one of the four _ Samuel, Abul Einein and the two lawyers _ jumped in the back seats of all four Humvees. The four vehicles drove on a dirt road for just a few minutes before they came to a grim-looking building that resembled a prison ward from the outside. It was.

"We've arrived," said a cheerful army captain who rode in the lead Humvee as he approached Samuel, who rode in the one right behind. "Let's do this, gentlemen!"

The party walked inside, through a metal detector and a body search that was so thorough it bordered on intrusive. Everything was meticulously checked. Belts and shoes were taken off and X-rayed. The four were checked for any residue of explosives, with soldiers extracting samples with a small swab from their hands and mobile phones. That exhaustive process alone took ten minutes to complete. It bothered Samuel that he, a former army intelligence captain and a top dog in a major American news organization, should be subjected to the same security procedure that, say, the Egyptian Mohammed Abul Einein, received. Throughout the search, the captain and three soldiers standing with him watched from about five meters away, looking smug and maybe enjoying the sight of three Americans and an Arab being put through one of the most thorough security checks anywhere in Baghdad.

"Sorry about that, gentlemen, but I am sure you understand," said the captain, still looking smug.

"That's fine," Samuel said, unconvincingly.

The captain led them down the hallway with the three soldiers walking behind the four visitors. He stopped outside a door halfway down the hallway.

"There are some rules and guidelines that must be observed during the visit," he began. "You will have complete privacy, but please don't do anything that will arouse suspicion. Don't whisper and don't try and make any physical contact with the suspect. Don't try and pass on to him anything, anything at all. Are we good?"

"Yeah, we're good," Suleiman said, looking inquisitively at Samuel, who responded with a nod.

On hearing this, the captain opened the door and stepped aside to let the visitors enter the room. Omar was there, seated on a chair behind a small table. There were four other chairs in the bare room, which had white walls and a tiny toilet and a washbasin at the far end. Omar looked pale and disoriented. Of the four visitors, he had only met Abul Einein before, when they both rode back to Baghdad from Fallujah with Sinan, the driver, at the wheel. He did not know who the three other men were.

"Hello," said Omar timidly as he stretched his hand to greet his visitors.

"Omar, you probably don't remember me since we only met once. It's Mohammed Abul Einein, the journalist from Egypt. This is Samuel Kennedy, the head of the company in Baghdad and these are lawyers Mohammed Suleiman and Jim Spencer. They are here to defend you and secure your release, God willing. They will want to ask questions to get information that could help them understand the case better. They've already asked me to tell you that you need not and must not conceal anything from them. They want to know everything, even the things that you think might be used against you. This way, they have a better and more comprehensive understanding of the case."

"God willing, I have nothing to hide from anyone," said Omar, affecting a confident tone.

"Omar, *salamou aleikom*," Suleiman said, trying to break the ice with the greeting of Islam. "First things first: Are you being well treated? Is there anything that you need?" he asked in English.

"They treat me well here, but I am in prison and I am away from my family. My mother came to see me a few weeks back and she's heartbroken. I fear for her. Anyways, I don't speak English, so I have not had much chance to talk to any of the guards. They seem ok, though. The food is not bad either and we get enough water to drink. But all that does not matter! I just want to go home."

"And that's why we are here," said Suleiman, a tall and heavy-set man dressed in a navy-blue blazer and khaki pants, topped off with brown shoes and a white shirt. "Now, tell us, what was going on the night the Americans detained you?"

"I was just back from a mission by the jihadists that I photographed for a photo essay I wanted to do. The Americans later came to a house we took refuge in, killed four of us and took me and the leader of the mission. That's all that happened."

"Did anyone in Baghdad know that you were going or who you were going with?"

"No, I wanted to surprise them with the photos. I viewed the mission as the chance of a lifetime to get photos that no one can dream of getting."

"Yes! And look where that got you!" Suleiman said, failing to suppress his anger. He immediately gestured to Abul Einein not to translate to Arabic. "Did you think it was OK to do that? Did you have personal knowledge of the people you went with on that mission? I mean were they childhood friends, relatives or just people you knew, like acquaintances?"

"No, I did not know them. Some of them were not even Iraqi, but their commander was."

"Alright," said Suleiman, who chose not to use Arabic when interviewing Omar. He could have. His Arabic is good enough but he decided to speak in English, maybe to distance himself from his client out of a sense of superiority, or because he wanted the accuracy of Omar's comments to be someone else's responsibility if it was ever questioned.

"You knew that the mission was to kill and destroy, right? I mean, it was not a rescue mission or a mountain climbing expedition, was it?"

Omar was silent for a few seconds. He stared at Suleiman and then the ceiling. He finally looked back at Suleiman. He was seething with anger.

"I did what I thought any photographer would do. Don't American and other photographers sometimes join American soldiers here in Iraq and go out with them on missions? Don't photographers join one side or another in any war to take photos? What did I do differently?"

"Well, for one thing, you never informed us in advance of your plans. You knew that they were going out to kill American and Iraqi soldiers. Every conflict has its own caveats and nuances. In this one, we cannot embed with people who film themselves slitting the throat of innocent hostages and post the video online for everyone to see. We cannot embed with people who blow up others because they are different. So, yeah, there is a difference and I am surprised that you did not consider or know that. Did you? I mean, did it even cross your mind?

Omar fell silent again. After a pause, he said: "I never hurt anyone, directly or indirectly. I just took photos."

"That might be true, but the Americans say you may have been responsible for the loss of American lives. They never shared with us why or what evidence they have to support that claim. Do you know why they think that?"

Omar again paused. He thought of what the American officer told him the day he was detained. Giving the jihadists heads-up that the Americans would attack in a few hours. Does this lawyer know what the Americans told him?

"No, I don't. I wish I knew what they have against me. I did nothing wrong."

"Listen, I need you to answer a few questions for me," chipped in Jim, sounding impatient. "How well did you know the jihadists up to the time when the Americans attacked to retake the city?"

"Some of them are my friends, people I grew up with."

"Ok, let me rephrase. Did you at any point do any work for them? Anything at all?"

Omar paused again. His mind quickly turned to the Egyptian he interrogated and tricked into confessing that he worked for the Americans and who was later executed by the jihadists. He did not execute him: but did he indirectly pull the trigger of Ibrahim's silenced pistol when he shot the Egyptian in the back of the head?

"No, I did not," Omar said.

"Take your time. Think hard and try to remember even the smallest thing," said Jim, who was more impatient now.

"No, nothing. Nothing at all."

"Are you sure?"

Omar did not answer. He just nodded.

"Ok. Here is what we are going to do now," interrupted Suleiman. "We will try and expedite your trial so you are not in prison longer than you have to be. You will plead not guilty to any of the charges and we will see where that takes us. We have hired a top lawyer to defend you. But I am afraid that the emergency court that will try you will have no time or tolerance for a good argument by a lawyer, even if he is the best lawyer in the country. Still, his big name may have a mitigating effect on a judge who, like many others, does not answer to anyone these days. Do you understand? So, if you are a good Muslim, and I believe you are, pray 10 times a day, not five. I will say even 20 times a day. You have all the time in the world here, so do it."

Omar was speechless when he heard the translation. His silence turned into rage at what he perceived to be condescending advice. Is that all that the company was going to do for him?

"When do you think I will go home?" he asked.

"Have you not been listening?" Samuel interjected, speaking for the first time since the visit began. "Abul Einein, have you been translating everything?" he yelled at the Egyptian.

"Everything boss, honestly."

"Then what the fuck is he going on about? Jesus Christ!" he screamed before he looked down at the floor, clearly trying to calm himself.

"Listen, there is going to be a trial. You are facing terrorism charges. This is a serious matter. It's not a joke. We are doing everything we can. And it's costing us a hell of a lot of money and a hell of a lot of time. But we cannot control the process. I wish we could take you home now to your mother and brothers, but we cannot. You will have to stay put and hope for the best. Getting caught with a bunch of bad guys after they killed American and Iraqi soldiers is not a fucking joke, is it, son? So, don't ask dumb questions like when you'll go home. You'll go home when you are acquitted or when you get a suspended sentence. And if you do, then please don't forget to thank us, because it will be us who pulled it off for you."

CHAPTER TWENTY-ONE

Hassan did not think it was a good idea for him to stay at the same place in Baghdad with Ibrahim and the other men. The authorities were alert to anyone moving into rented apartments anywhere in the city and landlords were now obliged to report any new tenants to the police or face a heavy fine. This was one of a number of methods used by the government to track down jihadists infiltrating the city with the intention of carrying out attacks. But reporting new tenants did not really help much in reducing the number of attacks, since jihadists did not stay in rented apartments. They stayed in safe houses mostly located in Sunni-dominated areas.

Hassan moved into one of those houses, while Ibrahim and the others found different safe houses to stay in.

Hassan's was on Saadoun street in the heart of Baghdad, in an area known as Rusafah on the east bank of the Tigris. The apartment was in a poorly-kept, three-story building that dated back to the 1970s. It was a five-minute walk away from Fardous square, where U.S. soldiers used a military crane to bring down a bronze statue of Saddam on April 9, 2003, the day Baghdad fell.

Hassan found food, water, tea and sugar in the apartment. It was generally much better supplied than the one in Mahmoudiyah. The most useful item he found was a Nokia phone with an active Syrian SIM card. Having a non-Iraqi SIM card, the jihadists thought, would be safer than using a local chip whose provider could easily be controlled by the Americans. The roaming charges were high, but it was money well spent.

For hours on end, Hassan relied on his memory to dredge up the numbers of family members in Baghdad. He wanted to know whether Safiyah was there. He did not know for sure but guessed that this is where she was most likely to be. He tried her mobile number countless times, but it was not ringing. The recorded message said it was either switched off or out of the coverage area. She must have lost it and the battery eventually ran out, he thought. But he kept trying in the hope that it might still ring and she would pick up. How delightful it would be to hear Safiyah's voice again after such a long time. He was missing her terribly. He had never been away from her for this long since they got married. He missed everything about her and felt lonely without her. Almost incomplete. She'd been such a big part of his life for years. But what would he do if she was indeed in Baghdad and they were alone together one more time? He knew, of course. But what else? The apartment he lived in was depressingly bare and there was little in the kitchen that he or she could turn into a nice homemade meal. But these were not ordinary times: the main thing was to make sure that the bed linen and the pillow covers were not dusty or dirty. Safiyah would be uncontrollably coughing for hours if they were.

His phone rang hours after he went to bed. It was a voice he could not immediately recognize, but he eventually realized that it was one of his Baghdad cousins.

"We know where you are and she will be coming to see you in the morning," said the voice.

"Good. Tell her to be careful."

"Don't worry, it has all been taken care of. *Salamou aleikom*," said the cousin before he hung up.

Hassan grinned. He was fully awake now, wondering how early in the morning his wife would arrive. What could he do to celebrate her? Should he shower? Of course he should!

Hassan drifted in and out of sleep before he was finally awakened by the call for the dawn prayers. He got up, washed and prayed. He prayed so hard that he teared up. He asked God for so many things. Things for himself, for Safiyah, for his family and for the faithful. His heart was filled with so much joy that he would shortly be reunited with his wife. He felt that God would grant him his wishes. He was convinced that God loved him. If God did not, why then would he make his imminent reunion with Safiyah so easy to arrange?

He heard a knock on the door hours after the dawn prayers. It was late morning. He rushed to the door to open it. Safiyah was standing there in all her divine beauty. She wasn't wearing a niqab or an abaya. To blend in with the women of Baghdad she wore black pants and a matching jacket that went down all the way to just above the knees. She wore a white headscarf, but it was much in the category of what was wryly known as "Islamic light." Not too tight. Showing a little hair on her forehead and the temples. She carried a large plastic bag in her right hand.

Hassan reached out for her left hand, held it, and used his right hand to take the bag off her before he gently pulled her inside the apartment. He closed the door and locked it.

"That's heavy, what do you have in there?" he said as he put the bag down behind him and returned to stand right in front of her. He held both of her hands and brought her closer to him. They hugged. She started to sob. Her chest heaved as she began to cry uncontrollably.

"I am here! I am safe and so are you," he said in a soothing voice as he gently pushed her away from him so he could look into her eyes. "God willed that we part and then he willed that we be reunited here. I prayed so hard for so long that God fills your heart with peace and contentment while we are apart. I wanted Him to give you the strength to endure our separation. I asked him to give me the same but he has not answered my prayers for I missed you more than I can put in words. Being away from you was like an open and painful wound that refuses to heal."

They kissed. She stopped crying. She breathed heavily and let out a sigh that laid bare both her joy and angst over being with Hassan again. She could no longer stand on her feet. It was too much to bear after so long. She nearly collapsed, but Hassan's arms were there to support her. He had his left hand around her waist while his right one held her left hand as he led her to the bedroom. They headed straight for the bed, which had a clean set of sheets and pillow covers that he had found at the bottom of the wardrobe in his bedroom.

It was a while before they spoke again.

"Hassan, praise be to God that you survived the war in Fallujah. I hear many of the jihadists were killed by the Americans. People in Baghdad were saying they were not taking any prisoners. May God curse them and curse the day they came to our country."

"They are evil and God will soon exact revenge on them for killing so many Muslims."

"They killed my parents the night you left," Safiyah said, trying hard not to be dramatic about the news she just broke or show her conviction that he was partially to blame for their death.

But, in the end, she could not resist.

"It was just minutes after you left me. I think the missiles were meant for you, but my parents were killed instead. It's God's will. It cannot be helped," she said unconvincingly.

Hassan recited a brief prayer asking God to bestow his mercy on his in-laws before he turned to Safiyah.

"May God have mercy on their souls and grant them an eternal stay in paradise," he said choosing to ignore what she said about the target of the airstrike.

"I, too, almost died, Hassan! I was making my way out of Fallujah on foot when an American plane bombed a house I was close to. I was injured and bled for a long time before I was taken to hospital."

"What hospital?"

"I passed out and when I regained consciousness I was in an American hospital in Baghdad. It's called Ibn Sina."

"God have mercy on your father, how did that happen?"

"I passed out after the Americans found me lying on the street bleeding. They wanted to give me first aid. I refused, but then I passed out and the next thing I knew I was in a hospital bed."

"We are believers, Safiyah. It was God's will that they find and treat you. God wanted you to live and he sent you those infidels to deliver his will. Sometimes, we, God's slaves, just don't know what is good for us, but He does."

Safiyah was taken aback by her husband's unusually moderate rationale. She did not think he had it in him to see God's hand in something that he would normally reject out of hand. But Hassan, she'd learned over the years, sometimes departed, albeit briefly, from his extremist beliefs, something that she interpreted as a sign of the conflict raging inside him despite all appearances to the contrary.

She did not need any convincing herself that the Americans, primarily the medic John and the Palestinian-American doctor, Khater, saved her life and treated her as something of a celebrity while in hospital. That may have been in part due to her exceptionally good looks, but still. They did everything they could to make her comfortable. With the help of a Muslim male nurse, they found out and informed her of the direction of Mecca for her prayers. They provided her with a small rug that a hospital worker bought from a souvenir store inside the Green Zone to take home to America but agreed to lend it to Safiyah to use as a prayer mat. They helped her wash before the prayers and brought her a copy of the Quran although she never asked for one.

"Some bedside reading that you'll enjoy for sure," the blonde nurse, Bridget, told her when she brought her the book: she had literally snatched it from an Iraqi soldier she spotted standing on sentry duty outside the prime minister's Green Zone office. The soldier was so surprised when the nurse walked up to him and just grabbed the book he kept on a chair next to him. He did not protest, nor did he utter a single word.

"It's the Quran, right? I am just borrowing it, you'll have it back!" she cheerfully told him as she walked back to her white SUV. Her words, which he did not understand, only deepened his bewilderment.

Khater showed Safiyah so much care she was left with no choice but to thank him profusely every time he visited her. He checked on her at a frequency that went way beyond the call of duty. On some days, he visited four or five times; and every time he came into her room he wanted to have a conversation. He would check on her wounds after the nurse removed the bandages and then administer the antibiotic ointments himself. He did not have to, clearly, since it was the nurse's job. And he would not stop talking to her while doing that.

Safiyah, to her own surprise, did not mind. In fact, she looked forward to his visits and enjoyed his conversation. He would talk to her about his childhood growing up in Brooklyn. He told her of his parents' struggle to make ends meet while he attended a rough high school in their poor, immigrant neighborhood. He told her about medical school in Chicago and how he had to take up part-time jobs to reduce the financial burden on his family even though he had a near-full scholarship.

Safiyah was fascinated by his stories, their details and his struggle to carve a future for himself. His conversation allowed her to discover a world she knew nothing or very little about. To her, America was so far away; and so evil. It had never crossed her mind, not for a second, to visit America. Her travel daydreams did not take her beyond Iraq's immediate neighborhood: Jordan, Syria and maybe Saudi Arabia.

When they talked, their eyes met, and remained steady. "You know, Safiyah," Khater told her one day. "I am learning so much here and gaining a lot of experience. When my time in Baghdad is up, I will be able to get a surgeon's job in any one of the biggest hospitals in the United States. The more experienced doctors here have revolutionized emergency surgery. We have saved the lives of so many. So many! But some of those we saved will almost entirely depend on care for the rest of their lives. Some of them say they would have been better off dead than lead the difficult life of an amputee or someone with special needs. I disagree. Life is priceless."

"You're right. Every sunrise that ushers in a new day is a blessing from God," said Safiyah who, in her conversations with Khater, was rediscovering a part of herself that marriage to a jihadist had suppressed. In Ibn Sina hospital, she talked with almost complete ease to an American doctor who was unrelated to her, something that she had not been able to do since she reached puberty back in Fallujah. Unlike when she was with Hassan, she did not have to quote from the Quran or the hadeeth to argue a point. With Khater, she did not have to edit herself so she did not sound too worldly or secular. She was able to get through entire conversations with him without bringing God into it. Was that the side of her whose growth was arrested when she married Hassan as a teenager? Was that the side she developed before that by reading fiction and history by the greats of Iraq and Egypt? Was she really meant to be the wife of a jihadist?

And she began to wonder whether she would have been better off if she had married a cultured man from Baghdad.

Hassan, on the other hand, fought a foreign occupier and was ready to make the ultimate sacrifice for his cause. He was a brave and dedicated defender of the faith. He was the only man to have ever touched her. His lovemaking was passionate, although at times it bordered on the violent. But there was always, she felt, something missing; and it was not just that they had no children. That really bothered Hassan, but it was much more than that. It was like Hassan was never enough for her, or that what he lacked bothered her. She wanted much more from life; and being married to a jihadist stopped her from getting what she wanted.

But what did she really want? She did not know exactly, but she knew that it was something that Fallujah could not give her. Not even Iraq could give it to her. As she spoke with the foreign doctor, she began to realize that what she really wanted was freedom, unfettered and boundless. She did not want to be let loose on the world. No! She wanted the freedom to make her own choices.

Lying now next to Hassan, she recalled how often she wondered about what he was hiding from her. Did he kill in cold blood? Did he, as the sheikh of the mujahedeen in Fallujah, play both judge and executioner? People outside the ranks of jihadists in Fallujah feared him. They were terrified of him, in fact. In many ways, she thought, he was something of a Saddam Hussein. A dictator with a radical religious narrative who forced everyone into submission, at least publicly. After all, who in his right mind would challenge the rule of God? When he and his fellow jihadists took over in Fallujah, people fell back on old habits developed and honed during Saddam's rule, but which they briefly discarded when the Americans toppled his regime: they started whispering again when they spoke about the jihadists, just as they had about Saddam's Baathists. They were paranoid about being spied on by admirers of the mujahedeen. They never aired their grievances about life under their rule when their children were around lest they repeat what they heard to friends. Men made a point of praying at mosques at least once a day rather than pray at home as most of them normally did. When there, they went out of their way to ensure that they were seen by the jihadists who happened to be there too.

Friday prayers was a must, especially since the sermon was always given by a senior jihadist or a sympathetic imam. Listening to the sermon was no longer a passive act. Men felt the need to show vocal admiration for or appreciation of what was being said. "*Allahou Akbar!*" or "*Yaa Allah!*" the worshippers would now cry out, to show they were paying attention and appreciating what was being said.

Many rumors circulated about the fate of local men who disappeared. People whispered that they were executed for spying for the Americans, the government or that they were closet Shiites. Many believed they were quietly executed and buried in unmarked graves at the backyards of abandoned houses or at the industrial area on the outskirts of the city. When families of the disappeared asked the jihadists about the fate of their loved ones, they either denied any knowledge of what happened to them or suggested that they might have left town to seek refuge in Baghdad or Ramadi.

Khater, Safiyah frequently thought, came from a different world, one that's kinder and less oppressive. He was pleasant, charming, smart and ambitious. She caught him several times looking at her affectionately when she was being attended to by one of the nurses.

Sometimes, she would look back and he would quickly look away shyly. But there were times when they both looked at each other and lingered. And, for a fleeting moment, Safiyah would feel something. She did not exactly know what it was, but it was delightful. It made her feel guilty, but also like she was in a sweet dream.

She found Khater's stories interesting and rich in detail. Each one took her on a journey away from the life of austerity and hardship in Fallujah, whether during Saddam's days or under American occupation.

A man like that, she thought, would be so rich and successful a few years down the road. He was a surgeon in America, after all, she thought. He would afford a nice big house, maybe with a swimming pool, an expensive car and holidays anywhere in the world. He would also be a good husband and a great father.

But these fantasies never lasted long. She felt guilty for allowing herself to dream of a life with a man other than Hassan. A man she knew so little about. She felt her fantasies were a betrayal of sorts of Hassan, the love of her life. The only man she ever knew. But, curiously, she kept returning to the same fantasies about life in America with the Palestinian-American doctor. They offered her a temporary escape from the misery and trials of life in Iraq. But she knew they were just fantasies that would never become reality. She was married to Hassan and that was that. Was she falling for Khater? The question drifted into her mind several times before she immediately banished the thought as sinful or untrue.

But her confusion over her feelings for Khater vanished the day she was discharged from hospital. She was scheduled to leave around three in the afternoon. She and Khater spent most of the day chatting in her room. They were both saddened by the imminent end of their friendship and yet happy to be together one last time.

"Do you plan to stay in Baghdad or will you try and go back to Fallujah?" he asked her.

"I think I will be in Baghdad for a little longer. I have no one left to go back to in Fallujah and my two sisters and brother are here. So, I will join them."

"You will be so close, yet I won't be able to see you, you know!" he said, "We have strict rules about leaving the Green Zone. I mean if there is official business for me to leave, I will, but that will be in a convoy and I won't be able to go anywhere other than the places listed on an official itinerary."

"But why would you want to see me?" Safiyah asked with a mischievous smile.

"Well, wouldn't you like to see me again?" he asked, embarrassed by her question.

There was a brief pause before she replied. "I would," she said. "Of course, I would. You have been so kind and good to me during my stay here. You are the only one I could speak to. And I enjoyed the time we spent talking with each other. You opened my eyes about a world I knew nothing about. I am grateful and happy to have met you, but how am I going to see you again? Don't you know what it's like in Iraq? You cannot just drop by to say hello, even if you can. What am I to tell my family? That you are a friend I met while in hospital? You should know all this," Safiyah said, giving him an answer that totally omitted that Hassan, her husband, was still alive and that, as a married woman in Iraq, receiving an unrelated man at her house was a social taboo that, if broken, would carry serious consequences.

"I know all that, I do. I grew up as a Muslim in a conservative family. You know, back in Palestine, there are still honor killings. I guess there would have been similar killings in America among some Arabs if they knew they could get away with it," he said, reminding Safiyah that, regardless of all appearances to the contrary, they belonged to the same cloth.

"So, what am I to do? How can I ever see you again?"

Safiyah was taken aback by the question. There was only one explanation for it: he had grown attached to her, maybe even fallen in love with her. Could he fall in love with her in just ten days? Her heart felt heavy. She had opened the door to this when she lied and said her husband had died in a car accident. The guilt sank deeper. But the joy was far greater.

She was almost in tears. She thought for a moment that he deserved to know the truth, but then again how could she be sure of how he would react? He would not report her to the military or the Iraqi authorities, she thought, but what would he think of her? Would he continue to love a woman he once thought to be a widow but who turned out to be the wife of a jihadist with blood on his hands? Should she have told him the truth, in confidence, earlier on to avoid this situation?

"I don't know, Khater," she said, doing away with the "Dr" for the first time since she met him. "Let us leave it in God's hands and see what he plans for us. Whatever it is, it will be what's best for us. I don't know what else to say, really."

"Maybe we can keep in touch by phone," he suggested, pulling out a small notepad from his white coat pocket. He scribbled numbers and tore off the paper and handed it to her. "These are my Iraqi and U.S. numbers. I have them both on me all the time. Call me whenever, please. If I don't pick, then I am either in surgery or very busy with patients, but I will call back as soon as I can."

Safiyah reached out for the paper, but Khater did not let go. Their hands met and he folded hers in his. Taking a step forward, he brought her hand slowly to his face and kissed it, still looking into her eyes. She tried to pull her hand away, but he held on to it and moved his face closer to hers while his eyes remained fixed on hers. He wanted to kiss her. She closed her eyes and seemed to be surrendering, but turned her face away at the last moment before their lips met.

"I cannot! Khater, I just cannot," she said, breaking down in tears.

Now facing Hassan after a long absence, she cried: "I know, Hassan, I know," she said in response to his notion of how God worked in mysterious ways. "But does not that make you think of how strange and unnecessary wars are? Sometimes, I feel that we humans share a bond that is so strong we should not be killing each other at all and instead resolve our differences through dialogue. I feel that we are all the same, Iraqis, Americans, English, Indians."

"Safiyah, in this world, there are Muslims and non-Muslims. As Muslims, that's the only way in which we can see and deal with our world."

"And what should we do with the non-Muslims?"

"We invite them to convert. If they don't, they can keep their faith and become people of the book and pay us tax in return for their protection. If they don't, we go to battle against them until they do."

Safiyah knew that the conversation had at this point reached a dead end and it would be better if she changed the subject. It was not a case of her being shocked or dismayed by her husband's harsh interpretation of Islamic laws. She knew Islam's rules on non-Muslims just as well as Hassan did, but her commitment to them was not as strong or unshakable as his. Unlike him, she did not think they were applicable now. Safiyah had always tried in her mind to find a way to soften some of the harsher Islamic rules. She was not as well versed or as widely read on Islamic jurisprudence or the interpretation of the Quran as Hassan. But she was a thinking Muslim, and her ten-day stay at Ibn Sina confirmed her rudimentary belief that there are strong bonds that unite humans, bonds that rise above nationalism, race and religion.

The kindness, professionalism and compassion shown to her by the nurses who had come from the other side of the world touched her and chipped away at her rigid perception of the Americans as unmitigated evil. Khater, being an Arab American, showed her a side of America she had not known before. A Muslim of Arab descent who gets to be a surgeon with the American army in Iraq was both unfamiliar and surprising to her. And to show her so much kindness while doing his job so well left her in awe.

All of that did not shake her belief that the Americans had no right to be in Iraq. They were occupiers and needed to be driven out of the country, by force if necessary. But her stay in Ibn Sina offered her the opportunity to see beyond that; to nuance her once categorical rejection of America.

But even then, she remained, out of ignorance or confusion, unable to grasp the complexity of her encounter with Khater and the world of Ibn Sina. She barely scratched the surface, but that was enough to confound her or nudge her into adopting naïve views. She was, after all, a simple woman from Fallujah.

"Why are you here? I mean what motive did you have to volunteer to come here?" she once asked Khater during one of those days when he just sat himself down on a chair by her bed and made conversation.

"I am here to try and help the soldiers who get hurt," he said. "I did not make the decision to invade Iraq. I didn't. Someone else did that. So, my being here is an attempt to try and bring down the number of soldiers who die here. Do you understand what I mean, Safiyah? Whether I like it or not, the war started here and my coming to Iraq helps save lives not lose them."

"I know what you mean, but why are you not doing anything to stop the war?"

"Like what?"

"I don't know. Talk about its cruelty? Talk about the innocent lives lost every day here? Do or say something, anything!"

"I am in uniform here, Safiyah. I am not a pacifist or a peace campaigner. I am here as a member of the military, yet I am not shooting anyone. I am a doctor. I value life and I try and save lives if and when I can. I fully understand why you saying what you're saying as an Iraqi, as someone who lost her parents in this war, but honestly, this is not my war, but it's very much my war in the sense that I treat its victims."

Safiyah fell silent. She stared at him not knowing what to say. For a moment, she wanted to hug him and tell him they were both victims of a war they had nothing to do with. Even that would have been an oversimplification of what they both stand for or symbolize.

He stared back, expecting her to say something. She did not. She just kept staring at him.

He could tell that her mind was filled with ideas that she wanted to share but was reluctant to. He firmly believed in his own moral rationale for being in Iraq, it was part of his own narrative of who he was and what his role in life was. Safiyah might not be convinced of much of what he was saying, he thought, but maybe one day she would. It would be too late for him, though, he thought.

Was he falling for Safiyah? She was unquestionably gorgeous. Has a disarming voice and eyes that he's lost himself in many times. And she was available. A young widow who might be looking for a man to spend the rest of her life with. But, how? It was so very complicated. She would shortly be discharged from hospital and out in Baghdad or back in Fallujah, both of which were outside the Green Zone. She would be in a place where he could not possibly go, let alone be with her. It's futile, he thought. But Safiyah, he comforted himself, would always have a special place in his heart, but not in the big house he planned to buy in a Chicago suburb with the money he was making in Iraq. She would forever be associated in his mind with his tour of duty in Baghdad. She injected a generous dose of happiness into his grim and challenging life in Ibn Sina hospital. A bright spot amid the blood, severed limbs, screams of excruciating pain and the deafening noise of ambulance Blackhawks landing and taking off.

Now out of Ibn Sina and back to the grim reality of life with Hassan, major issues, none of which was easy or safe, needed to be dealt with.

"Hassan, what are you going to do now?" asked Safiyah, who was still naked in bed next to her husband under the sheet. "We go back to Fallujah?"

"That will be very difficult. But I also cannot stay in Baghdad for too long. The government has eyes and ears everywhere."

"So, what do we do? I am not too happy at my aunt's place in Azamiyah. I really want to go home."

"I think you can go home, Safiyah, if that's what you want, but I won't be able to join you there any time soon. There are ways of getting into Fallujah without going through the checkpoints, but I must see how it can be done. But even if I am safely inside, the city is no longer the same after the battle. It will be crawling with the Americans for months to come. So, really, I don't know what to do. But God will guide me to what is best for me."

"I am also thinking of staying here for the time being. There are many restrictions facing displaced people who wish to return to Fallujah. I am worried that I might be recognized as your wife and they detain me as a hostage to pressure you to surrender to the government. Better stay in Baghdad."

They paused, each looking away from the other. Hassan was pondering his displacement and what he could do next. Safiyah was thinking of whether her life and the love and marriage that tied her to Hassan for years have changed since they left Fallujah, the only place she knew, the place where they both grew up and got married.

"Hassan," she said pleadingly. "Was it worth it?

"What was worth it?".

"Fighting the Americans in Fallujah."

Hassan's face suddenly darkened and he fixed his wife with a stern look. He felt her question belittled his cause, made a mockery of the course God had led him to champion. Why would his wife, the closest person to him after his mother, ask a question like that? But he wanted to answer her. This, after all, was Safiyah.

"Was it worth it? Safiyah, how could you ask a question like that?" he said, sitting up and looking down at her. "Have you allowed the devil, God's curse on him, to shake your faith? It was more than worth it. We are fighting for the cause of God against infidel invaders who crossed oceans and seas to kill us here."

"Hassan, I meant whether it was worth it to take on an enemy that's superior to you in weapons and numbers. Was it a kind of suicide?"

"Did not the prophet and his companions triumph in their first battle against a much larger number of infidels? Didn't God send his angels to help them? If God did not send angels to help us against the Americans, then he wanted to test our faith and our commitment to him and his cause. We may have been defeated, Safiyah, but we fought bravely like the prophet and his companions did. We did not run away.

We stood our ground and screamed '*Allahou Akbar.*' The Americans are cowards. Whenever they felt they were about to lose a position or get more of their men killed, they would withdraw and ask for help from their planes or drones. Our dead are martyrs in heaven, Safiyah, their dead will languish forever in hell."

Safiyah went quiet again. Hassan stared at her, waiting for her to say anything to suggest she agreed with him. But she remained quiet. Her head remained on the pillow as she turned on her side. Silently, she began to weep, feeling the warmth of her tears streaming down her cheeks. She sat up and moved closer to Hassan, holding on to the sheet to cover her breasts. She rested her head on his left shoulder and wept.

Hassan did not move, made no attempt to console her. She had changed, he could sense that much. She did not accept what he had to say without question like she used to. Her faith was not as strong as it once was. What happened to her, he wondered. Who influenced her? Was it the Americans in the hospital? But, how? They did not speak Arabic and she did not understand English.

He lifted her head off his shoulder and looked her in the eye. She was still weeping. He pushed her down and rolled over and mounted her. She let out a cry of pain and anguish when he penetrated her. She was not ready for him, but he did not care. Hassan was claiming back his wife.

"Bear me a child, Safiyah! Give me the child I have wanted for so long."

CHAPTER TWENTY-TWO

Hussein, the Iraqi reporter, had to do all the talking, and it was all in Arabic. But Samuel went along because he wanted to bear witness to the deal, if one were to be reached. He also wanted to be there to rubberstamp it. He did not want Hussein to promise anything the company could not deliver. Hussein was briefed and coached by Samuel and the two lawyers on how to handle the meeting with Ali Kareem, a career judge from Kurdistan whom the Americans had taken a shine to when they overhauled Iraq's legal system after the invasion. He was among dozens of judges trained by the Americans to try to make sure that due process was introduced to the country after decades of Saddam's rule.

Ali Kareem had lived in Baghdad all his life and only visited Irbil in Kurdistan to see his family. He studied law at Baghdad University, where he graduated with high enough grades to join the chief prosecutor's office, first as a researcher and later as an investigating judge. He was embraced by the Saddam-era judiciary made up of loyalists because he was Sunni and was not known to hold nationalist Kurdish views. Married with two children, judge Ali Kareem enjoyed the trust and confidence of his new patrons in Baghdad: the U.S. military's prosecutors and legal counsels placed in charge of reforming the Iraqi legal system. He was an active participant in the seminars and workshops held at the Conference Hall inside the Green Zone across the street from the Al Rasheed hotel. His English was basic to begin with, but he worked hard to improve it, hoping that he would be able to land a scholarship to do a postgraduate degree in the United States. His American mentors were impressed by his progress and he was extremely pleased with himself when he spoke to them at some length without the assistance of the interpreters swarming around them.

"My dream is to go to America and study law at Harvard or Yale," he once told a U.S. military prosecutor during a coffee break.

"You're very ambitious, sir. Only the very best of us get to study there. It's not easy to get into those two schools," replied the American.

"I will get in if I have your support," he said.

"Trust me, it will take much more than that to get you into Harvard or Yale," the American said, letting out a laugh and walking toward the coffee table.

Ali Kareem would not give up. His ambition knew no limits. He would say the same thing about Harvard and Yale to any American willing to listen. He was never disheartened by their response, the gist of which was always the same: Too tough to get in, so you had better lower your expectations.

It's not that Kareem was not smart. He was. He had ingratiated himself to the hardcore Saddam loyalists in the judiciary before the American invasion, but he trod a fine line. He did not go as far as making distasteful gestures of devotion to the regime, like using his own blood to mark the "yes" box on ballot papers during the sham referendums that forever renewed Saddam's mandate. He never broke into chants of "We sacrifice our lives and blood for you, oh Saddam!" Instead, he would smile and clap quietly while the people around him broke into chants, showing his approval but keeping a measure of decorum worthy of a member of the judiciary. It worked. Colleagues known to be active members of the then-ruling Baath party never questioned his loyalty to the regime or his love for the country's dictator.

With Saddam gone, Ali Kareem was concerned about the fallout from the regime change. He had been heavily invested in the old order and had been on track for a dizzying climb to a top job in the judiciary. He had to seriously revamp his career strategy and goals. The landscape was confusing and foggy. It took him a while to figure out who was who in the new Iraq and who really held the reins of power: not the fifteen-man Governing Council appointed by the Americans soon after their arrival, nor was it the president or the prime minister. It was the Americans.

That, he thought, posed personal challenges to him, with his broken English, cobbled together in Iraq's collapsing education system and with almost no contact with the outside world. He also knew that, under the new order, Iraq's Shiite majority would hold sway over the country's minorities. That he was a Sunni, he thought, could be an impediment, but could also serve as an opportunity for the new order to show how inclusive it was, by giving a promotion to a token Sunni and a Kurd. But first he must win over the Americans and convince them that he could be an embodiment of the "new Iraq" they were seeking to create.

Hussein and Samuel met judge Ali Kareem at one of the handful of restaurants that reopened after Saddam's removal at Baghdad's Arasat district. It was an expensive restaurant for Iraqis, but quite affordable for expatriates or Iraqis with access to dollars. They sat at a table at the far end of the restaurant not far from the kitchen door, working their way through plates of appetizers before moving on to heavy courses of grilled meat and chicken. Samuel declined the beer that the waiter – seeing a westerner – suggested. He needed to stay one hundred percent alert, and did not want to risk offend any sensitivities the judge might have about alcohol.

The restaurant was a typically Iraqi affair, with busily decorated walls and dozens of the Chinese-made plastic flowers that Iraqis are so fond of. But by Baghdad standards it qualified as a classy joint.

After an exchange of pleasantries and the consumption of a large amount of food, Hussein thought the time had come to talk business.

It had taken him days and endless calls to find out that Ali Kareem would be the presiding judge in Omar's trial. He used his sources in the government, the military and the intelligence and security agencies to identify him and find out how to reach him in person. Many of his sources cautioned him against approaching members of the judiciary to plead for leniency for Omar. Some warned he could be charged and prosecuted for unlawfully interfering with legal proceedings. But Hussein was under considerable pressure from Samuel to find out who the judge would be and to approach him with a view to winning him over.

Hussein had found out that Ali Kareem's office was at one of the smaller of Saddam's old palaces inside the Green Zone. He could not go alone to see him: the judge's assistants and security personnel would not let him get close. So, after days of exhaustive research, he discovered that someone he knew well at the prime minister's office was friends with Ali Kareem during their college days. It was not difficult for Hussein to persuade his contact to accompany him when he visits Kareem under false pretenses. The contact called the judge to say he missed him and it was time for an overdue catch-up. It worked. The judge gave Hussein's contact an appointment two days later.

"This is my friend Hussein, a trusted journalist who works for an American news organization here in Baghdad," said the contact to Ali Kareem. "He has a favor to ask of you."

"Tell me, Hussein, I hope I am able to do whatever it is that you want," Ali Kareem said politely.

"Thank you, your honor. My boss, who is an American, would like to meet you and discuss an issue that is of great concern to our organization. Is that possible?"

"I am always happy to help, especially the Americans, who have helped us Iraqis to be rid of a shameless and brutal dictator," replied the judge, in a tone more suited for a public speech than a private conversation.

And so they agreed to meet the following week for an early dinner at the Arasat restaurant, which the judge knew of but never patronized.

"Judge Kareem, we have a colleague who has been unjustly accused of terrorism and we know for certain that he is innocent. He was just trying to take photos in Fallujah when the Americans detained him. We believe that he will soon appear before you. We know that it may be inappropriate that we've asked to meet with you, but I am sure that you will forgive us when you realize that he is innocent."

"This makes me feel very awkward. I thought you were meeting me to offer me a visit to America or a grant to study there. This, as you said, is very inappropriate. You'll have to excuse me. I must leave now. I will not report this meeting to the authorities and that's out of the kindness of my heart," Ali Kareem said, placing the napkin that was on his lap on the table and getting ready to get up.

"Just give us a few minutes, sir! We can explain," said Samuel, realizing the gravity of the situation he and Hussein were in now. "I think we can do this in a way that does not take anything away from your integrity and your devotion to the law. Please, sit down, sir, I beg you."

"Ok, I will stay, but just for another five minutes."

"That is more than I need," said Samuel, trying to reassure the judge. "We are not part of the American government. We are an independent news organization. What we have on our hands here is the case of an innocent man who has been wrongly detained. I can vouch for his innocence. If he's convicted of terrorism, his future will be destroyed. In fact, his entire life will be ruined. I have total confidence in your sense of fairness, but I also realize that you are under a great deal of pressure from the government …."

"I am under no pressure," the judge protested. "The law and the evidence before me are what I consider, not pressure from the government or anyone else."

"Sir, the climate in the country is against the jihadists; and rightly so. They are not just killing Iraqi and American soldiers; they are bombing innocent people everywhere. But our man is innocent, we just want to help him take his life back and resume his career."

"And what do you expect me to do?"

"Nothing, except that you give him the benefit of the doubt."

"What is that? I don't understand."

"That if there is some doubt in your mind that he might indeed be innocent, then you acquit him."

"I routinely do that. It's a legal principal not to convict someone if there is a chance, however small, that he might be innocent. By doing that we eliminate the possibility of locking up innocent people," the judge said, showing off the sort of legal knowledge that is rarely applied when a country like Iraq is effectively torn apart by a civil war.

"That's great. I am glad we are on the same page, judge Kareem," said Samuel, beaming an affected smile before he took a large sip of water from the glass sitting on the white tablecloth.

An awkward silence descended on the three, with the judge, a slender man with a bushy moustache in a dark blue suit, held his fork and moved around the final bits of salad on his plate.

Samuel, in his hallmark dark blue blazer and khaki pants, looked ahead of him past the judge. He gave Hussein a look, signaling that he should break the silence, but the judge did so himself.

"You know, I am a great admirer of the law. It's my passion. I love what I do and I aspire to do more for Iraq through my love of the law. My dream is to go to Harvard or Yale to do a master's and a PhD in law. That will enable me to come back and maybe, given the chance, reform the entire legal system in Iraq."

"That seems to be a good plan, sir," said Samuel, faking interest.

"Well, it's hard to get into these two universities, but another big problem is the tuition fees," said the judge, repeating what he had heard from American officials countless times, and thinking that by doing that he would sound knowledgeable. "They want tens of thousands of dollars. I don't have that kind of money and I don't think I can secure a full scholarship. Can you help me get a scholarship?"

"I doubt it, sir, but we can contribute toward your tuition fees. It will not cover your entire time there, but it will get you there and give you the opportunity to prove yourself and maybe earn a full scholarship."

"This is very kind of you Mr. Samuel. Very kind. You are doing a great service to me and Iraq."

"It's the least we can do for you, sir," said Samuel, flashing a triumphant look at Hussein.

CHAPTER TWENTY-THREE

Hassan's stay in the Baghdad apartment on Saadoun Street was nerve-wracking. He knew it was too dangerous to stay in one place in Baghdad for longer than just a few days, but he could not do anything to change this. He had limited contact with other jihadists in Baghdad, where checkpoints constrained their freedom of movement. Adult males with typically Sunni names were scrutinized much more closely than anyone else. The jihadists resorted to the wide use of forged citizenship documents with Shiite names to navigate the checkpoints undetected.

Hassan knew of Omar's arrest from a text message sent to him by Ibrahim, who had decided to stay in Dora on the Karkh side of Baghdad. Confirmation came from the emir of Baghdad, who also reported the arrest of Saadoun, the former army officer and the only other person beside Omar who survived the marines' raid on the house that night in Fallujah.

Hassan was surprised and confused by news of Omar's arrest. He knew nothing of the circumstances of his detention and did not know who to ask to find out. Isolation was his worst enemy in Baghdad. No one was calling him and the text messages he received were very few and mostly not addressed to him. There were two messages on the arrest of Omar and Saadoun. Most other messages were Quranic verses, sayings of the prophet or prayers.

It was a time when the jihadists were seemingly able to strike with near impunity at Iraq's security forces and members of the Shiite majority. Attacks on the Americans were less frequent, but enough to make casualties an issue for both the military on the ground and the politicians back in Washington. Roadside bombs and rockets were the most frequently used methods of attacks. Suicide bombers and car bombs also were used, killing mostly civilians at outdoor food markets, weddings, funerals or at mosques. The stepped-up violence heightened tension in the city and fueled sectarian violence between the Shiites and Sunnis.

Hassan's despair deepened as his isolation stretched on. Even Safiyah could not visit him a second time. She was concerned that she might be detained at one of the checkpoints and recognized as the wife of the former emir of Fallujah. If that happened, the police would hand her over to the domestic security agency, which would publicize her detention with the intention of persuading Hassan to surrender in exchange for her freedom.

With the passage of time, Hassan's despair had become so profound he was prepared to take a chance just to be with other jihadists. His primary target was to meet up with Ibrahim, his lieutenant in Fallujah and now the closest person to him in Baghdad. He knew that he had much easier access to other jihadists because he was in Dora. Much of the area was a de facto no-go zone for the Iraqi police or their American backers, something that allowed the jihadists considerable leeway to meet, stockpile weapons and explosives as well as levying an informal tax on small businesses owned by loyalists.

Hassan had shaved off his long Salafi beard before he had made his escape from Mahmoudiyah to Baghdad. Now, before heading to Dora, he made sure he was once again clean shaven. All he needed to do was to come up with a convincing story to tell the policemen and soldiers at the checkpoints why he had to get to Dora, and where he was coming from. These were the two most likely questions he would be asked and which he must answer convincingly.

Taking a serious risk, he called Ibrahim on his mobile. He needed to brainstorm with him to come up with a good story. Ibrahim was helpful, giving him the names of people who lived next door to him. It was a family whose patriarch was about Hassan's age and had roots in Mahmoudiyah, Hassan's birthplace, according to the fake citizenship document he traveled on to Baghdad. The man next door, Ibrahim explained, worked in the Dora power station and had three children. Hassan could say he was on his way to visit him.

Hassan changed into gray pants and a black sweater, with plastic sandals and dark socks. He wanted to look rural and poor. He left the apartment after a brief prayer, one that pious Muslims often recite when they leave their homes. It has been years since he walked the streets of Baghdad. He headed directly to Tahrir square in the hope of finding a ride to Dora on one of the minibuses Iraqis generically call "KIA" regardless of their make. It was shortly before 8 am and a pleasant cool breeze moved the air. An hour or so later, it would be baking hot in Baghdad.

Hassan found his ride just a short distance off the square near the Shorjah market. The minibus, a Toyota Coaster, was almost full. He sat on the last of the foldable chairs in the row before last. He silently recited verses from the Quran as he looked out the window. The first checkpoint was at the beginning of Al Goumhoriyah bridge. The soldiers, members of an elite unit that guarded the Green Zone just across the Tigris, signaled to the driver to move on as they quickly glanced at the passengers while the vehicle slowly moved by. They passed through two more checkpoints without any trouble. But things were not so smooth at the next checkpoint, set up at an entry point through the concrete blast barriers encircling the entire neighborhood of Dora. Ostensibly, the walls were there for the protection of Dora, but they effectively locked its residents inside.

The line of cars at the checkpoint was not long, five or six vehicles. That gave the federal policemen manning the checkpoint time and space to carry out more thorough checks of passengers and car registrations. Hassan kept his cool as much as he could. His eyes shifted from looking out the window at nothing specifically to glancing at the policemen in their camouflage blue and gray fatigues and black helmets. The policemen began with the driver, with one of them standing by his window demanding to see his driving license and citizenship certificate and those of the two passengers seated next to him. Another one stood outside by the vehicle's sliding door, popping his head in and demanding documents from the rest of the passengers. Hassan's anxiety grew. He was not sure that his story would be convincing. Even though his documents showed his birthplace and home address to be in Mahmoudiyah - which was hardly on par with Fallujah or Mosul, when it came to insurgent attacks - it was bad enough for the police to closely examine the documents of a fighting-age man like him.

When the police asked Hassan for his papers, he made an effort to stop his hand from shaking. He handed it to the policeman, who looked carefully at it, twice raising his head to look at Hassan to see if he matched the photo.

"What's your business in Dora?"

"I am visiting an old friend who, like me, comes from Mahmoudiyah."

"Your friend, what does he do?"

"He is a technician at the power station here."

"Can you step out of the bus?" the policeman demanded.

"Why?"

"Step out of the bus, now," the policeman said impatiently, raising his voice.

What could have aroused his suspicion, Hassan wondered. He was rising slowly from his tiny fold-up seat when he felt himself being jerked off his feet. His head slammed into the ceiling of the bus. The policeman who had just asked him to step off the bus was no longer visible. He was groaning from pain as he lay on the ground next to the bus, bleeding from his arm and left side. Hassan lifted his head, running his fingers through his hair, now sticky with his own blood. He had seen the aftermath of enough suicide bombings – the smoke and the smell of burning human flesh filling the air – to recognize that the insurgency had just targeted the Dora checkpoint.

Despite the pain throbbing through his head, he knew he had to act quickly.

The other passengers were either dead or more seriously wounded than he was. Policemen who had survived the blast were frantically firing in the air.

His vision blurry, Hassan staggered out of the vehicle and looked for the policeman who had his citizenship document. He found him, bleeding profusely from his arm and side but miraculously still clasping the paper. As Hassan bent down to take it from his hand, the dying policeman gave him a look of utter hatred. He tried to spit at Hassan but did not have enough life left in him to do it. Hassan stood upright and placed the document carefully in his pocket. He then kneeled down by the policeman, pretending to help him: he put his right hand firmly over the man's nose and mouth and pressed as hard as he could. He kept it there, his eyes fixed on the policeman's, until the man's chest stopped moving. Then he got up, took off his sweater and placed it on the bleeding gash on his head. He walked slowly away, through the blast walls.

He had finally arrived in Dora.

***

Ibrahim became worried when he heard the blast. He knew that the aftermath of any blast, especially a deadly one, would mean the arrival of more policemen and troops as well as random house searches. But there was little he could do except wait inside the small house he had rented on a crowded street of tiny homes overlooking an open sewage drain running in the middle. He made himself a pot of tea and took it to the front yard where he pulled up a chair and sat waiting.

Ibrahim was hugely relieved when Hassan showed up a little more than thirty minutes after the blast. He was sweaty and both his white undershirt and the sweater he'd placed on his head were soaked in blood. He'd had to ask for directions from the few pedestrians reckless enough to be out on the streets of Dora shortly after the blast with ambulance and police sirens wailing across the district. Walking around the streets in just your undershirt, blood dripping from your head and stopping to ask strangers for directions was not something anyone wanted to do soon after a deadly suicide bombing. But Hassan felt safe doing that in Dora, a Sunni stronghold crawling with jihadist cells.

By the time he reached the house, Hassan had lost a great deal of blood and was struggling to keep his eyes open. But he was overwhelmed by his relief and happiness to finally see Ibrahim, who sprang out of his chair to meet him the moment he appeared at the door.

"Thanks be to God for your safety. What happened to you?" he asked as he helped his former commander in Fallujah to the chair he had been sitting on.

"I was hurt by the blast, but it's nothing serious. Can I have some water?"

"Of course," said Ibrahim, dashing inside the house and emerging seconds later with a jar of water and a metal cup.

"Here," he said, offering Hassan the water. He drank the water slowly and then threw his head back and closed his eyes. He was exhausted and felt weak.

The day was quickly becoming warm, but Hassan was seated in the narrow shady area provided by the lone palm tree standing in the tiny yard. Ibrahim went back inside the house and brought a bowl filled with hot water, a bottle of rubbing alcohol and a face towel. He went back again and brought out another chair and a cushion. He lifted Hassan's legs one at a time and placed them on the second chair before he gently lifted his head and placed the cushion beneath it. He then added some of the alcohol to the water and dipped the towel in it. He began to clean Hassan's head, first around the cut and then the wound itself. The gash was deep and needed stitches. Ibrahim had done the procedure back in his army days, but it had been a while and he did not have any anesthesia. He called the owners of the house and was told there was a medical kit in one of the kitchen drawers. Hassan groaned in pain as Ibrahim began to sew the wound: he was breathing heavily but did not open his eyes. It took Ibrahim a minute to realize that his friend was asleep. Relieved, he put in five stitches.

Hassan did not wake up until late in the afternoon. He was hot and sweaty again. The white sheet Ibrahim had used to cover his head did not offer much protection from the heat. He felt weak, with a splitting headache and his joints ached from the uncomfortable position he'd slept in. He was very hungry, too. It was a few minutes before Ibrahim emerged from the house where he too had been napping.

"How do you feel?"

"Thanks be to God. I feel better now, but I am hungry."

"I have cooked some meat and rice. Let us go inside and eat."

"Let us pray first before the afternoon prayers are upon us."

"Sheikh Hassan, you need to eat first. You lost a lot of blood. I am worried you could keel over and hurt your head again while praying. I will bring you some raisin juice I bought from a Kurdish man who sells it in the market. That will give you a shot of energy and then we eat."

"May God bless you and fulfill all your wishes."

Hassan drank a small glass of the sweet juice and sat on the floor to eat with Ibrahim, who made a simple salad of cucumbers and tomatoes to go with the rice and meat. The food was almost tasteless, but Hassan was so hungry he did not even pause. He just kept scooping the rice with a spoon, which he also used to cut the meat. After eating he felt sleepy again. Ibrahim offered to make him tea, but Hassan politely declined and asked him instead where he could lay down inside the house. Ibrahim showed him to a sparsely- furnished room with one large bed, wardrobe and an electric fan.

Hassan walked straight to the bed, took off his sandals and lay down.

"Ibrahim, what did you do to my head?"

"I stitched it. The wound was deep."

"Thank you. It hurts so much. I could use a painkiller if you have one."

Ibrahim went out and fetched one, together with a glass of water. Hassan sat up and washed the pill down with a large sip of water. He lay down again and a few minutes later, the sound of his snoring filled the entire house.

He did not wake up until late in the evening. He found Ibrahim in bed in the room next door, not quite sleeping but almost there.

"Ibrahim, we need to do something to avenge Fallujah. We cannot just let the Americans get away with it."

Ibrahim rubbed his eyes and ran his fingers through his hair.

"Like what?" he mumbled, still half asleep.

"I don't know," said Hassan. "Something with the will of God needs to be done and it has to be big. We want the world to write and talk about it for a very long time. We used to have someone at the American embassy here in Baghdad. Do we still have him?"

"I am not sure, but I can check."

"Do that. If we are going to hurt them, we need to target one of their masters, not Americans that no one cares about. If we can get the ambassador, that would be worth becoming a martyr for. How many men can we get to do this with us? And how easily can we get weapons?"

"God is great, Hassan, and if we have him on our side, we will do it and live to tell the story to our children and grandchildren. I will start asking around and see who will volunteer, but I must go through the emir of Baghdad first. Now, let me get you a towel and a pair of slippers so you can wash and pray. I have missed listening to your sweet voice reciting from the Quran. God bless you Haji Hassan, may you always be my imam."

CHAPTER TWENTY-FOUR

Omar's brief trial took place inside the Green Zone at a makeshift courthouse exclusively designated for terrorism-related cases. He was brought to the courthouse with two dozen other defendants, all of them were in yellow jumpsuits, plastic slippers and handcuffs. Omar was pale and disoriented. He had barely slept the night before and could hardly eat. The little sleep he did manage to catch was interrupted by nightmares, visions of being led to the gallows or reading the Quran in a cell as he awaited execution. He'd had such nightmares from time to time since being detained, but they seemed to be on a loop the night before his court appearance. He would wake up sweaty, eyes wide open and totally disoriented.

He had been kept in isolation for weeks, questioned almost every day. He did not have just one or two interrogators. There were many and they took turns questioning him. The questions were repetitive: At least half of them assumed he was an active member of Al Qaida, which Omar at first vehemently protested and denied, but as the questioning dragged on and on and he became tired of arguing his innocence he began to make do with "I am not a member of Al Qaida," delivered impatiently and emphatically.

Sometimes though they asked him about topics that weren't just about him: what were relations like between the jihadists and the women of Fallujah, how was food distributed among the fighters and what were the habits and customs of the foreign fighters, and how did they interact with their local hosts?

The serious questions, he thought, were those pertaining to jihadists he knew, like Saadoun, the leader of the cell with whom he was captured in Fallujah. They asked him repeatedly about Hassan and the fate of the Egyptian man executed by the jihadists for spying for the Americans. They wanted to know who exactly pulled the trigger in the video of the execution that was posted online with a brief statement from the Fallujah "emirate." Omar made no mention of his role in the case of the Egyptian spy. He claimed that he had never met him, let alone questioned him or extracted a confession from him.

It seemed that the Americans were determined to find those responsible for the death of a man who was apparently of immense use to them as an informant. Omar was terrified every time his investigators brought up the case of the Egyptian, but he stuck to his story. He had never met him nor even knew of him.

As for Hassan, Omar insisted that the top jihadist in Fallujah was a friend and nothing more. He sought to make that a little more plausible to the Americans by saying he met him a few times after he was named the emir of Fallujah, but that their interactions were mostly social. He had suggested that Omar join the group, but he had declined.

"I wanted to be a news photographer. That was my dream," he repeatedly told the skeptical Americans through their interpreters.

The investigators only once brought up the charge they tailor-made for him soon after his detention. It was to do with passing on to the jihadists the heads-up he received from the office about the imminent start of the American offensive. He vehemently denied that he had sent a message to Hassan or anyone else saying the attack was about to start.

"I received word about the attack from my boss, but I kept the information to myself," he told an investigator who affected a smile of disbelief.

Omar lost considerable weight while in detention despite the three daily meals he was getting and the little physical exertion he made. He shared a large room with another fifteen or sixteen inmates after they were done questioning him. While incarcerated with the others, he spent much of his time reading the Quran. He was praying regularly, always with the rest of his cell mates. They rose before dawn to pray. Some of them preached to the rest after the sunset prayers. They lectured on the interpretation of the Quran and Hadeeth and explained Islamic jurisprudence. Very often, there would be some talk about the merits of jihad as laid out by the Quran and the Hadeeth. The preachers, however, were careful when speaking about jihad not to deviate from what was in the Quran and Hadeeth. They feared that bringing up what the jihadists were doing in Iraq would be misconstrued as incitement by the Arabic-speaking guards hired by the Americans to guard and spy on the prisoners.

Still, time passed agonizingly slowly. Omar started to look forward to the little breaks he and his cellmates would get, like a visit every fortnight from his mother or the daily exercise break when he could pace up and down a small yard for half an hour, a routine that allowed him to stretch his legs and enjoy the fresh air outdoors.

Finally, his day in court had arrived. Omar and the other accused were kept in a room at the end of the hallway outside the courtroom. They were given water to drink and a bucket to urinate in. They all had reeked, and their hair was almost white with dandruff. Their arms and necks showed white spots, some sort of skin infection caused by their detention conditions. Omar was handed over to the Iraqi authorities about two weeks before his trial. He was kept in a 3X3 meter cell with seven other inmates. Hardly any space to lay down and sleep, so they slept in turns. Food was inedible most days. The stench from the small toilet and washbasin they shared was overwhelming. It never went away, not for a second.

"State your name and date of birth," Judge Ali Kareem instructed Omar as he was led into the defendants' wooden cage.

Omar shouted back his name and date of birth, his eyes darting around the courtroom to see if there was anyone there he knew. He recognized Mohammed Abul Einein, the Egyptian reporter he had met in Fallujah. He also recognized Samuel. Both men wore blazers and ties and sat there timidly, avoiding eye contact with the judge.

Judge Kareem read out the list of charges leveled against Omar, to which he pleaded not-guilty as instructed by his lawyer, Mohammed Allawi, one of Baghdad's best known criminal lawyers. Allawi only met with Omar once before his trial, for a two-hour sit-down at his detention facility, when he spent most of the time coaching Omar on how to answer the judge's questions. Allawi was kept in the dark about the deal struck by Samuel with the judge. Looping him in, Samuel thought, would complicate things, and maybe even discourage Allawi from doing his job as best as he could. He also could not trust Allawi who, for one thing, could have demanded more money for his services or who might have acted suspiciously during the trial, knowing beforehand that Omar was likely to get acquitted or receive a suspended sentence.

The charges against Omar were serious. Membership of a terrorist organization, collusion in the murder of American and Iraqi soldiers and deliberately failing to inform authorities about an impending attack against government forces and those of an allied nation.

Ali Kareem gave Allawi permission to speak. Puffing himself up like a peacock, Allawi appeared to relish the chance to show off his public speaking skills. He politely greeted the judge and used flowery language to extoll what he called the importance and relevance of maintaining a just and fair legal process even when Iraq was being consumed by a deadly conflict.

"Your honor, my client is innocent. But he is guilty of bad judgment. He allowed his professional ambition to blind him. He crossed the boundary that separates professionalism from liable recklessness. There is not a shred of evidence that suggests that he was involved in any act of violence. None," Allawi said, delivering his words in an articulate and deliberate manner. Just minutes into his little speech, he realized from Ali Kareem's expression that he had likely reached the limit of the judge's tolerance and that he had better wrap it up.

In courts like Ali Kareem's, judges hear at least a dozen cases a day. There was no time for the kind of speeches seen in courtroom dramas. This was almost mechanical justice. Or maybe random justice. No witnesses were called and no cross examinations. The judge read the case file at home and came to the courtroom to go through the pretense of giving defendants a fair trial. His mind had already been made up whether the defendant was guilty or innocent based on what was in the file.

"I move to acquit my client of all charges," said Allawi.

"Thank you," said Ali Kareem. "Will issue a verdict after consultations," he added before he moved Omar's case file to one side and picked up another file from the heap sitting on a trolley next to him. He called for the next defendant to be brought to the courtroom.

Samuel and Abul Einein stepped out of the courtroom and walked slowly to a nearby waiting room where they sat down.

"Glad this is almost over," said Samuel. "It wasn't an easy deal to arrange. Finance could not believe that top editorial management asked for 200,000 dollars. I guess there is a first time for everything. I'll be so glad when this is finally over. What a fucking nightmare this has been. You know what we told finance? We said we needed the money to spend on teaching young Iraqi reporters multimedia skills. They were incredulous, but the big boss told them to let it slide. Oh, yeah! They let it slide alright." Samuel said, letting out one of his evil-sounding laughs that made his beer belly wobble up and down.

"An hour or so now, boss, and it will all be over," volunteered Abul Einein.

"Well, I don't really give a rat's ass. Fuck it! I've had enough of this dog and pony show. If he doesn't walk free today, then that's just too fucking bad. We will make sure his mother and brothers are taken care of while he serves his time. That way we'll all feel we have done what we could and sleep peacefully at night."

CHAPTER TWENTY-FIVE

It had been long in the planning.

They wanted it to be spectacular. An attack that would top news bulletins the world over for days. But it was not easy. Hassan spent days brainstorming with other jihadists about how to get to the target and how to get their weapons and ammunition there undetected. It took them weeks to find jihadists willing to be martyred for the cause of Islam. To wear those explosives belts and blow themselves up. When they found about a half dozen, they had to put them through a selection process to identify two or three who are smart enough to avoid detection at checkpoints, not to panic and prematurely detonate the explosives and make sure that they did it at the right spot.

They also needed to be firmly indoctrinated about what awaited them when they were dead. Their memories had to be refreshed about going to heaven, the rivers of milk and honey there and, of course, the virgins.

Ibrahim, after countless telephone calls, found out that their spy at the American embassy was still active. He briefed his handler on the information they needed to obtain: the itinerary of the ambassador outside the Green Zone on at least three or four different days. The spy was told in no-uncertain terms that the information must be 100 percent reliable and actionable.

The weapons, the ammunition, grenades and RPGs were all available in Dora. The assembly point for the men and the hardware was at the house Hassan and Ibrahim were staying in.

There was nothing to be done until the embassy spy fed them the information they requested. So, to kill time and stay fit, the men _ Hassan, Ibrahim and four others _ exercised twice a day. They did pushups, sit-ups and skipped rope. They took turns cooking lunch and dinner, using vegetables, red meat and chicken delivered to the house by boys not older than 10 who were the children of fellow jihadists or sympathizers in Dora.

The wait was long and tedious despite the effort they made to stay busy and fit. They read from the Quran together and discussed verses and Hadeeth. Ibrahim made daily inquiries about the embassy spy and whether he had any information for them. The answer was consistent. He had not been in touch.

It was not until weeks later that Ibrahim received the answer he had been waiting for. The ambassador and his top diplomats planned to eat an early dinner at the villa housing the American news organization that Omar worked for. The information, however, lacked a precise time for the visit and the number of vehicles that would be used. The spy promised to find out the exact time but said he could not be certain he would get the required information. The house, he said, was on Abu Nawas street, on the banks of the Tigris and a stone's throw away from the Sheraton Hotel. The house, the spy said, had armed guards and was sealed off by concrete blast barriers. The guards were Iraqis led by British security consultants.

The visit would likely take place on a Friday afternoon, when traffic in Baghdad thins out before slowly picking up at nightfall, when the city becomes congested with people heading out to eat in restaurants, visit family or stroll in the parks on the banks of the Tigris. The lack of traffic could either be a blessing for quickly getting away from the scene of the attack on nearly deserted roads or a curse because pursuing police cars would be able to catch up easily or have a clear target to shoot at with a little chance of collateral damage. Also, light traffic could very well mean much more thorough questioning at checkpoints.

The consensus was to give it a try during Friday prayers when most soldiers and policemen would be praying at nearby mosques. That meant they needed to find a temporary shelter somewhere near the target until it was time to stage the attack. They abandoned plans to transfer the weapons and hardware from Dora to Rusafah on the other side of the Tigris as too risky, given the multitude of checkpoints between the two sides of Baghdad. The weapons had to come from elsewhere in Rusafah, which would be easier. Ibrahim and Hassan were told that there was a cache of all the hardware they needed hidden at an abandoned store in the Shorjah market, a short distance from where Hassan hid on Saadoun street.

On the Friday that the US ambassador was supposed to make his visit to the news agency, the six men involved in planning the attack rose at dawn. They prayed together and read from the Quran. The two designated suicide bombers were kept in seclusion with a senior jihadist cleric who had not left their side for a single minute over the past two days. They had made their farewell videos the previous day at the house, assuring their families that what they intended to do was for God and Islam and asking them not to mourn them for they would be martyrs in heaven.

The men ate around 11 in the morning and prayed one more time before they left. They traveled with forged documents in two beat-up sedan cars to avoid drawing attention. The bombers were to leave later with the cleric who would watch them from a safe distance to make sure they didn't chicken out at the last moment.

The six men crossed to the other side of the river without any hindrance, since most of the security forces were at prayers and the checkpoints were manned by just one or two service members. They arrived at the Saadoun street apartment and, to their surprise, they found the weapons they needed there already, complete with spare magazines, grenades and RPGs. Someone must have decided to offer a bit of extra help and moved the weapons from the store in Shorjah to the apartment.

Each one picked up an AK-47 and checked it before they inserted the magazines. There were two extra magazines for each of the six men. Then they sat and waited, each man murmuring verses of the Quran they had memorized by heart. Hassan and some of the men began to sweat. The anxiety was intense, and the sudden quiet lent an eerie sense of foreboding.

"Sheikh Hassan, shall we brew some tea? We have time," said Ibrahim, trying to sound excited about such a small domestic task.

"Yes, let us do that. Anyone of you a smoker?" asked Hassan, addressing the four other men, all of whom were in their late 20s or early 30s. "No," answered the men in near unison.

"Then let us make that tea and have it together. Today's mission, by the grace of God, may end with all of us martyred. It will be a blessed death, one that will raise high the banner of Islam and send us to paradise, God willing."

Two of the younger men rose from the floor where they were squatting and headed to the kitchen to make the tea. Once there, they shouted back to Hassan asking where the tea, cardamom and sugar were. They crushed a handful of the cardamom and added it to the water in a stainless-steel kettle. When the water boiled, they added the tea, turned down the heat and let it brew for a few minutes. They fetched four tiny glasses from a cupboard and placed them on a small tray that was too small for the kettle. One man took the tray with the glasses back to the living room and the other one brought the kettle, holding its hot handle with a kitchen cloth.

"You drink first and we will follow when you're done," said one of the two men who made the tea. "There were only four glasses there."

"No," protested Hassan, rising to his feet. "We will drink this tea together and we will pray and then leave," he said as he walked to the kitchen. He emerged seconds later with two water glasses. "These should do."

The men poured the tea, added plenty of sugar and noisily started slurping. Once done, they took turns going to the bathroom where they washed and later fell in line behind Hassan, who led them in prayers.

"*Allahou Akbar*," he said in his melodious voice before he began reading the opening verse of the Quran, followed by another verse that spoke of Islam's martyrs who continue to live in the eyes of God. Ibrahim began to weep, followed by the other men. Hassan chose that verse to remind his crew that they should not fear death, but instead relish and embrace it. But one of the two men who had made the tea began to shake visibly during the final part of the prayers.

Hassan went and sat near him as soon as he finished his prayers and took the younger man in his arms.

"We will only be faced with what God has written for us," said Hassan in a soothing voice, paraphrasing a Quranic verse. "Be brave. If we fight hard and courageously in the name of God, we will either be victorious or martyred. These are the two paths open to us as good Muslims who believe in God and his Prophet."

The man's shaking began to subside. He raised his head to look at Hassan, tears on his cheeks though he was no longer sobbing. "God is against the oppressors," he whispered to Hassan. "I will seek martyrdom today and, when I fall, I will be seated by God's side in heaven."

Clasping each other's right hand, Hassan and the man helped each other rise off the floor. They went straight to their AK-47s, which were leaning against the wall by the apartment's door.

"*Allahou Akbar, Allahou Akbar*," the six men shouted as they raised their rifles in the air.

It was time for jihad.

***

They concealed their rifles, magazines, RPGs in black trash bin liners and each stuck a grenade in his pocket. They left the building, got into the cars and headed to Tahrir Square, from where they took a side road to the right just before the Goumhoriyah bridge. They made a left at the end of the street to come out on Abu Nawas street, where the final checkpoint before their target was located. They waited patiently in the slow-moving line of cars. Federal policemen were manning the checkpoint. There was only one car ahead of them when a strong blast shook the ground and their cars. As planned, one of the two suicide bombers had just blown himself up some 20 or 25 meters behind the two cars in which Hassan and his men traveled. The ground in the immediate vicinity of the explosion was charred. The policemen began to fire in the air. The car in front was unscathed and it sped off, escaping a possible secondary explosion. Before Hassan and his men followed suit, the second suicide bomber jumped into the back seat with them as planned.

The distraction plan has worked perfectly. The first suicide bomber knew exactly where to blow himself up. The spot he chose was far enough from Hassan and his men to ensure that they didn't get hurt, but close enough to the line of cars to create enough carnage to distract the policemen from paying attention to the two cars waiting to pass through the checkpoint.

The cars sped forward towards the target, believing that the American ambassador and his top diplomats were already there.

In fact, the ambassador's convoy was delayed by fifteen minutes and was halfway across the Goumhoriyah bridge, headed to the dinner party, when they heard the blast. The ambassador's security detail instantly ordered the convoy of black armored SUVs to turn back. Of course, Hassan and his men did not know their designated target was already fleeing; and so they sped onward toward the house where Samuel and staff were waiting for the VIP guest and his company.

The suicide bomber stepped out of the car and casually strolled up to the compound's metal gate, where many of the Iraqi guards were still trying to figure out what had just blown up. The bomber walked straight up to them and started telling them about what happened at the checkpoint. More guards joined them, keen to hear an eyewitness account of what just happened. The bomber waited until enough of the guards had gathered around him before he blew himself up. Almost everyone _ eight armed guards in total _ were killed, cut down by the blast and the nails packed around the explosives.

As soon the blast cut down the guards, Hassan, Ibrahim and the other four men rushed out of the two cars and ran straight for the compound. The street gate remained shut and bolted from the inside. Hassan took aim at the middle of the gate with an RPG and fired. It ripped a wide hole through which Hassan's men fired into the compound. The surviving guards inside returned fire but failed to hit any of the attackers. The gate remained firmly shut despite the gaping hole left behind by the RPG blast. One of Hassan's men jumped through the hole as others covered him with bursts of gunfire. He managed to slide the bolt back but was shot dead as he pushed the heavy metal gate aside to allow the rest to pour in.

The moment they entered the compound, they were met with a hail of bullets from the roof, where one of the British consultants took position with two of the senior Iraqi guards. Ibrahim was hit in the head and fell dead to the ground. Two more men were seriously wounded.

Hassan and the only other man still on his feet rushed inside the building, firing blindly to deter anyone from tackling them. Already ambulance and police sirens were filling the air as they drew closer to the compound. Hassan went quickly through the ground level floor, desperately hunting the American ambassador, but there was no one there. He had no idea what the ambassador looked like, but he was confident that he would be a white man in a suit. He ran upstairs, several steps at a time. Again no one was there. Thwarted, he ran back downstairs and paused for a second before he noticed a narrow staircase at the end of the hall. He jogged toward the staircase and went down. In the kitchen, three cooks were squatting under the wooden table they used to prepare food.

"Where is the ambassador?" Hassan shouted, pointing his AK-47 at them.

"He never came," said one of the cooks in a trembling voice. "We were expecting him, but he never came."

"Where is everyone?"

"In the room just outside the kitchen on the left," said the cook, hoping Hassan would immediately act on the information rather than pause there and maybe decide to shoot him and his two co-workers.

Hassan took the bait and left the room. He primed his RPG with another shell he carried in a back bag, took shelter inside the concrete stairwell, turned his head away and fired at the metal door of the safe room. The thunderous explosion was deafening, causing his nose and ears to bleed and his body to uncontrollably shudder. The impact did not pierce the metal door, only separated it from its frame. There was enough room for Hassan to throw a grenade inside. The explosion brought the door crashing down. Hassan peered through the smoke and could see that everyone inside was either dead or seriously wounded. He sprayed the room with his AK-47 before he rushed back upstairs. There he found the dead body of the last member of his group sprawling halfway up the staircase. He knew that he had been pursued to the inside of the house.

He rushed back downstairs to the basement and went into the kitchen.

"Is there a way out from here?" he asked the cooks, his voice even more threatening now.

"Through the window of that room," said the same cook, pointing to the adjoining dining room where only minutes ago the entire staff had been celebrating Samuel's 35th year at the company.

Hassan, now nearly deaf and bleeding from several parts of his body, rushed through the second kitchen door to his left and walked through the shattered glass window that opens into the back garden. He headed directly to the wall separating the garden from the Alawiyah club, the one-time exclusive hangout for Baghdad's rich, powerful and trendy elite. With energy fast seeping out of his bloodied body, he began to climb the wall when a helicopter flying just above treetops appeared overhead, violently shaking the lawn and the handful of trees dotting the garden. Hassan could not see much of the aircraft because of the blinding searchlights fixed on both of its sides. He had no time to think or react. A single high-caliber bullet to the head took care of that.

Hassan was dead before his body hit the ground with a thud, his brain splattered on the lawn.

The helicopter lingered for a minute over the house, then gained a little altitude and made a sharp turn to the side before it flew away.

CHAPTER TWENTY-SIX

Life in Beirut was not easy for Omar.

He had never left Iraq before, so when he arrived in the Lebanese capital knowing that that was where he was to start a new life, his heart sank. It was just so different from Baghdad or anywhere else in Iraq. To him, it was like landing on another planet. It was an Arab city, but seemed far from it to him. He marveled at what the women wore and how much flesh they showed. The people spoke an Arabic that was so different from his, and he had to listen hard to understand everything that was said to him. The Lebanese were also different from the Iraqis. They were much savvier, much more entrepreneurial and their women far prettier than those back home.

Most Iraqis quickly feel homesick when they travel abroad, regardless of where they go. Omar was no different.

The police kept summoning him for questioning after the company applied for his residency permit. He was asked repeatedly about Al Qaida, Fallujah and whether there were any Lebanese jihadists in Iraq. Throughout, Omar insisted that he had no information. But they would not stop. He was summoned at least once a week. The Lebanese officers who interrogated him were less than pleasant, but not outright rude. They seemed to be after any information that would allow them to detain anyone with links to Al Qaida in Iraq. They wanted them detained upon their return home, most likely via Syria, the obvious transit point to and from Iraq for jihadists.

They were growing impatient with Omar's claim of ignorance. They suspected he knew a great deal more than he was telling them, but they could not use nasty methods to extract the information since he was linked to an international news organization with a globally recognizable name.

Omar found a small apartment in Beirut's Hamra district, a commercial area popular with Arab tourists and packed with cafes and restaurants. He also liked the fact that Hamra's residents were a mix of Sunnis, Shiites and Christians. The proximity of the American University of Beirut gave the area an additional flavor, with hundreds of students renting apartments across the neighborhood. Its proximity to the sea was another plus.

Omar was now a photographer in the Beirut bureau, a reward given to him by the company for the time he spent in jail. He had been acquitted of the more serious charges but convicted and given a suspended one-year sentence for his failure to warn the authorities of an impending and potentially deadly attack on government troops and their allies. The prosecution did not appeal the verdict and he was set free the day after his one-hearing trial. The company pulled strings to get him a passport as quickly as possible and he was put on a plane to Beirut after visiting his mother and brothers.

Everything happened so fast that Omar did not have time to stop and think about the huge changes that were about to come into his life. Still, he was immensely relieved to have been freed from prison, though not so happy about having to leave Iraq.

"Put all this behind you and show us what a good job you can do in Lebanon," Samuel had told Omar when he stopped by the office to collect his passport and a one-off, 10,000-dollar payment to help him settle in Beirut.

To Omar, the Beirut office was his refuge. It was there where he felt at home among colleagues he had just met but who went out of their way to accommodate and help him.

Omar learned of the attack on the Baghdad office from his Beirut colleagues. He did not know what to make of the news. Most of the people who perished or were seriously wounded he had met only once or twice. He did not have a relationship with any of them, but the news saddened him and, for a fleeting moment, he wondered whether he had anything to do with it.

The attack made front-page news everywhere in the world. Many reporters in Iraq found out about the planned visit to the Baghdad office by the American ambassador that never happened and figured out that he was to have been the target. But the death of so many reporters in a single attack was enough to make headlines and top news bulletins the world over for a couple of days. Some newspapers and online news sites published brief biographies of Samuel and his staff.

The company refused to release photos of the victims' bodies, only making public general images of the building and the gate that was hit by an RPG. But photos of the pile of the dead bodies in the safe room were circulating on the mobile phones of some of the Baghdad office staffers who survived the attack.

The photos were believed to have been taken and shared by Iraqi policemen who arrived at the scene soon after the attack ended.

The company held a wake for the victims in the New York headquarters, inviting several senators and congressmen as well as the families of some of the victims. The company's chief executive ordered operations in Baghdad temporarily suspended and commissioned a U.S.-based security company to investigate what led to the breach of security at the compound, and whether the security plan that was in place had been properly thought out. The local staffers continued to work from their homes, filing their stories to a special desk set up in Beirut to handle the Iraq war. An exhaustive and complicated discussion was underway on the best location for a new office in Baghdad.

The story in Iraq was so big, the company could not simply walk away from it, not even if it had lost so many employees in the attack.

Omar went home early the day he heard the news of the attack. He was burdened and worried. He was not enamored of Beirut, the same way so many Arabs are about the Lebanese capital. In reality, he just wanted to be home in Iraq even if it was to live in Baghdad rather than Fallujah. He could bring his mother and brothers to live with him there. But there was a major drawback with that dream. He was on the radar of the local counterterrorism agency and would most likely be picked up and detained if he was ever to return. But the next piece of tragic news he heard made him reconsider.

It was a few days after he heard of the attack on the company's Baghdad office that his mother phoned to say that Hassan had been killed and that all the Iraqi television networks were showing images of his body. Safiyah, she told him, was still in Baghdad, but could not publicly organize a wake for her husband or publicly mourn him because she did not want it known she was his widow. She feared arrest, his mother explained.

She did not know how or where in Baghdad Hassan had been killed, but Omar soon found out from friends in Fallujah that he died in the attack on the news agency's office. He did not find out until a few days later that the target was the American ambassador. The news provided some comfort, but Omar was still baffled by it. He decided he must return to Baghdad and offer his condolences to Safiyah and Hassan's family in Fallujah. He also wanted to see his Baghdad colleagues who survived the attack and hear their first-hand account of what happened.

There were daily flights to Baghdad from Beirut, a fact that helped Omar quickly make up his mind to go.

He decided to leave the next day. He told his boss at the Beirut office that he had urgent business to attend to in Baghdad. The Lebanon photo editor knew better than to keep Omar's planned trip to Baghdad to himself and immediately informed his boss in New York, John, the global photo editor. John went ballistic and demanded that the Beirut office stop Omar from returning to Baghdad.

"He could easily be picked up at the airport by the police and then we will have to go through everything again," John yelled on the telephone. "This is not a matter to be taken lightly. We jumped through hoops of fire for that guy and it's time he respects and appreciates that. Returning to Baghdad is disrespecting us. Tell him that I said that. I swear I am going to fire his ass if he goes and you can tell him that, too. We are in enough shit as it is without this imbecile piling up more shit on us. For fuck's sake!"

The Lebanon editor, Mohammed Hassan, listened patiently. His English was rudimentary, but he figured out what John wanted. He did not know how he would go about it though. He told John a few reassuring words and hung up. He immediately called Omar.

"You cannot go to Baghdad, Omar. The big boss in New York is dead against it. What do you say?"

"I will be alright. I don't understand why you are so worried."

"Omar," Mohammed said impatiently, "These are my instructions from way above me. You listen to me and we will all be fine and we can get on with our lives. You go to Baghdad and you and I might very well lose our jobs. This is how serious it is."

"Then so be it. But I sincerely hope, God willing, that you don't lose your job on account of me. I must go. Losing my job is something that I can tolerate. God does not forget the faithful and provides for them. He will make another job available to me."

"This is it? You still want to go?"

"I have no choice, Mohammed, I must."

Mohammed did not respond. He was so angry with Omar he just hung up. "May God curse that Iraqi," he screamed.

The Middle East Airlines flight to Baghdad at noon the next day was half empty. A few irate infants, however, shattered what could have been a quiet one hour and forty minute flight. They seemed to take turns screaming, but that did not interfere with Omar's deep thoughts as he gazed out of the window. He had no idea what was in store for him in Baghdad, and wasn't even sure he would get out of the airport without being arrested.

He ate the in-flight meal and dozed off. He woke up slightly disoriented as the aircraft began to circle over the airport before finally landing. He felt a little sick, so he drank what was left of the bottle of water that came with his food. He burped and felt a little better.

His fear of arrest proved to be baseless. No questions at passport control, just like everyone else traveling on an Iraqi passport. He collected his bag from the conveyor and took the communal taxi to the famous statue of Abbas ibn Fernas, the medieval Arab who had tried and failed to fly. From there he hired a yellow taxi to central Baghdad.

He was home. Kind of.

That feeling was reinforced by the warm reception he received from his uncle, his aunt and their children when he arrived at their home in Baghdad's Waziriyah district. It was afternoon when he got there and they served a late lunch of meat, rice and white beans in tomato sauce. The food was not particularly good but Omar, happy to be back and eating a homemade Iraqi meal, ate a great deal. For the rest of the evening, he chatted endlessly with his relatives over rounds of tea and a homemade sponge cake.

The next day, Omar went to Azamiyah to look for Safiyah. He had a few leads to follow and it did not take long to find her aunt's house. He knocked on the door and her uncle answered. Omar introduced himself and asked whether he could speak to Safiyah. The uncle instantly told him that Safiyah could not see an unrelated man until 40 days had passed after the death of her husband. It was something that escaped Omar's mind and made him feel stupid. But before he responded, the uncle told him that he could speak to her from behind a wall or a curtain, but he should not see her in person.

As he was talking, Safiyah herself emerged from behind her uncle and pushed the door wide so she could see Omar. "I can see him and talk to him, uncle. If the intention is pure and honest, then there should be no harm in that," said Safiyah.

Her uncle, a skinny man in his late 60s, was clearly angered by her forwardness. He said nothing and angrily walked away, mumbling something about leaving everything in the hands of God.

"*Salamou aleikom*, brother Omar, come inside," said Safiyah, wearing a black abaya over a house dress and a black scarf that left much of her hair uncovered.

"*Salamou aleikom.* I came to offer my condolences. Hassan died a martyr and he is now in a better place, seated with Islam's early converts and the Prophet's companions."

"*Inshallah*, thank you, Omar," said Safiyah, her voice almost a monotone. "He died attacking the company that hired you as a photographer. But I heard you are living in Lebanon. Why did you come back?"

"I came back to offer my condolences. Hassan was more than a brother to me. He was closer to me than my own brothers," said Omar, fighting back tears.

"Let me make you some tea," offered Safiyah. She did not wait for his answer, just got up and disappeared inside the house, leaving Omar alone in the room, where the curtains were made of a loud red fabric, a jarring contrast to the sofa and chairs that were upholstered with green velvet. There were photos on the wall of a younger version of her uncle. There were other men, too, in separate photos, but he could not recognize any of them.

"Here we are," said Safiyah as she made her way back to her chair. Omar rose from his chair and lifted a small table to where she sat so she could place the tray on it. Safiyah poured a glass for him and sweetened it. She was about to get up and take it to Omar but he rushed to her to take the glass off her hand.

Mourning had done nothing to diminish her beauty: in fact, she looked even more beautiful than ever, just a little tired in her deep brown eyes. Omar had never really had a chance to take a good look at Safiyah before, out of respect for his old friend. But now he did look, and what he saw made him catch his breath. He was amazed and surprised by how beautiful she is. He scrambled to find some justification for what he suddenly found himself feeling: Islamic tradition encourages men to marry the widows of martyred Muslim men. Surely, he thought, Safiyah was familiar with that tradition and, who knows, she might even welcome it. The idea, as Omar understood it, was for Muslim men to keep those widows immune to temptations.

Omar decided there and then that this was as a good time as any to approach Safiyah.

"Safiyah," he began, "The Prophet and his companions and followers married widows of martyrs to safeguard their virtue and compensate them for the companionship and love they no longer had."

"Yes, I am aware of that tradition, of course," said Safiyah in a stern, almost business-like tone.

"It will be my honor if you will accept me as a husband after the forty-day mourning period is over," Omar said, trying to keep the imploring tone out of his voice. "We can go and live in Beirut, away from all the bloodshed and misery here and maybe have a child or two. What do you think?"

He was excited by the idea of him and Safiyah living together in Beirut, where he often felt lonely. There was so much more to do there than in Baghdad. Definitely more than what's in Fallujah. The idea gave him butterflies.

"My husband died not too long ago," she began, her voice disapproving. "I am not at all ready to even consider your offer, kind as it is," said Safiyah who in reality had not given his offer even the most fleeting thought. In reality, all it had done was make her think of Khater and how much she missed him. She was saddened by Hassan's death, but a subtle sense of relief laced with joy had also crept in over his demise. She was free now to be with Khater. It was a delightful thought, not without some burden of guilt, but not enough to make her think less of it or admonish herself.

But how could she get a hold of Khater? She knew exactly where he was. He was literally just a 20-minute car ride away if the traffic was light. But did he really want her? Maybe it was just a passing infatuation or a crush that the passage of just a little time had already taken care of. She knew, though, that she needed to act quickly if she wanted to see him again. The end of his one-year tour in Iraq was fast approaching.

"I may have made my offer too soon," Omar said apologetically, worried that Safiyah's response was essentially a "no". But he still had some hope, so he continued. "But, as you know, well-intentioned deeds must be done as soon as possible. But take your time. Think about it. I am in no hurry at all."

"It's a kind offer and I will think about it," said Safiyah, this time impatiently. She rose from her seat, signaling her wish to see him leave. "It was good to see you after all this time. I wish you the best in your new life in Lebanon. May God be with you in every step you take."

It did not take long for Omar to realize his offer had indeed been rejected. Safiyah did not want him but was being polite about it. He was disappointed. True, it had been worth a shot, but the timing was unfortunate. Disastrous. Surprisingly, he found that he was not sad or heartbroken. He had acted on a whim when he asked her to marry him.

Or was he thinking with his penis? Was he truly smitten by her that he instantly fell in love with her? A case of love at first sight? Hardly. It must have been his penis. The whole thing began and ended in a matter of minutes. She must have thought he was stupid, an immature young man at best, he thought.

"Thank you, sister Safiyah," Omar said with stung politeness. "*Salamou Aleikom.*"

Omar did not know what to do next. It was afternoon and he did not have the energy to make calls to find out where his colleagues could be found in Baghdad. He wanted to know from them what happened the day of the attack. He specifically wanted to know how Hassan died, and who killed him. He took a taxi to Karadah. He thought he would just walk round to clear his mind and maybe grab a bite to eat.

It was almost dark when he arrived at Karadah after a long drive through heavy traffic. He got out at Fardous Square and walked. The area was crowded with shoppers. Store lights were just coming on and parts of the street looked almost festive. He stopped by a sidewalk food stand and bought himself a falafel sandwich, which he took to a nearby juice store where he bought a large cup of orange juice to wash down the sandwich with.

Omar did not feel like sitting down on one of the stools at the juice shop. He wanted to take a walk around Karadah, one of the busiest parts of the city. No matter how many suicide bombings hit the area, it always bounced back quickly. Some of the bombings had killed dozens and injured many more, but it would only be a week or so before the site of the bombing went back to how it used to be. Even during that week, adjacent businesses would carry on like nothing happened. It was the kind of resilience Iraq had become renowned for, and which might not have an equal elsewhere in the world.

For Omar, Karadah was the place he visited whenever his parents took him and his siblings to Baghdad to visit family on weekends or during the summer holiday. In his mind, it was associated with ice cream, cocktail juices and kebab eateries where he ate until he could eat no more. It had been years since he was last there. The place had clearly changed since then. Anything could be found in Karadah after the fall of Baghdad. The country's gates have been flung open since the U.S. invasion, with all kinds of consumer goods pouring in. No custom tariffs and no taxation and a population hungry for anything after 13 years of crippling U.N. sanctions.

Omar punctuated his walk with bites of his sandwich and sips of juice. He had not thought he would enjoy being in Baghdad so much. Karadah was the closest thing to the main commercial street in Hamra in Beirut, but it had the added value of being home. It was such a dramatic improvement on Fallujah. It was nowhere as conservative as his hometown, where fundamentalist Muslims had enjoyed significant influence even before the militants took the reins there.

He thought of the marriage offer he had just made to Safiyah and lamented that he rushed it, blowing whatever chance he might have had. Will she ever marry him, he wondered. But what made him do it? Did he betray Hassan by offering to marry his widow so soon after his death? Was he really trying to keep alive the tradition of Islam's early days by proposing to Safiyah, or was he rushing to snap up a prize before others did?

Omar walked while these thoughts of self-admonishment and regret raced through his head. The busiest part of Karadah was now behind him. He was close to the exclusive Jadriyah district. The streets were dimly lit and only a few people were on the streets. He was suddenly startled by the sound of a roaring engine. He stopped and turned to look. The speeding motorbike was coming fast toward him. He jumped on the sidewalk to avoid it, but it stopped when it reached him. Two men wearing ski masks were on the bike. Omar froze. The passenger on the bike slowly removed his ski mask and gave Omar an examining look, as though making sure he had the right man. "*Salamou Aleikom*, you are Omar Al Rawy, right? The photographer?" said the man. He had a thick mustache and his thuggish expression made Omar very nervous.

"Yes, that's me," said Omar, heart pounding and his legs weak. "Do I know you?"

Still seated on the bike, the man's right hand reached to the back of his pants, sliding under the track suit top he was wearing. When it re-emerged, he had a gun fitted with a silencer pointing at Omar's face. "This is from Saadoun, remember him, you dog? He was sentenced to death because you led the Americans to him with your phone."

Omar was about to say something, to challenge the accusation, but his time was up.

The man pulled the trigger. The bullet went straight between Omar's eyes and he instantly fell backwards on the sidewalk. A pool of blood started to blossom beneath his head and it quickly grew bigger.

The man driving the bike removed his ski mask and tucked it inside the front of his pants. The job was done.

The assassin gave him a gentle tap on the back of his right shoulder.

"He will languish in hell, by God's will. Let's go."

CHAPTER TWENTY-SEVEN

"I am, of course, sad that he died. We had been together for many years. How could I be otherwise?" Safiyah told her aunt's husband a few days after she received Omar's marriage proposal. "I only told you about Omar, because I felt that you needed to know as my uncle, especially after my parents died," she said in her defense against the man's not-too-subtle suggestions that she appeared rather relieved by Hassan's death.

"Grief is in the heart," she said.

Safiyah may have been overstating her sense of loss over Hassan's death.

She was indeed sad to have lost him, but somehow she had known for years it would come to this: a violent death that would make headlines as a victory for the Iraqi government and the Americans. She never approved of the path he took, but she had very little say in that, if any. From time to time she had delicately aired her misgivings, but he always used religion to justify the violence. And when he cited Quranic verses commending jihad, she fell silent. How could she possibly argue with that?

That they could not have babies had also been something of a time bomb ticking away, ready to explode at any time and bring the marriage down. It was Hassan who could not impregnate her. His sperm count was too low and his sperms were deformed.

"Unable to navigate their way to the target," was how the doctor in Baghdad described the sperms' condition after he had seen the test results. Safiyah was fertile, of course, and her desire to be a mother was overwhelming, but she had to tread carefully. Hassan could have received treatment to increase his sperm count, but he was too proud to do that.

"If God wills it that we have children, then we will," he told Safiyah once, concealing his anger.

Normally, even in conservative Fallujah, a husband's inability to impregnate his wife would be sufficient grounds for a woman to ask for a divorce. In all likelihood, a family court would grant it, too. But Safiyah was married to the sheikh of the jihadists in the city. Even if she could have mustered the courage to take such a step, it would have exposed her to the wrath of a husband who had no qualms about taking lives with his own hands. All in the name of God and Islam, of course. Safiyah knew better than to do that.

Somewhere deep in her heart and mind, she knew she had hoped Hassan would meet the fate he had, so she could be free to try her luck with another man who could give her the children she so wanted.

Now he was gone, all she could think of was Khater. She wanted to see him or at least contact him. She had his numbers, but every time she called he did not pick or she got a recording saying the phone was turned off or out of the coverage area. Her messages went unanswered.

She was despairing and she knew that time was running out fast. What if he left before she could see or contact him? Maybe she could get inside the Green Zone and make her way to the hospital. But how? Entry was severely restricted, enforced by grim-looking American and Iraqi soldiers who were usually reluctant to cut anyone any slack at the gates. There must be a way, she thought hopefully. She kept on trying his Iraqi mobile, but to no avail.

She tried her luck one morning at the Green Zone gate near the Goumhoriyah bridge. She pleaded with the Iraqi soldiers, telling them that she wanted to see a relative who was an American doctor of Iraqi origin. She gave them Khater's name, but they would not listen.

"Call him and ask him to come and pick you up from the gate here," one soldier told her. She would not give up though. She stood there waiting for the soldier to take pity on her and let her go in, but he would not relent.

"You must leave now," the soldier finally ordered her after three hours of standing at the gate. He used the sort of "or else" tone of voice that left her no choice but to leave. In tears, she began her journey back to Azamiyah on the other side of the city.

She felt depressed for days after her failed attempt to enter the Green Zone.

It was days before a ray of hope appeared. It was a long shot, but definitely worth a try. And it was unexpected.

Of all the people who could have been the source of that glimmer of hope, her aunt's husband was the last one she had expected. A man who had over the years perfected the art of leading a quiet life on the sidelines, earning a salary from a tedious administrative job at the Health Ministry, minding his own business and keeping everyone except family at an arm's length. Her aunt, his wife, was a woman only slightly younger than he was but who has been bed ridden for years by an assortment of chronic diseases, including severe diabetes.

"I am thinking of visiting my brother here in Baghdad next week," he said, starting what appeared to be an attempt at small talk with Safiyah, who did not react to his mundane statement. "Come with me. A change of scenery might help you."

"I am Ok!" Safiyah said, trying to suppress her frustration with the entire conversation. "I am fine, thanks be to God. You can take my sisters and brother if you want."

"It's you that I want to come. My brother and his family live in the Green Zone. It's a great part of Baghdad. You can go … "

"The Green Zone?" Safiyah interrupted, screaming in excitement. "Can we go tomorrow?"

"No, my brother must submit our names to the Iraqi authorities there along with copies of our citizenship certificates so we can enter the Green Zone. It takes two to three days."

"Not possible to do it faster?"

"I don't think so. We will be lucky if it's done in three days. There are delays sometimes when they have intelligence of impending rocket attacks or whatever," he said. "Why are you so excited?"

"Nothing. I just need the change," She said before she got up and walked to her uncle and gave him a kiss on his bald head. "Thank you, thank you!"

The man was stunned.

He was right. It took the permit four days to be processed. The relatives living in the apartment blocks caught up in the Green Zone when the Americans drew its boundaries in 2003 had to submit the names of their expected guests along with copies of their citizenship certificates to the military and police. In theory, the Interior Ministry's security agency examined the applications before they issued their verdict. But the process was in reality just a routine that did not include thorough checks. The thinking was that carefully searching visitors and the vehicles they travelled in was more than sufficient. The visit must take place on the designated day and its duration had to be specified, too. Most such visits took place on a Friday or a Saturday. Relatives and friends mostly chose Friday, the first day of the Iraqi weekend.

Her uncle broke the news of the approval to Safiyah, who could not contain her excitement.

"We will be going tomorrow, God willing," he said, still bewildered by Safiyah's joy. "If I knew this would make you so happy, I would have suggested we go and visit them a long time ago. But God wills things to happen when He sees fit."

Safiyah did not respond. She was deep in thought but with a hint of a smile on her face. All she could think of was what she would wear and how would she get from the relatives' home to Ibn Sina hospital. On the question of what to wear, she needed to strike a balance between showcasing her beauty and maintaining a level of reserve befitting a Muslim woman in Iraq.

She decided to start with a pampering session at the women's *hamam,* or spa, in Azamiyah. She wanted to remove unwanted body hair, get a scrub and a massage. The place was not far from the mosque and shrine of Imam Abu Haneifa. The spa was old and not very neat, but her mother used to go there every time she came to Baghdad to visit her sister. Besides, Safiyah did not want to leave Azamiyah to go somewhere better equipped or cleaner. As a Sunni out-of-towner, she felt safer in Azamiyah than anywhere else in Baghdad.

Next was the question of what to wear and where would she get the money to buy new clothes. She had not left the house since the day she visited Hassan at Saadoun street, when she had worn clothes borrowed from her sick aunt. But those clothes would not cut it this time. She wanted to show Khater what he could not see when she was in her loose hospital gown. Her idea was not to seduce or dazzle him, just to show him what she was really like. She would still have to cover her hair, but she had no intention of covering all of it. She wanted to show him what her body looked like, but not to cheapen herself by wearing something too tight or revealing. She wanted to wear heels, so if he watched her walk from a distance he would notice a slight but enticing swing, but the heels must not be too high. She could fall flat on her face and hurt herself, but that would not be too bad, in fact: then she could be admitted back to Ibn Sina and get to see more of Khater!

But, now, where would the money come from for all that?

Her aunt's husband? Could she actually ask him?

She did. And he was more than generous. For years, he and Safiyah's aunt tried to start a family but could not. He was happy to have Safiya and her two younger sisters and brother staying at his house. He liked the noise they filled the house with. All four were grief-stricken by the tragic loss of their parents but were doing better with every passing day. He took pleasure in cooking for them to give Safiyah some rest. He frequently took her two sisters and brother walking around the commercial part of Azamiyah across the street from the Abu Haneifa mosque. One afternoon, he took all three across the bridge to Kazimiyah, where they visited the shrine of the Imam Al Kazim and strolled around. They stopped at an eatery on the pedestrian street that leads to the shrine and had a kebab with salads and rice. He later took them to the famous Kazimiyah gold market and bought the girls earrings.

"Take the money, Safiyah, I cannot think of anything more fulfilling to me right now than to make you happy," he told her as he opened the small safe he kept at the house. "It's just money sitting at the house not doing anything."

Safiyah teared up. She was filled with both gratitude and remorse. His generosity and his kind words moved her, but she also felt she was deceiving him by not sharing why she needed the new clothes, the shoes, the handbag and the money for the *hamam*. She wanted to share, but was scared she would be misunderstood, even judged harshly.

She decided against sharing. How could she? Hassan died not too long ago and she was already thinking of being with another man? And an American man! No, she would only share if she absolutely had to.

The day of the visit finally arrived.

Safiyah woke up at dawn, prayed and showered. She prepared breakfast for her aunt, her husband and siblings, but she herself ate very little. She was too excited, anxious and afraid. After breakfast, she tried Khater's number again. The same recorded message came on: "The number you have dialed is either switched off or out of the coverage area".

Her heart sank a little although that was exactly what happened every time she tried to reach him. She quickly stifled her disappointment and started planning the day ahead.

She wore a black skirt that went down halfway between her knees and ankles. Matching the skirt was a white blouse and a gray blazer. She covered her hair with a black silk scarf, with her forehead partially covered with hair that was artfully allowed to escape. Her black shoes were plain. They had five-centimeter heels, just enough to give her a little swagger.

Her uncle drove his black "Brazilian," the name Iraqis gave to the Volkswagens manufactured in the South American country and imported by Saddam's government in the 1980s. The uncle rarely used it but kept it in pristine condition, covered and parked in the garage on one side of the house.

The late morning drive to the Green Zone from Azamiyah was pleasantly smooth, with very little traffic on the streets. It was a sunny day with a cold breeze and a slight chill in the shade. They headed to Abu Nawas street and continued until they came to the point where the street was blocked for everyone except those headed to the Green Zone. They were stopped at a checkpoint, their documents checked and allowed to proceed to the next one, where they were told to get out of the car so that sniffer dogs could do their work. The guards told them to leave their citizenship certificates and take visitors' passes they needed to pin on their chests. Only then were they allowed back in the car to resume their journey.

"You know where the house is that you're going to, Haji?" asked the friendly Iraqi soldier, addressing the uncle.

"God willing, yes," he replied with a smile and drove away, slowing down at the endless speed bumps and checkpoints.

They arrived at the apartment block, a grey four-story structure dating back to the 1980s. It was in a cluster of identical structures built by Saddam for employees of the presidency and his palaces, but many of the apartments had been passed on over the years to new owners, traded off by the original tenants who wanted to live in more authentic neighborhoods, away from the prying eyes of the dictator's feared security agents. They were now suffering from neglect, covered in damp spots on the outer walls and with countless missing tiles at the entrance.

Safiyah got out of the car and ran around to the driver's side.

"Uncle, I must go somewhere here in the Green Zone. I will come back as quickly as I can and we will return home together, God willing."

The uncle was speechless, not knowing which question to ask first. He chose the obvious one after a long pause, during which he looked like he might be about to pass out.

"Where are you going?"

"I will tell you everything when I am back, but not now. I need to go. Please, I don't have much time and I must find what I am looking for."

Her uncle said nothing, just murmured a prayer that only he could hear. He got out of the car and gave Safiyah a fatherly hug. It felt like a goodbye. Safiyah hugged him back and turned around and walked away without as much as a word.

She did not know where the hospital was, but she somehow convinced herself that it could not be far. She asked an Iraqi who happened to walk by the apartment blocks. He told her where it was, but also warned her that she would not be able to easily get inside. She ignored the warning, thanked him and walked in the direction he suggested. The distances seemed greater than they looked from a moving car and she could not walk fast because of the heels. But she kept going, breaking a sweat and sensing that her hair had gone from carefully groomed to unkempt and then crossed the line into totally messy. But she could not care at this point of the search. She was desperate and her heart was beating fast.

"Woman, where are you going?" shouted an Iraqi soldier at a checkpoint in a side street that she had not noticed as she hurried past.

Safiyah stopped and searched for the source of the voice.

"Woman, come over here," the soldier shouted.

Trembling with fear, Safiyah started walking slowly toward the soldier. This is it, she thought, her desperate attempt to see Khater was doomed to fail. He would return to America and she would never see or hear from him again. By the time she arrived at the checkpoint, the soldier was joined by three more.

"Where are you going? You cannot just wonder around here. What is your business in the Green Zone?" asked the soldier as the other three examined Safiyah with hungry eyes.

She felt uncomfortable and it occurred to her that their unwanted attention could be due to her somewhat liberal clothes. Would they have behaved like this had she been wearing an abaya? Unlikely.

"I am heading to the Ibn Sina hospital to see a relative who works there. He is an American who is originally from Iraq."

"What's his name?" he asked, no shred of sympathy visible on his face.

"Dr Khater."

"What is the rest of his name?" he asked impatiently.

"I don't remember," she said.

"Your pass is for visiting Iraqi civilians living in the Green Zone, not visiting the hospital," he said, his tone turning suspicious.

Safiyah did not know what to say. "There must have been a mistake at the gate," she began, hoping he would believe her lie and let her go.

"No, no mistake! We do our work very carefully here. I will check with the gate," he said, signaling to the other three soldiers to step back, since they were moving uncomfortably close to Safiyah. One of them pretended to be sniffing her.

"Are you from Baghdad?" he asked. "Your accent tells me you are not."

"I am from Azamiyah here in Baghdad," she lied.

"I don't think so, you don't at all sound like you're from Baghdad. So, tell me."

"I have lived in Anbar for a few years when my father, a former police officer, was posted there."

"When was that?"

"When I was still at school," she kept on lying as her hands shook and her heart raced.

The soldier gave her a look of contemptuous disbelief, then fished his phone out of his vest pocket. He typed his pin number and pressed on an icon. There was a display of photos, mostly grainy and some in black and white. He began to scroll up. Barely ten seconds passed before he seemed to have found what he was looking for. He stared at Safiyah and then looked back at his phone. He did that several times.

Safiyah's entire body began to shake. She ran her hand nervously over her head, accidentally pushing her scarf farther back. She did not realize that most of her hair was now showing. What she did realize was that her dream of being reunited with Khater was gone, and that was just one small part of the nightmare she would now have to endure.

The other three soldiers began to move slowly back towards her, sensing an opportunity. That horrible leering look was back on their faces again.

"Safiyah Hamad Salah?" said the soldier victoriously. "A terrorist and the widow of Fallujah's biggest terrorist!"

Safiyah's head began to spin and her vision became blurry. Drops of sweat dribbled from her forehead into her eyes. She collapsed. Her scarf was now completely off her head and her skirt rose a few inches above her knees. She did not pass out, not completely. Her head was filled with images of prison, torture, Khater leaving Iraq to launch a prosperous career in America and Hassan returning from the dead to call her a whore.

She screamed, barely audible at first but growing louder until it sounded like she was begging death to come and claim her.

THE END

ABOUT THE AUTHOR

Egyptian-born Hamza Hendawi is a prize-winning journalist who covered the news from nearly 30 countries in the Middle East, Asia, and Europe for Reuters and The Associated Press in a career stretching back to the 1980s. In those years, Hamza covered nearly every Middle East conflict, from South Sudan's civil war and Iraq's invasion of Kuwait to the 2003 US invasion and subsequent occupation of Iraq and the Israel-Hezbollah war in 2006. Hamza won several journalism awards and honorary mentions for his work, including the AP Managing Editors prize for the capture of Saddam Hussein and the Deadline Club for his Middle East coverage. In 2013, his stories from rebel-held areas in Syria were part of an AP package placed as a finalist in the Pulitzer's international reporting category. He also authored two, non-fiction books on the Iraq war in Arabic. Hamza is currently the senior correspondent in Cairo for The National, a UAE-based, English-language daily.

NOTE FROM HAMZA HENDAWI

Word-of-mouth is crucial for any author to succeed. If you enjoyed *The Wife of the Emir of Fallujah*, please leave a review online—anywhere you are able. Even if it's just a sentence or two. It would make all the difference and would be very much appreciated.

Thanks!
Hamza Hendawi

We hope you enjoyed reading this title from:

www.blackrosewriting.com

Subscribe to our mailing list – *The Rosevine* – and receive **FREE** books, daily deals, and stay current with news about upcoming releases and our hottest authors.
Scan the QR code below to sign up.

Already a subscriber? Please accept a sincere thank you for being a fan of Black Rose Writing authors.

View other Black Rose Writing titles at www.blackrosewriting.com/books and use promo code **PRINT** to receive a **20% discount** when purchasing.

www.ingramcontent.com/pod-product-compliance
Lightning Source LLC
Chambersburg PA
CBHW060716190726
48289CB00002B/711